MW00964304

ALASDAIR

MASTERS AMONG MONSTERS

ELLA FRANK

Copyright © 2015 by Ella Frank

www.ellafrank.com

Edited by Mickey Reed

Edited by Candace Wood

Cover Design © By Hang Le

No part of this book may be reproduced or transmitted in any form or by any means, electronic or mechanical, including photocopying, recording, or by any information storage and retrieval system without the written permission of the author, except for the use of brief quotations in a book review.

This book is a work of fiction. Names, characters, places, and incidents either are products of the author's imagination or are used fictitiously. Any resemblance to actual persons, living or dead, events, or locales is entirely coincidental.

flaccid cock he found inside. When a soft groan left the human, Alasdair used his other hand to capture his captive's wrists like iron shackles and pin them above his head. Before the man had a chance to wake, he delved inside his head and projected an image of where this hunt would finally end.

It was somewhere he hadn't thought of in a long while, but after having spotted that book, he suddenly had an intense urge to revisit there with this fair-haired specimen.

The bathhouses.

Yes, it's perfect. He had him exactly where he wanted him.

Not a thing on Earth could save the poor soul now, and as his teeth cracked into deadly formation, Alasdair dove inside his mind and goaded, *"Run."*

THERE WAS A bright, blinding light, and again, Leo dreamed.

It was an odd sensation to be reliving the same dream sequence over and over, but that's what had been happening—until tonight. Tonight, something was different. Something was out of place.

Over the last few weeks, he'd been imagining himself alone in front of an altar while clutching something in his hand. The altar had resembled those back in ancient times—an oblong podium constructed from marble—and he'd chalked his imaginings up to the project he and his coworkers had been working on at the museum.

Tonight, however, the light that usually shone so brightly around him had been snuffed out, and he was pulled into the darkness by someone or something.

HE HEARD HIM before he saw him.

A hypnotic voice instructed him to, "Run," and some inner instinct told him to listen. Leo bolted to the left, recognizing his surroundings as the bathhouses he'd been researching for an upcoming exhibit at work. Several white pillars flanked an enormous rectangular pool, which was carved into the stone ground, and he darted behind one of them.

As he tried to catch his breath, his body started to heat. He felt flushed, as though he were aroused, and when he looked down to his cock, he noticed it was as hard as the pillar he was resting against.

What the hell is going on?

The thought quickly dissipated, though, as a low groan left his lips.

He scanned the area, taking in everything he could about the place. The classic architecture of the Doric columns made it clear where he was, but...

How is this possible?

It felt as though he'd fallen inside one of his textbooks and woken up in Ancient Greece—with a fucking hard on.

A mocking chuckle echoed inside his head like a chain rattling against a steel trap. He shook it, trying to banish the sound, as he squeezed his eyes shut. He was breathing in heavy pants now, the odd sensation of being given one hell of an amazing hand job more obvious than it had been two seconds ago, and his lungs tried to pull in extra oxygen as he waited for...

What? What am I waiting for? *He wasn't even sure.*

He moved his hand, about to press it against the erection throbbing between his legs, and that was when he realized he was still dressed in his pajama pants.

So this is definitely some kind of nightmare.

"Almost."

Leo jerked back against the pillar, quickly moving his hand by his side again, when the stranger belonging to the voice appeared from out of nowhere.

"You're still in bed. That's the 'almost' part. But this isn't a nightmare, and you want to know a secret?" the stranger asked.

Then he felt it again—a strong fist stroking up the length of his erection—and Leo's entire body shuddered, reacting from the sheer pleasure of it.

"What happens in here also *happens out there."*

Leo searched the stranger's face, trying to recognize something about the man he'd conjured up in his dream. But nothing about the short, dark hair and piercing emerald eyes were familiar. Neither was the way he was making him feel.

"I can hear your pulse," the stranger informed him in a silky tone. "Thump, thump, thump. It's a beautiful melody. Is it

from fear, I wonder? Or perhaps something more basic in nature. Something more…sexual."

Leo tried to speak, something he usually didn't have a problem with. But he couldn't get anything past the lump that had lodged itself in his throat. The man taunting and touching him was extraordinarily attractive. More so than anyone he'd ever met. And even if his words and the situation hadn't been alarming enough, being this close to such male perfection would've likely rendered him—

"Mute? Oh, that won't do. Thelo na se gamiso," his dark fantasy said, slipping into another language.

Greek. And he'd interrupted Leo's thoughts as if he'd said them out loud.

"But I don't want your silence when I do it. I want to hear you scream."

The way he'd said the word scream could've been taken as it had been delivered. Full of sensual promise in the haze of Leo's sexed-up state of mind. But as a contemptuous smirk drew the man's lips back to reveal two gleaming fangs, the hair on the back of Leo's neck stood tall. Any attraction he'd been feeling seconds ago drained away and was replaced with dread.

He'd just been reading about this—the monsters of Greek mythology—and he'd come across *The Scriptures of Delphi* and the origins of vampires. That had to explain this bizarre dream he was having, the reason for this monster in his head.

"This can't be happening," he finally managed to say, hearing the disbelief in his own voice. *"You're not real. I'm imagining you. This is a nightmare."* It was the only logical

*explanation as his lips fell open on another sigh of pleasure and he
stared into the face of a…vampire.*

*Before he could think beyond that, the fist around his cock
vanished, and a solid pressure pushed on his shoulder. Then cold
fingers pressed against his temple, shoving his head to the side to
expose his neck, and he heard,* "If that's true then this shouldn't
hurt at all."

*The patent lie ghosted over his ear as the blinding sting of
what felt like a thousand knives sank into his throat. A shout tore
from his chest as the vampire plastered itself to his front and let
out a feral growl.*

*The hand on his shoulder ran down his bare arm to his
bicep and jerked him forward. He tried to put up a token fight,
raising his other hand to shove his attacker, but it was as effective
as trying to move a boulder. The vampire was as solid and cool as
the column he'd been pressed against, and Leo knew that his effort
to escape was a futile one.*

*As his vision dimmed and his heartbeat slowed, he
wondered if what the vampire had said earlier was true.* "'What
happens in here *also* happens out there.'" *If it was, Leo only
had seconds until—*

*The teeth devouring him ripped free, and the hands
holding him released him with a hard shove. His knees gave out,
and as he collapsed at the feet of the dangerous creature, he heard it
say,* "This cannot be happening," *which mirrored his own thought
from earlier.*

Then everything faded to nothingness.

ALASDAIR BLINKED, SEVERING the connection between him and the man, and yanked himself from the mind he'd been immersed within.

What the fuck is going on?

He tried to focus on the human pressed beneath him on the bed, but all he could see was a crimson pool of blood seeping from the wounds he'd inflicted. That wasn't anything out of the ordinary. But the acidic burn racing through his own extremities was.

He wasn't supposed to feel that. The pain wasn't supposed to be his. But as he tried to gather his keen hunter senses, he couldn't locate them. Instead, his vision was starting to blur.

As quickly as he could manage, which was infuriatingly slow at that stage, he pushed away from the human. But his arm gave way and he lurched downward instead.

What is happening to me? he thought as his legs fell slack and useless against those lying prone beneath him.

Then he heard it. A moan of pain. The sound of stirring. And as the sounds filtered inside his head, the scorching sensation in his veins hit his joints and seemed to detonate, locking them into place. His canines retracted with bone-fracturing precision, and his flesh continued to burn.

That was when the man beneath him opened his pale, grey eyes.

What the fuck? For the first time in over two millennia, Alasdair was completely captivated. He couldn't move a single muscle, nor could he will himself to fade out. And as his eyes locked on to those staring up at him, all he could think was, *What are you?*

It all happened in a matter of seconds, but before he could try to ascertain what he was experiencing, his name, though faint, managed to infiltrate his dazed mind.

Alasdair?

The second time around, the echo of Isadora's voice came through much clearer.

Alasdair? Where are you? You're about to be summoned. And we both know it won't be pretty if that happens.

Even in his current state, Alasdair knew that to be true. If he lived through whatever was happening here, the price he would pay for having thought he'd had time to hunt tonight would be extreme.

But when the man beneath him dared to move, Alasdair gathered some semblance of strength and tightened his grip around the wrists he was holding. The stormy grey of the man's irises seemed to swirl as the will to survive blazed to life—then Alasdair's name sounded again.

This time, however, it was like a cannon blast.

The summons.

The pull.

The directive to return home had been issued.

Time stopped, and he and the human faded into the night.

Two

"DAMN IT, ALASDAIR. What the hell happened to you?" was the first thing he heard as he and the man faded in at Isadora's feet. They landed in an unceremonious tangle of arms and legs on the large, rectangular rug in the Adjudication Room.

The human, whose wrists he was still holding tight, had passed out cold from the transport, which wasn't unusual for a mortal. It *was* unheard of, though, that *he* was just as disoriented.

Isadora crouched by his side, the long line of her leg flawless and her patent red Louis Vuitton stilettos eye level with him. Then she let out an exasperated sigh and rolled up the sleeve of her black chiffon blouse.

"Feed, you arrogant ass. And don't give me any trouble. You need it."

Since his legs were continuing to disobey direct orders, he didn't bother arguing. And when Isadora thrust her dainty arm between him and the man, who was flat on his back, Alasdair listened.

His fangs extended over the smooth skin, and without hesitation, he struck. Biting down hard, he pierced through the layer that, for most, was impenetrable, but to their own, it was easily punctured. She cursed at him, and as he siphoned the blood from his cousin's vein, his lips curled against her wrist, his message clear.

Don't get used to issuing the orders, Isa. I'm still your superior.

The ever-eternal flush of immortality rejuvenated him, and as it coursed through his body to every joint and extremity, his strength began to return. The force of it vibrated through his limbs, and once the full potency of it had hit, another response did also.

A more primal one.

Primitive.

One that often, but not always, followed a feed. And as his cock stiffened against the man underneath him, he knew exactly who the cause was.

Able to now move, Alasdair retracted his teeth, and Isadora snatched her arm back.

"You asshole," she accused. "What's your problem?"

Alasdair ignored the question and, instead, placed his palms on either side of his prisoner's head. He inspected the wounds on the human's neck and then faced the pissed-off female who'd moved to the massive chair on the far side of the room.

"I need you to watch him while I'm gone."

"Excuse me?" Isadora scoffed as she crossed one of her bare legs over the other. Her black A-line skirt slid perilously high up her shapely thigh. "I'm not babysitting a human."

"You will do what I tell you to do," he stated. Then he returned his attention to the unconscious man. "He incapacitated me tonight. We both know that has never happened. Not to one of us. I want to know how he did it."

"You want a lot more than that if your cock is any kind of indicator."

Alasdair whipped his head around and pinned her with a look that dared her to say more. Wisely, she chose to keep her mouth shut.

"I have to go to the Chamber. The summons was clear. I have fifteen minutes."

"I know. Thanos and I were...instructed to recuse ourselves from the hearing they called for you."

Of course they were. This was to be a punishment—allies were not invited.

Before he could change his mind, Alasdair leaned down so his mouth was poised over the gash in the strong throat he'd attacked. Then he ran his tongue over the wounds and sat back. The skin stretched and then drew together until it seemingly stitched itself back in place and tightened into a smooth patch of healed flesh.

"We both know whatever happens to me in there is likely going to take days—"

"Or weeks," Isadora interrupted.

"—to recover from," he finished as he got to his feet. He stepped over the man and saw that his cousin was staring at him as if he'd lost his mind.

"I don't know what's going on with you lately, Alasdair. Or what happened tonight. But you need to get it out of your system. You've never ignored a direct order from Vasilios. And he is pissed that you chose to tonight. "

"*He* happened," Alasdair said, gesturing to the body on the floor. "Just watch him, would you?" He was about to leave, but at the last minute, he pivoted around as Isadora was getting to her feet. "Isa?"

She stopped where she was and turned her head in his direction. When her midnight-blue eyes found his and her raven hair spilled in loose curls over her shoulder, Alasdair ground his teeth together.

Isadora was a beauty. A deadly one, at that.

"You are to keep guard from the *outside* of the room. He will heal. You will keep him alive. And when I return, I want to know what is running through his blood and how someone such as *he* was able to defeat someone like *me*."

Three

"ENTER!"

THE BELLOWING order was issued with the force of a sledgehammer. The weight of it coursed through Alasdair's veins as he stood outside the closed door where the three Ancients had gathered.

He'd committed a grievous transgression tonight. He'd missed a meeting, and as one of the first sired, he was expected at all that were called—unless dead.

Two of his Ancient's brainless minions flanked the massive doors, waiting to bring him inside, and as he glared at them, he held his chin in lofty disposition. They knew better than to challenge him. He'd have them defeated and dead in the blink of an eye if they tried. This show of muscle was merely a formality. An insult to him, because he now had to wait until he had permission to enter the Chamber.

As one of them opened the door, the tether that bound him like an anchor to his maker strengthened, and Alasdair had no choice but to walk forward.

How ironic. To have the entire world at your fingertips and one word or thought from one being will bring you the fuck home.

He entered the cavernous hall, one foot in front of the other. However, unlike other times he'd been inside the Chamber, he had no control over his motions. He was being brought to heel, and he knew what was about to come— punishment.

Many times over, he'd borne witness to one who'd disrespected the Ancients. Most didn't live to see another night. But death would not be the ultimate, or swift, ending to this particular session.

The scrutiny of the council members was intense as Alasdair continued inside, his eyes trained on the three sitting on the elaborate stone dais at the far end of the monolithic room.

Each one of them was a striking specimen in his own unique way. He was always somewhat shocked when he had the privilege to be in their presence—even more so tonight, dressed as they were in their ceremonial garb.

They were remarkable. The high, black-collared empire jackets with brass buttons that held the fitted garments in place drew one's eyes down the flawless proportions of the body it concealed. It was a body both mortals and immortals craved the second they were within eyesight.

The Ancients had mastered a most effective disguise. Civilized and outwardly appealing, they resembled nothing more than extremely handsome men in their prime. A form no one in everyday society would question but, instead, would want to be near. But if one were unfortunate enough to procure their wrath, the creature that emerged from within that polished shell was a most frightening fiend to behold.

"Alasdair."

His name echoed down the extensive aisle, but it was as clear as if his sire were standing by his side.

"How gracious of you to find the time in your busy schedule to join us." The words were delivered with an air of authority only an Ancient could pull off.

Muffled whispers came from the pews lining the aisle, where the council members of each brood had gathered to await his punishment. Deriving pleasure in another's torture was an inherent trait of their kind—and there was no way they would miss out on it being inflicted on an Ancient's sired.

As he continued up the walkway, his jaw fused shut, which was standard at a punishment hearing. He couldn't open his mouth to speak, and he wouldn't be given the opportunity until his opinion or thoughts were deemed necessary.

His eyes remained on the figure at the center of the platform—his Ancient, Vasilios, who was more breathtaking to look upon than Michelangelo's *David*. His coal-colored hair was cut close to his head, accentuating a face that was a model study of sculptured angles and bones. It made one want to reach out and trail their fingers along those lines. But, as Alasdair knew firsthand, that deceptive allure was a façade, and a most potent one, at that.

As usual, there was no indication to judge what Vasilios was thinking. The stony expression on his unflinching face didn't flicker. But then Alasdair caught it, the way his eyes narrowed a fraction of an inch. It was the only movement in the otherwise still room—until he spoke.

"I have to confess. You have disappointed me tonight."

Vasilios halted Alasdair's movements when he was within a few feet of the three and found himself fixed to the spot.

"I never expected you to be one who would show such disrespect. Thanos, perhaps, but not you."

The inability to speak was frustrating as fuck. But even if he'd had the capability to do so, he wouldn't have responded. One didn't do that—not unless they wanted their tongue ripped from their head.

"I wonder what could have been so pressing tonight that you would have dismissed a meeting so blithely? Especially when you knew this one held such importance."

As the word *importance* left his tongue, Alasdair's kneecaps cracked and he fell to them with a muted grunt of agony.

"You will kneel as we ruminate your misgivings. Do you understand?" Vasilios's eyes glowed with the question, and Alasdair's jaw loosened enough for him to speak.

"I live to serve, my sire."

"I am delighted to hear that. But not quite convinced of your sincerity."

The perverse excitement building en masse was obvious from the muttering amongst the council members, the anticipation of blood and violence starting a frenzy amongst the natives as the one-sided trial played out before them.

"Perhaps we need a token of good faith. Proof that you weren't thinking clearly when you disregarded a mandate over a thousand years old. It's been a long time since I have thought about my own beginnings, Alasdair. The whys of it all. Like…why do we share a bond that binds you to me if you are going to *ignore it*?" Vasilios's voice had built to a thunderous roar, and then he ceased talking altogether. The silence was eerie as he glared down at him. Then he clasped his hands together and asked, "Do you need a reminder, Alasdair? I wouldn't think you would need to be re-schooled on how we came to exist. However—"

"Ambrogio," Alasdair forced out between taut lips.

"Ahh, yes. See? You *do* remember your history."

"Of course," he said through the crushing bite of pain in his knees. "He turned the three of you after years of isolation. That is why, with him in a state of transcendence, you three reign as the almighty. The most powerful vampires to exist."

"Quite right you are, *agóri*."

Deciding he might as well try everything to get in his Ancient's good graces, Alasdair continued. "That is also why he made a vow to you three. A promise that you would not share the same lonely fate as he. He allowed you to choose one you would bind yourself to. Creating an eternal bond between you and your first sired."

"Yes. One I am seriously second-guessing since you deemed it within your right to disregard my wishes this evening."

Alasdair opened his mouth to continue but found he could no longer speak.

"I think it is time you prove yourself to me once more. In front of our friends and family."

The splintering shards of broken bone in his knees were a crushing reminder that he had no choice of what he wanted or could do. But the humiliation that accompanied the position was what really smarted, not so much the shattered bones. So, with the expected respect, Alasdair lowered his eyes to the ground and answered.

"I would enjoy nothing more than to prove my obedience to you."

Mumbled speculation swept throughout as the council played onlookers to a day they never thought they would see: Alasdair Kyriakoús on his knees. It truly was a first.

"Quiet!"

The word thundered through the hall, and the silence that followed could have only been achieved by those who had the ability to exist without breath—those who were already dead.

"It would be remiss of us not to give Alasdair a chance to defend himself before we decide what should become of him. And how are we to do that with all of your inane chattering? The next to utter a sound will take up and play his proxy, and unlike for him, I hold no affection for any of you. Do I make myself clear?"

Alasdair wondered if the others were thinking just what would happen to them if the affection he was currently being shown was two smashed kneecaps and fuck only knew what was to come.

"As for you… You are going to help me understand why you would *ever* think it was acceptable not to show your face when I command you to do so."

Metal scraped across stone—pointed nails extending from deadly fingers. Nails that could slit a throat open, puncture a vein, or stab an eye out.

Before he had a chance to speak, though, Alasdair's head was thrust up by invisible fingers to face his sire, who was now on his feet. His eyes locked with the angry, black orbs that had replaced the green they both shared.

Alasdair had never seen him so enraged—at least, not at him. In that moment, the true majesty of Vasilios's power washed over him, and a rush of adrenaline raced down his spine, followed by the icy tendrils of true fear.

"Are you frightened of me right now, Alasdair?"

Vasilios was able to sense his fear as easily as he could rip his heart out with no more than a thought. But part of his punishment, Alasdair understood, was the humiliating process of bringing him down a peg or two.

"Yes, my sire."

He figured the next thing that happened would be painful and horrendous, but instead, he heard in his head, *You should be, omorfo mou agóri. You have hurt me greatly. And now, though it pains me to do so, I must return the gesture.*

When his right hand was wrenched behind his back between his shoulder blades, a curse tore from his throat. His arm had been dislocated from the joint and left to swing down by his side. Then, invisible, ironlike tentacles wrapped around his spine and arched his chest out at a warped angle so his upper body bowed. Next went his coat and his shirt, both ripped free so they fell on the floor behind his useless frame, exposing his torso to the crazed eyes surrounding him.

The temperature in the room skyrocketed from frigid to fevered as the lust and hunger of a kill, or a taking, was presented. Alasdair wondered for a brief second which direction it would go—until fingernails scoured his chest as they dragged down his ribs to his pants.

"Understand, Alasdair. Although I need you to exist, I can still *break* you."

The words were calculated. They were issued as a way to inform the others of exactly who was the puppet and who was the master. But there was no mistaking it, and Alasdair knew that the words were also being stated for Vasilios's own warped pleasure. He was enjoying showing the council what was his. That was soon confirmed as the next thought was forced inside his mind.

If you try to resist what I am about to do to you, I will let these animals feed on you until you are so weak it will take a good year to heal. And they're hungry for you. Look at them.

The threat was the most effective one he could've issued.

Alasdair was known for three things.

One—never slaking his needs within his own brood. Fight-or fuck-wise.

Two—his selective nature when it came to *whom* he fed and healed from.

And three—his unnatural self-control.

All things his sire was aware of.

The welts now rising down the length of his torso festered from the liquid silver the nails had been tipped with, searing like an iron poker being pressed directly into his veins.

He couldn't help the tormented snarl that roared
from his gut as those same nails found the button of his
pants. His eyes were still locked with the malevolent being
controlling every fucked-up second of this power exchange,
and a flash of raw, sexual desire entered Vasilios's eyes.

Before Alasdair could begin to imagine what was in
store for him, a memory hit with blinding force, and even
through the pain, a frisson of lust shot through him...

Ancient Athens – 47 BC

*HE WAS BEING followed as he wove his way between the
columns of the deserted bathhouse. He slipped into the shadows
cast by the moonlight, and as he waited there, Alasdair realized he
enjoyed the feeling of being chased.*

*The baths were a favorite place of his. They were where he
went if he wanted to be seen, be heard, or to participate in delights
of the flesh. At this time of night, he was most certainly there to
partake in the last of the three, and he suspected that the man who
had been watching him for days on end was there for the same
reason.*

*He pressed his back to the pillar he'd moved behind, and
his cock swelled beneath the heavy wool of his toga. It had been a
long time since he'd felt such excitement over a rendezvous.
Usually, one was too busy watching their back for knives to enjoy
any kind of lead up to a fuck at the bathhouse. But ever since the
celebratory feast two days past, where he had beheld the most
heavenly man he thought to exist, he had thought of little else.*

It had only taken a glimpse, and still, Alasdair was not certain the vision he had seen was real. He'd appeared godlike. Ethereal. And as quickly as he had seen him, the man had vanished.

From that moment forward, Alasdair had felt him like his very own silhouette, could sense when he was near. And when the sun disappeared and the dark desires rushed to the surface, the hunger to be touched consumed him with the need to come face-to-face with he who was responsible for his state of sexual longing.

"Alasdair..."

As the bewitching voice floated through the air and entered his mind, Alasdair's heart thumped. It was as if the word had been whispered right by his ear.

"You really should not walk alone in the night, omorfo mou agóri."

Alasdair licked his lips as a breeze ruffled through his long hair and the material of his garment where it brushed his calves. In all of his thirty-one years, he could not remember feeling such anticipation, such build to a moment of meeting. And as this man, being, or night angel continued to taunt him, the thrill only intensified.

"A lot can happen when the sun dips down and the moon comes out to play..." The seductive voice trailed off, and as he mourned the absence of it, a delicious pressure surrounded his swollen shaft.

A strangled moan fell from his lips as he pressed his head to the column and looked from left to right. No one was there. No one was even near him. But he could feel—oh gods, yes—he

could feel fingers stroking his turgid length, and then the voice…
It was back.

"Things you cannot even begin to imagine. I can give them to you."

Alasdair tried to take a hold of himself to ease the ache throbbing between his thighs, but he found his hands immobile by his sides, held prisoner by some kind of invisible force he could not fathom.

"Ti mou kanis?"

"Let go and enjoy. Give yourself to me," the voice cajoled.

Alasdair wanted to do nothing more. For, whatever kind of magic was being weaved, it continued to bring him pleasure beyond his imagination.

"I have been waiting for you for some time, Alasdair Kyriakoús, son of Lapidos. Ise poli omorfos. A man worthy of my attention, if ever I saw one."

Alasdair's breathing accelerated with every word and stroke of his flesh, and he wanted — no, needed — to see. "Show yourself," he demanded on a ragged groan.

The sound that reverberated in his mind was unquestionably immoral. A laugh that he swore was as effective as a siren calling him to the jagged edges of a cliff.

"Are you so sure you wish to see me?"

"Yes," he panted, positive he'd never been more certain of anything in his life. And as the stroking between his legs changed to slow, languid pulls, his eyelids fluttered shut. "I desire your presence."

"Understand, Alasdair. Once you really see me, you can never unsee me again. You will be of my blood. Your life—tied to mine," his angel explained.

At that stage, Alasdair was willing to give anything to get another glimpse of the wonderment he had so briefly witnessed. "I understand. And still wish for nothing more."

With his hands still trapped and his shaft being deliciously manipulated, a warm tongue licked his ear as that melodic voice invited, "Then open your eyes."

AS THE MEMORY was brutally expelled from his mind, Alasdair was brought back to his painful reality. His traitorous cock stiffened between his thighs as his sire's lips twitched. His response had been wanted and noted.

This wasn't anything new between the two of them. It'd been that way from the moment their paths had crossed and he'd been offered eternal life. He'd only had to promise one thing in exchange—eternal devotion.

What *was* new was the declaration about the intimate side of their bond. It'd been rumored over the centuries, but never confirmed, and it was due to the humiliation he'd brought upon Vasilios that he was making such a spectacle now.

I felt you return to the baths tonight, but then the feeling disappeared. So I thought I would remind you. Did you forget that I would sense when you entered them? You are my property, Alasdair. That is where I made it so. You belong to me, agóri.

The possessive words were shoved into his mind with a force belying the velvety tone, which served as a balm for the confused emotions pulsating through his body as he was forced to submit in a way he'd never done before.

"Please, Diomêdês," Vasilios invited aloud, turning to the Ancient on his right—Isadora's sire. Eton, Thanos's sire, was sitting quietly to his left. "Tell my Alasdair what he is charged with. I'm too perturbed to deal with him any longer."

When several witnesses snickered, Vasilios roared out, "Enough!"

Without so much as a glance in the direction of those who'd dared find enjoyment at his displeasure, Alasdair watched his sire's fangs descend in a vile snarl that distorted his handsome face.

The air practically vibrated from the tension weighing it down—and then the coil snapped. A vacuum sound of…*one, two, no—three hearts* being suctioned from their chest cavities echoed off the walls, and then they hit the floor with the dull thump of dead weight.

"Does anyone else find my vexation amusing? If so, please make it be known so we can continue."

The Chamber remained deathly silent.

"Sorry, Diomêdês. Please, begin."

As Vasilios took his seat, his eyes returned to their usual color, and the desire that had been humming through Alasdair vanished so he was left only with the searing pain.

Nothing was more insulting to an Ancient than not showing upon command, and it was considered the highest and most punishable offense. And whatever was about to take place was something he would most certainly live to regret.

"Alasdair Kyriakoús, first sired to Vasilios. You are charged with disobedience, indifference, and contempt. Do you refute these claims?"

"I do not," he managed, his gaze still held by the man he'd failed. His face wasn't giving anything away, and the only way this would end was with his ultimate submission.

"You admit to dismissing a direct summons from your Ancient without offering up perhaps a reason?"

What reason could he give? Certainly not the truth.

"I do," he pushed out through clenched teeth.

"Then you are willing to accept the punishment of Veinious Peeling."

Fucking hell.

The malicious streak his sire was renowned for was in full effect tonight. But he'd be damned if he cowered more than he already had. Instead, Alasdair addressed his Ancient as only he ever did—the same way he did when he entered his bed.

"It would be my pleasure, as the blood of your blood, to give to you my body to do with as you please, my king."

Those jewel-toned eyes gleamed with satisfaction, and a surge of pride flooded Alasdair, that he'd put it there—right before his arms rose involuntarily, palms up and outstretched, and the veins from each were stripped like ribbons to the elbow.

That was when the incredible agony of near death dropped him to the ground like a fucking rock.

Four

LEO STARED AT the wall and wondered for the millionth time, *How do I get myself into these situations?*

He had no idea how long he'd been wherever the hell he was, and it was making him crazy. It could've been days or weeks. There was no way to be sure, but he did know that it'd been a damn long time.

Ever since he'd woken up, he'd been trying to work out where he was. He'd waited hours on end for someone, *anyone*, to walk through a door so he could ask—but no one ever came.

He'd racked his memory to think back to the night he had been taken. Tried to remember when and how it had happened. But nothing was clear. All he had was a distant jumble of memories that made no sense.

The last thing he knew for certain was that he'd walked home from the train station, climbed into bed exhausted, and read for a while about the work he was finally close to completing at the museum: Greek gods, ancient times, and myths.

Then had come the nightmare.

The one where he had been chased and attacked.

Jesus, I've got to be losing my mind, he thought, scrubbing a hand over his face. He was definitely suffering from sleep deprivation, and after having been locked away—*God knows where*—it was no wonder he was starting to believe the unbelievable.

While he'd had nothing to do but think, he'd come to the conclusion that his long hours and perpetual single status must've finally caught up with him to produce someone so damn hot that, even when he'd morphed into a vampire, he hadn't had the desire to run away.

But do I really believe that? That a vampire is holding me captive? Come on, Chapel.

That seemed too ridiculous to even contemplate. Yet, as he sat there, hour after hour, scanning the opulent room he'd been locked inside, the only answers he had come up with were the impossible. His former life and any sense of normalcy seemed like such a foreign concept in his current reality that he wondered how much more he could take.

How many days? How many hours would it take until his mind would start to play tricks on him? Tell him lies?

Hell, maybe it already has.

Because there was no way he would've kept envisioning what he was without having had some kind of snap in his brain synapses.

Over the course of his captivity, he'd begun to catalog in great detail the objects and appearance of the room he'd awoken in. And he'd locked it away for that moment when he would escape and tell the authorities everything he could remember.

The first thing would be: black and gold. He could register those colors in the muted light cast from the three flickering candles that were secured in iron candelabras around the wall. Candles that never seemed to go out.

The second would be the wall itself—and that was the only way it could be described. It was seamless, save for the small en suite off to the side. No entry. No exit. And it was covered with studded, black leather. When he'd finally gotten brave enough to look closer, he'd noticed that each stud was actually a golden coin from the ancient Greek Archaic period—something he never would've known if it hadn't been for his chosen profession.

They were very old and very expensive. And the sheer amount of them had him wondering where the owner had acquired them. It also got him thinking that maybe that was the reason he'd been taken, something to do with his job.

The room had no bed, but there was a massive chair in the center of some sort of raised stage. It looked like a mighty throne with wooden sides carved into flames that swept up towards the high ceiling. When Leo followed the line of them to the center peak, where the metallic roof struts met, he saw the one object that was causing him the most alarm.

A thick, metallic hook hung from a dangling chain. A chain that was threaded through a pulley system and attached to a crank over on the far wall. It was menacing in its silent surveillance.

He stood up on the black rug he'd been sitting on and walked over to where a tray of food had been deposited. The latest of many. He wasn't sure how the meals were being delivered since he never saw anyone enter or leave. But every few hours, a new tray with fresh food and water was left on the floor under one of the flickering candles.

The entire situation was so unusual that he was starting to think maybe he'd never woken up. Maybe *this* was still part of the nightmare he'd been having.

As he looked down to the most recent tray of food, the fleshy thigh of the roasted chicken called to him as his stomach rumbled. He'd decided on the first night that, if he didn't die from eating the food that was left, he would take anything they gave him. That way, he would be strong enough to escape when the time came.

He'd never had to fight a day in his life. Never had cause for it until now. But if it came down to it, he could be as determined as the next guy, and he wouldn't go down without kicking, punching, and inflicting as much damage as possible to the asshole who'd taken him.

As he leaned down to pick the plate up, he heard voices for the first time on the opposite side of the wall. Forgetting the food, he took a step closer and pressed his ear flush against the wall, trying to hear what was being said.

"Christ, Alasdair. I couldn't believe it when I heard."

Leo was surprised to hear a high, feminine lilt to the voice. It'd never crossed his mind that he might've been locked up by a woman.

As if it makes a difference in the end, he chastised himself. *Focus. What do they want?* He wasn't anyone important. He led a normal, everyday life and worked at the National History Museum. No matter how hard he tried, he couldn't think of any reason why someone would take him.

Then the woman started talking again. "It's been—"

"Thirteen days. Trust me, Isa. I am aware."

Leo's entire body tensed at the second voice. He would have recognized it anywhere. It was the same voice that had rendered him mute. The one from his nightmare.

"Diomêdês even seemed baffled over how unmerciful he was to you."

"He showed mercy. We're still alive, aren't we?"

"Hilarious. But still, you can't believe what he did was justified. For one misstep? After all these years."

"I humiliated him. Disobeyed him. Are you trying to tell me that Diomêdês would not do the same?"

Leo thought he heard a shuffling sound, and then that all-too-familiar voice stated, "I'm lucky that's all he did."

Before Leo could wrap his head around the words being said, a voice behind him asked, "Didn't anyone ever tell you that it's rude to eavesdrop?"

Shit. Oh, shit.

That voice—it was much closer now. In fact, he would say that it was inside the room with him.

But how is that possible?

Leo didn't dare move other than to swallow the nervous gulp of air he'd taken. He didn't want to turn around, didn't want to know who, or what, was now with him in a room that had no doors.

"I apologize that it took me so long. I've been somewhat...*detained* these past few days. I trust that Isadora has kept you fed."

The one-sided, oh-so-polite conversation was odd, to say the least, and as Leo remained facing the wall, he wondered if it would be his last.

"Could you perhaps turn around, *file mou*? It would make this much more civilized."

Greek. Leo instantly recognized the words—*my friend.* The man addressing him had slipped into Greek—just like he had in the nightmare. Which might explain the coins on the wall. He filed that piece of information away and slowly turned, not wanting to be "punished" for disobeying.

When he came to a stop, he found himself face-to-face with the stranger from his nightmare. His breath caught in his throat, but this time, it wasn't from nerves. *No.* This time, it was because he was allowing himself his first real look at the man.

Attractive wasn't nearly the right word to describe him. This man—he was divine.

"There. That's much better. I always prefer conversing face-to-face. Don't you?"

Leo continued to stare as he took in every feature that he could see.

A brooding brow emphasized the catlike shape of his green eyes but didn't detract from the strength of his face. Rather, it added a predatory feel as the eyebrows narrowed on him while he continued his inspection.

Leo anxiously licked his parched lips. He knew on a fundamental level he should be afraid of this man. He'd been holding him prisoner for nearly two weeks. But as he continued to look at him, his body was having different ideas altogether.

Stop it, he admonished himself. *Stop thinking with your dick, Chapel. Just because he's hot as hell doesn't mean shit. He's not a good guy.*

But his body wasn't listening.

The classic Roman nose caught his eye next. It was perfectly proportioned for the man's face and sat between high cheekbones that might have made some look feminine, but not this guy. They only enhanced an already stunning appearance. His lips were exactly how Leo imagined the devil would create them—so a lesser man would be tempted to sin. He had a full, pouting lower lip and a bowed top one, and the stubble lining his jaw and upper lip highlighted them in a way that made Leo *very* aware of his unwanted desires.

"Are you choosing not to talk to me, human? Or do you need an extra minute to decide if talking is what you actually wish to do?"

Leo blinked, snapping himself out of the trancelike state he'd been in. Then he lifted his chin and forced himself to speak for the first time in days. "Who are you? What do you want?" And then it occurred to him to ask the one question of utmost importance. "Are you going to hurt me?"

The eyes pinning him to the wall like a thumbtack never wavered. "That's an interesting question. And a couple of days ago, I would have said, 'Wrong time, wrong place.' But things have changed since then."

"What do you mean?" Leo asked, well aware he hadn't answered his question regarding his well-being. "I don't understand any of this."

The man tilted his head to the side, and the coppery highlights in his dark hair shone when the candlelight caught them in their glow. "You don't remember, *file mou*?"

Without thinking, Leo said, "Stop calling me that."

"Calling you what?"

"Your friend," he stated. "We're not friends. I don't even know who you are or why I'm here." His voice got louder as the panic set in all over again.

"You understand Greek?"

Leo bit his bottom lip, deciding that he'd said more than he should have. That clearly hadn't been the right response, however, because with the accuracy of well-wielded whip, a frigid hand clamped around his throat and drew him forward, effortlessly raising him off the ground. His feet dangled, and his breath choked him in gasping pants as he flailed around, reaching out with both hands to try to free himself from the unrelenting hold.

"I asked you a question, human. Answer me."

The face Leo had been admiring only seconds ago began to morph. The forehead furrowed as suspicious eyes studied him, and then white teeth flashed in a cruel sneer as the man's top lip curled back and two wicked sharp fangs appeared. The sheer beauty of him altered to that of a deadly monster in the blink of an eye, and everything came crashing back.

It was true.

The nightmare Leo had started to believe had been a delusion hadn't been a delusion at all. He *had* been chased and attacked by a vampire. By *this* vampire. And as he stared wide-eyed at the creature holding him in midair, Leo knew that whatever he did next would either secure his survival or guarantee his death.

With an overwhelming sense of misplaced courage, he answered, "No."

Without warning, the hand around his neck hurled him across the room to the floor and the candlelight vanished, plunging them into complete darkness. Before he could get his feet under him to stand, a warm breath brushed by his ear.

"Wrong answer."

There was nowhere for him to go as his nightmare crouched in front of him and took his jaw between his fingers, bringing his face around to meet his. Those green eyes flared in the pitch dark and his teeth gleamed white, and all Leo could think was how utterly magnificent he was in his savagery.

THERE WAS A distinct shift in the air, and Alasdair immediately picked up on the emotion. The fear he'd sensed when the man had remembered what he was had vanished, and in its place was a much more curious one—one he could use later.

When he let his tongue come out and slide across the lip he'd pulled back over his teeth, Alasdair discovered that the man looking back at him wasn't scared. He was aroused.

"You continue to surprise me, for a human. And that takes some doing with the years I have been alive. I figured, after your realization, you would be either crying or praying. That's usually what occurs when one such as yourself discovers we exist." He could hear the rapid heartbeat thumping inside the chest inches from him, and as he shifted closer, the man remained rigid. "But prayer won't help you down here, and tears make mortals appear weaker than they already are. And our kind preys on the weak."

The human's face registered shock, and when their eyes clashed, Alasdair's own arousal started to surface. He'd made a vow during those agonizing hours following his punishment that he would unravel the secret as to how this man had debilitated him. And for that reason alone, he would not dispose of him any time soon. Neither would anyone else, for that matter.

"If you're going to kill me," the man said bravely, "just do it."

Alasdair tightened his fingers on the chin he was holding, silencing him. "I don't plan to kill you. At least, not yet."

He released his hold and backed away, bringing the candles back to life with a mere thought. Then he stared down at the man, who was still on the floor, and thought, *No…we have too much to discuss. And no one is going to touch you until I have my answers.*

LEO KEPT A wary eye on the unpredictable vampire as he paced back and forth. He was both fascinated and terrified as he watched him move about. He'd never been in the presence of something so ancient *and* alive. As an archaeologist and lover of history, he was in awe.

The creature walked as if he were gliding across the surface, his motions fluid and soundless. He had broad shoulders currently covered by a loose, white button-down shirt, and where Leo would have guessed him to be around six three, maybe six four, he now realized that wasn't the case at all.

This vampire, who had picked him up like some kind of rag doll, was six foot at the most. Like him.

"Get up."

Leo raised his head but remained where he was. *Maybe, if I stay still, he won't —*

"I said—" *Get. Up.*

This time, the order entered Leo's mind, and before he could even try to understand how that had happened, he was on his feet and toe-to-toe with the male. Almost like his brain was issuing an instruction that *he* was not giving. He tried to clear the fog swirling through his head, but it was no use. It was as if it were squashing down his own thoughts while being manipulated into doing someone else's.

Look at me.

Leo's eyes fastened on the face opposite him as he stood transfixed.

"There's something different about you," the vampire drawled as he left Leo's line of sight. It wasn't until he spoke again that Leo realized he was now behind him. "I want to know what it is."

Still unable to move or talk, Leo remained helpless to do anything but listen as he tried to sift through his blurry thoughts.

Who are you? Tell me your name.

The question was shoved inside his head, and he couldn't stop himself from answering.

"Leo. Leonidas Chapel."

"Ahh. That explains one thing. We have something in common, you and I. I, too, am of Greek descent. Wouldn't that be a stroke of ironic fate? If you were of my bloodline all those years ago?"

Leo's heart raced when he realized what was happening. He'd somehow lost complete control over his free will, and there was no way to stop himself from giving any and all information to the one who was demanding answers.

Tell me everything about you in less time than it takes for me to become bored.

Without a second thought, Leo rattled off, "I'm twenty-seven years old, an only child, and I lost my mother three months ago to cancer." His throat physically tightened around the words, practically choking him, even as the drive to continue talking remained. "I'm an archeologist, and I work as a curator at the National History Museum downtown."

His mouth clamped shut after that, his brain deciding that that was the right amount of information to give. The room was so incredibly still he thought he'd been left alone. That the vampire had done that thing where he vanished from sight—but a warm breath skimmed the back of his neck and a third question was asked.

That's everything? I don't think so. How did you stop me that night in your room? What are you, Leonidas?

Leo's mind started to whirl—as if it were sifting through every thought and memory he'd ever had. Like someone flicking through a filing cabinet in search of an answer to the question.

It wasn't until he saw a shadow out of the corner of his eye that he was aware that the one who was questioning him was walking back around to face him. He stared at the vampire, who was waiting with a look of dangerous interest on his face, and then his expression intensified when he finally replied, "I don't know."

Five

HE DIDN'T BELIEVE him—*the human.* Or perhaps he'd call him Leonidas now. As Alasdair circled him, he looked over his naked chest and back, checking for any kind of supernatural markings. Any indicator that he wasn't merely the human he claimed to be. But there was nothing.

"I don't believe you," Alasdair said when he stopped in front of him.

Leo watched him with the blank stare of someone under the force of compulsion, and Alasdair found himself disliking the dull expression on him. It was an odd thought to have since he'd never given much credence to any others' reactions in the past. But he quickly removed the fog from Leo's mind and watched the light of awareness spark back in the eyes focused on him.

Then Alasdair asked, "Are you telling me the truth?" He waited for Leo to regain control over both his mind and his body, and when Leo finally spoke, the words were not what he'd been expecting.

"It's hard not to when you're being forced. How did you do that?"

Well, well, Alasdair thought. *Isn't that curious. Remembering what happened after a full compulsion.* "I did something to you? What? Pray tell."

"You were in my head," Leo accused and took a wary step back. "Somehow controlling my thoughts. My actions."

"Was I?" Alasdair asked. Then he closed the distance between them, unable to fight the desire to be close to the human. "You felt me inside your mind?"

Those wary eyes of Leo's darted over his shoulder as Isadora appeared in the room. Alasdair had sensed her before she had faded in, but he hadn't wanted to turn away from the wired man. Leo's tense shoulders and fidgety hands gave him away. He was ready to bolt if given the chance.

Not that he'd get very far.

His hair was like it had been the first time Alasdair had seen him—sticking out at every angle, in complete disarray, as if he'd been worrying it with his hands. Considering his circumstances, Alasdair imagined that was exactly why it was a mess—but somehow, the mess suited this guy. As did the strong line of his jaw, which he had a sudden desire to scrape his teeth along.

His eyes were intelligent but jumpy as hell as they continued shifting between him and his cousin, trying to work them out like some kind of puzzle. Then a frown appeared between his eyebrows.

He asked, "How did she do that?"

Unfazed by the question, Alasdair forced his thoughts into Leo's mind. *It's nothing that concerns you.*

"Shit. I mean…" Leo shook his head. "How do you do that? It's…it's weird as hell, but totally fascinating."

Blindsided by the curiosity in Leo's voice, Alasdair actually found himself on the verge of explaining the finer workings of how he enters a mind, that he could only communicate inside his head this way because he'd fed from him. But that would have to wait, because suddenly, he felt *him*—Vasilios.

He twisted his head to the side to acknowledge Isadora for the first time. Her eyes flicked towards Leo and then back to him. The reason for her arrival was now crystal clear.

Fuck. Fuck. He'd thought he'd have more time. *What the hell am I going to tell him?*

Alasdair wrapped his fingers around Leo's bicep, holding him in place. "Listen to me very carefully. If you want to live past the next five minutes, do exactly what I tell you to."

The curiosity from seconds ago vanished, and a frown of concern formed between his brows. "I thought you said you weren't going to kill me."

Alasdair tugged him close and shoved his face in so their noses touched. "I'm about to be the least of your worries. If you want to live, keep your eyes down, your mouth shut, and your thoughts empty. I may be the only one who can talk inside your head, but all of us can *hear* exactly what others are thinking—so don't think at all."

Alasdair pushed him away before he could respond, and with lightning speed, he moved across the room to stand side by side with Isadora, who was glaring at him like he was certifiable.

"I can't believe you're risking us both. For *him*?" she hissed under her breath.

"He's uncommon for a human. Wouldn't you agree?"

"You mean he's appealing and you want to fuck him."

"Well, that too."

"He's far too curious, Alasdair. And stupid, for that matter. Talking to you in such a manner, asking all those questions. Who does he think he is?" she asked. "Not that it matters. He'll be dead within seconds. No mortal can control their thoughts when Vasilios is near. And I hardly think he'll be overjoyed to find out what his precious Alasdair has been up to this past month. "

"Shut it, Isa. If you stop acting as if there's something wrong, he will merely do whatever it is he's coming for and then leave."

The air in the room vibrated under the enormity of power that had entered it as she replied, "You're mad if you think he won't notice there's more going on here. It's as obvious as your cock every time that male looks at you."

"The only thing going on here is what you said: curiosity. A mystery. One I wish to get to the bottom of."

Isadora parted her glossy lips to retort, but she shut her mouth as Vasilios, striking as ever, walked over to them.

"Alasdair. Isadora. Finally, I have found you." He said it as if he'd been looking for hours. In actuality, it would've only taken him seconds to pin point the two of them if he had truly been trying to find their location.

"So you have." Isadora smiled tightly.

Alasdair stepped around her, deliberately pulling the attention to himself. He was the one distraction his Ancient could never resist.

"You're looking very debonair this evening," Alasdair told him as he ran his fingers down the arm of Vasilios's black suit jacket.

"I have an engagement to attend to. A meeting of utmost importance, I am told. Diomêdês called it. But I wanted to come and see you first since I heard you were...back on your feet, shall we say."

Alasdair extended his arms out to the sides and gave a slight bow. "As you can see. I'm in perfect health once more."

Vasilios drank in the sight of him. He inspected his body as if searching for any permanent damage after their last encounter. Alasdair could see the lustful desire in that gaze, but as those eyes traveled over his face and then lower, they creased around the edges in question.

Alasdair looked down his own body to see what the issue was, and that's when he spotted the three buttons missing at the bottom of his shirt. The white material was parted, showing the button to his pants. It must've happened earlier, when he threw Leo across the room.

"Did I interrupt something between you two?" Vasilios asked, glancing from him to Isadora, who was shaking her head vehemently.

"*No.* You certainly did not."

"You needn't sound so appalled," Vasilios assured her. "Alasdair has a spectacular cock, and he knows exactly how to use it."

Alasdair thought his cousin's eyes might fall out of their sockets with the fierce way she was glaring at him.

"I'll be sure to take that into consideration if, for some reason, there are no other options available and someone has chopped off both my hands, leaving him as the *last* person in the world I could go to for an orgasm."

Alasdair inclined his head when her spiel ended, thinking of the one time they'd been together. "Touché, cousin. Touché."

A playful but vindictive smile stretched her lips as she slowly stepped aside, drawing all attention towards the *other* occupant in the room. The one who was standing behind them exactly how Alasdair had instructed.

Silent, still, and with his eyes on the floor.

"Vasilios, have you seen Alasdair's…yielding?" She knew full well that Vasilios had not and that Leo was no such thing. "I thought he was going to send them all away as usual. But this one," she purred, "he seems rather taken with."

"Is that so?" Vasilios replied, the man across the room now becoming his primary focus.

"Isa has it wrong," Alasdair grit out, promising himself that she would pay for this. "He's not *my* anything."

"No? Then why is he here?" Vasilios asked as he turned back to face him. But before anything came to mind, Vasilios cupped his cheek. "*Ahh,* Alasdair. You do know how to please me. You brought me a gift after disappointing me last week." He stepped between him and Isadora and put a hand on his shoulder.

Alasdair caught his cousin's self-satisfied grin as she faded from the room. Then his attention was drawn back to Vasilios as he trailed his fingers down his chest while making his way towards Leo, who, thirteen days ago, was going to be a gift to *himself.*

"He's not a gift," he rushed out as he followed behind. "And certainly not fit enough to be presented to one such as you, Vasilios."

Vasilios halted his footsteps and then pivoted back in his direction. "He is not *fit* for me?"

Alasdair watched the male he'd been bound to for over two millennia look over at the man standing in the shadows cast by the candlelight—the one he couldn't seem to get out of his head. "That's right."

"He certainly looks fit from where I'm standing," he mused. "But I think I need to see him up close. What do you say?"

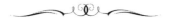

THE ROOM HE'D been locked in for the past thirteen days was full of tension. Fear or sexual, or maybe both, Leo couldn't decide as he listened to their voices.

Like the vampire Alasdair had suggested, he kept his eyes on the hardwood beneath his bare feet while the others conversed as if he wasn't even there. The third occupant who'd joined them, clearly a male, had a voice that Leo imagined would belong to angels, if they existed.

Deep and harmonious, it instantly caught and held his attention, urging him to raise his head and look into the face it belonged to. But Leo didn't dare follow that instinct after what Alasdair had told him.

Instead, he pressed his palms to his thighs and willed himself to remain still and think of nothing at all. Somehow, he knew in the pit of his stomach that who, or whatever, was now walking towards him was someone he should fear. He wasn't even looking at the individual, but he was smart enough to know when he was in a room with someone more powerful than he.

The shiny tips of black leather dress shoes stopped in front of him, and Leo heard, "Raise your eyes, human."

Leo's body reacted to the order with a shudder, and gooseflesh raised over his skin as he lifted his head, determined to do as he had been told. He wanted to live, and if what Alasdair had said was true, this was the man, *or vampire*, who'd decide if that would happen.

His eyes trailed over long legs encased in dress pants, and he wondered what exactly he would find when he...

Oh wow.

"Good evening, *agóri.*"

Before he could think not to, Leo's mind was flooded with thoughts. The first being that, if Alasdair was the most beautiful male he'd ever seen, then this man... He had no words. He was simply—

"Oh, Alasdair, you have a true admirer here."

A rush of heat hit Leo's cheeks as his thoughts were interrupted and the vampire addressed Alasdair.

"He thinks you are quite beautiful."

Alasdair's stare found his, and he ran his tongue over his top lip, causing Leo's pulse to thump. "Does he now?"

"Yes, he does," the other vampire stated matter-of-factly, returning his gaze to him. "But he thinks I'm indescribable. Of course."

The arrogance dripping off his tongue had Leo more than aware that this being, whoever he was, knew his effect on others. He had an aura about him that commanded one's attention. Not only from his undeniably good looks, but in the way he held himself.

With his black hair and jade eyes, Leo couldn't help but stare. He was dressed for a black-tie dinner, his broad shoulders filling out his jacket to perfection, and his trim waist was accentuated by the tailored cut of the suit. He looked sophisticated, worldly, and the very epitome of the word gentleman. But in his eyes lurked darkness, and it made Leo wary as hell as he waited, silent and unmoving.

It was quite obvious that, in this world, *his world*, there was none more deadly.

Ordering himself to blank out his mind, Leo thought of emptiness and black holes. As that filled his head, the vampire took a step closer and the hair on Leo's arms stood even taller, if that were possible. Even his body was aware of the danger it was in.

"You are quite the vision yourself. The light hair, those eyes. You remind me of someone…"

Knowing he wasn't to speak unless told to, Leo remained mute. He couldn't believe what was happening. He still didn't have any idea where he was, but he knew one thing for sure: He was in the presence of beings more powerful and destructive than he had ever known existed.

"Alasdair? Does he remind you of anyone we know?"

Alasdair stood beside the one now inspecting Leo like a bug under a microscope, and Leo's pulse jumped.

"Ahh, listen to his heart pound whenever you gaze upon him." The vampire laughed, the sound hedonistic. "Do it again, Alasdair. It's very amusing how affected he is by you."

Even though it went against his "question everything" nature, Leo let the two who held his life in their hands analyze him.

"Why is that so amusing? Do you not think I'm worthy of such a response?" Alasdair asked as if deeply offended by the taunting vampire's words.

The air in the room thickened with tension, clearly sexual in nature this time. The suited male turned towards Alasdair and placed a hand on his white shirt.

"I think you are worthy of a much greater response than a thumping pulse and an aching erection, *omorfo mou agóri.*"

My beautiful boy, Leo thought, again translating the Greek. He couldn't tear his attention away from what he was witnessing as Alasdair arched a perfectly sculpted eyebrow and asked, "Such as?"

The male moved even closer and ran his palm down Alasdair's abdomen to the visible skin at the top of his pants, where he drew his finger over the button securing them. Not only did Leo's heart pound at the seductive caress, but his cock stiffened as if he were the one being touched.

Several different feelings competed for dominance then.

Flight, fight, and—*yes, as a gay man watching the epitome of masculine sexuality and beauty*—fuck.

With his dick hard and sweat beading on his forehead, Leo suddenly had the urge to fuck someone or watch the act take place.

Christ. What's the matter with me? he thought as the one in the suit recaptured his attention by cradling one of Alasdair's cheeks. He then leaned in and dragged his tongue up the other side of Alasdair's neck and sank his teeth into the dark stubble on his jaw.

Damn, they're hot together. Dark, dangerous, and totally focused on one another. It was as though he were no longer in the room.

Alasdair tipped his head back, and the other male slid his mouth down under his chin and over his Adam's apple. Leo glanced at the hand on Alasdair's waist, and the fingers there unbuttoned his pants before the soft sound of a zipper being lowered echoed around the room. Leo then fisted his hands by his sides.

He wanted nothing more than to shove his fingers inside his own damn pants and grip his aching shaft. But he didn't dare move as the suited one dropped down to his knees. He parted Alasdair's pants, and when his thick, veiny erection came into view, Leo's knees weakened.

Fucking hell. He couldn't believe what was happening. It was unreal.

He'd been wishing for this very scene only moments ago, but he hadn't actually expected it to happen. Yet, as he stood there, feet away from the two horny-as-hell males, he was pretty fucking close to coming. No touch or stimulation required.

A raspy sound emanated from Alasdair as the one he'd called Vasilios circled his erection with his fingers. Alasdair clasped the back of the male's head and jerked it forward, cursing when the other vampire's hand came up to rest on his thigh.

"*Ypomoní agóri*. You're so eager," Vasilios said—right before he lowered his head and swallowed Alasdair's cock down his throat.

A groan ripped through the air then, and when Alasdair's eyes lifted from the one at his feet, Leo realized that the sound had come from between his own lips.

Oh shit, he thought and quickly shut his mouth. But he wasn't sure he could stop himself from masturbating to the scene playing out right *there*. He continued to stare, unwilling to miss out on what was going on only an arm's length away. If the punishing way Alasdair was fucking the mouth sliding up and down his shaft was any indication, he didn't care one way or another what Leo did as long as he got to come down the throat of the other male.

They were intoxicating together, and when a growl resonated throughout the room, Leo's focus shifted back to Alasdair, whose teeth were now bared to him. From the taut way the skin was pulled across Alasdair's cheekbones to the glow in his eyes, it looked as though he was closing in on his climax. Leo wondered briefly what had triggered the fangs.

And how would they feel against *his* skin. *Wait a fucking minute. What?*

His teeth, Leonidas. He's using his teeth on my cock, and it makes me fucking crazy. Just as you're imagining mine on yours now.

The impure thought was thrust into his head, and it had Leo's eyes seeking out the devilish ones of the man who'd put it there. When he found Alasdair fixated on him, Leo licked his lower lip.

He wasn't sure what he was supposed to do next. *Lower his head? Turn away?* But even as he ordered himself to look at his feet, he couldn't help himself from watching, wanting to see how this would play out. He was positive he would never be able to erase it from his mind.

Alasdair was pulling the other male to his feet now, and once he was there, he took his mouth in a brutal-as-fuck kiss. As the two began to devour one another, Leo told himself that it was just a kiss. Then Alasdair's hands gripped the ass of the suit and hauled him close so he could grind his naked erection against him.

He'd seen hundreds of men kissing in the clubs, bars, and parties he went to. But with the way Alasdair had pushed his thoughts into his head, it was like he was now involved.

Alarmed and aroused by everything he could see and hear, Leo dropped his gaze, and he was glad he did, because that was when the other vampire finally chose to speak. His voice was raspy and low, and it was seductive in its delivery as he vowed, "You, Alasdair, are worthy of pleasures you will *only* find in my mouth and my bed."

As a frustrated sound surrounded them, Leo had a feeling the pleasure portion of this evening was over and Alasdair was now being taught some kind of lesson.

"So keep your yielding. And when you mark him later, know that I am the one who made you need the release. But don't let his pretty face enchant you—you've always been so good about disposing of your food once you were done."

The jarring reminder of who they were, and who *he* was, slammed into Leo with the force of a wrecking ball.

Mark me? Dispose of me? With those teeth? That does not sound pleasant.

"You have my word," Alasdair murmured. "I'll get what I need from him, and that shall be all."

The words weren't a promise of his imminent death, but they still did nothing to bring any comfort to Leo as the two figures vanished from sight.

Six

"YOU HAVE CHANGED these past few weeks, Alasdair."

The serious tone in Vasilios's voice as they left Leo and reappeared outside the Adjudication Room had Alasdair bracing himself for whatever might follow. He already had a severe case of fucking blue balls after having been denied a release, and as he looked at Vasilios, he wanted nothing more than to be finished off by him—and his sire knew it.

"Always so sure. That was my *agóri*. A picture of contentment in who and what he is. But lately…" He paused, and his knowing eyes shifted to the wall Leo was behind. "Lately, you have changed."

Alasdair bowed his head respectfully. And when Vasilios placed a finger under his chin, raising it, and moved in so they were a whisper apart, he caught Alasdair's lips in a kiss designed to make him want to weep. He remembered a similar one from the night Vasilios had finally come to him. The night he'd made him his.

"What is so special about this one, Alasdair?"

Alasdair thought about that first night when he'd noticed Leo and tried to pinpoint what he'd felt the precise moment he'd seen him. But when Vasilios's lips brushed over his again, nothing was in his mind but the male seducing him.

"You are so quiet lately. In your mind *and* your voice. As if you are hiding something from me. I don't like you blocking me out. It troubles me."

It troubled him too. But he had nothing to say. All he had were questions, and he wasn't ready to share them yet. Or risk his life, for that matter, over a strange fixation with a human.

Vasilios moved his mouth over to his jaw and slowly kissed his way up towards his ear. Desire shot through him as those tantalizing lips continued to weave a spell over him, and his cock strained against the confines of his pants.

"*Se thelo, file mou,*" Vasilios rasped in his ear, and Alasdair's hands clutched at the arms of his suit. "But you want the one in that room, don't you?"

He thought about lying for a second, but when the tip of Vasilios's tongue flicked over his lobe, all other thoughts left his mind.

"I am not averse to the thought of the *both* of you in my bed, Alasdair. Although I am not pleased with how taken you are by him. I believe that is something I need to think on before I allow him to join us. Until then, if you choose to dip your dick inside him, do it away from this lair. Away from where I have to hear you."

The bite of jealousy in his sire's words was evident. Alasdair had never before taken a yielding on, so the emotions running through both of them were new and…unfamiliar.

"I have not yet taken him as a yielding."

"But you want to. Alasdair, with as long as we exist and thrive upon the Earth, it makes sense that we would need something different time and again. I understand that. What's important is that you know whom you come back to. Whom you *belong* to. I've never had reason to be concerned in the past. You've never doubted this before. Are you doubting it now?"

Alasdair shook his head. "No. Of course not."

Vasilios crossed his arms over his chest. "I hope not. You seem to be faltering of late. Do not forget: There are many degrees of closeness. Remember your promise the night you were turned. Remember your vow. That cannot change because something shiny has caught your eye. You and I, we live in a state of symbiosis. There's intimate, and then there's life. *We* are of the life variety. You live because of me, and I because of you. Try to remember that and things will remain pleasant for you."

As Vasilios walked down the corridor, Alasdair watched him go. The male still had the ability to arouse and put him in his place all at the same time, and as he rounded the corner out of Alasdair's view the words, *If you forget whom you belong to, ómorfo mou agóri, things will be unbearable,* lingered inside his mind.

Alasdair closed his eyes and tried to get his fucking head on straight. What was the matter with him? He needed to pull his shit together before he faced the human again.

Seven

ELIAS FONTANA, THE director of the National History Museum, glanced at the clock on the corner of his desk. It was a George III Walnut Bracket Clock, circa seventeenth century, one of his most prized possessions, and it currently read ten thirty p.m.

He scrubbed a palm over his face and stretched his neck from side to side in an effort to ease the tension knot that had formed there. For the past two years, he and his staff had worked nonstop to get their latest exhibit off the ground. He was tired and stressed, but they were now ready to unveil the exhibit: The Gods and Myths of Ancient Greece.

Any other time before an opening like this, Leo, Paris, and he would head over to The Dirty Dog to celebrate the long, arduous hours they'd put into creating a piece of history. At the same time, they'd commiserate over the social lives they'd neglected to do so. But the pub wasn't in the cards tonight because one key person was missing—Leo.

Elias stood from behind his desk and placed his letter opener back on the inbox tray. He'd finally finished catching up on his mail after having neglected it for the past week, his mind having been preoccupied. He buttoned his suit jacket then switched off the lamp that sat opposite the clock and looked at the date displayed. It was the last day in October, and it'd been nearly two weeks since his friend and colleague had disappeared.

He'd known Leo for a little over ten years, ever since he'd walked into the offices at the university he'd worked at and asked for a course outline for his bachelor's degree in archaeology. Elias remembered the fresh-faced kid like it was yesterday. He'd been young, seventeen at the most, while he himself had just celebrated his twenty-seventh birthday. Over the next four years, Elias had watched him become one of the brightest students he'd ever had the privilege of teaching.

Around the same time Leo had graduated, he'd finished his master's degree in ancient history and moved on to pursue what he really wanted: to work in one of the top museums in the country. It wasn't until a couple of years later that Leonidas Chapel walked back into his life and interviewed for a job as one of his curators.

Now, that man was missing.

Elias crossed the office to the door and took his coat off the antique rack in the corner. Then he folded it over his arm, and as he reached for the handle, the door was pushed open.

Standing in front of him was Paris Antoniou, the museum's head registrar. His wild, sable-colored hair was tied the best he'd been able to manage at the nape of his neck, and he had a pencil stuck behind his ear. His black T-shirt with his favorite band's logo across the front was covered in dust, and beneath the neckline was a quarter-sized hole. He had a white glove on one hand, and in the other, he was clutching a piece of paper in a death grip.

"I think I may have something," he said, pushing past him into the office.

Sighing, Elias replaced his coat on the rack and switched the light on.

Paris held the piece of paper out to him. "I was going through—"

"Snooping?" Elias interrupted.

"No. I was *going through* some of Leo's things while I was down in his dungeon packing up...well, you know. You're the one who told me to go and do it."

Elias took a step forward and reached for the paper. He'd hated giving Paris the task of clearing out Leo's office, but after two weeks of no phone calls and the police getting involved, it'd seemed time to box things up.

Leo's handwritten scrawl was all over the paper. There were three dates, all fairly recent, starting towards the end of September.

9/25/15, 1:13 a.m. — Strange dream tonight. I was standing in a huge room at an altar or something, and there was a light. A bright, blinding light. And I was holding something in my hand. A scroll? A map, maybe? Usually I wouldn't care about writing it down, but it felt so real that I want to keep a record. - Leo

10/02/15, 2:13 a.m. — Tonight I had the same dream. The light, the altar, the rolled-up paper in my hand. I still have no clue what it means. I need to look this stuff up online, see if I can find anything. Maybe I should've stayed at the pub longer tonight for my birthday. Then I might've dreamed something more exciting. Or sexy. I'm probably exhausted from the past few weeks finishing up this exhibit. Note to self: Tell Elias to pay me more. - Leo

Elias glanced at Paris, a wary look in his eye. "Okay. He was stressed and having dreams. I don't think the police can do much with 'huge room,' and 'a big, bright light.'"

Paris rolled his eyes and stepped beside him, turning so he too was facing the paper. Then he pointed to the final date. "Read that one, smartass."

10/09/15, 3:13 a.m. — Okay, this is getting strange now. Same room, same light, but this time, I recognized the scroll in my hand. It's the Scriptures of Delphi that I've been reading about. Vampires and gods... Hmm, sexy combination. Maybe I just need to get laid by a hot guy so I stop imagining strong, dominant males.

"Look at the date and the time, Elias," Paris said, pointing to each.

As the pieces of the puzzle Paris was pointing to started to fit together, Elias's chest tightened. Each date Leo had written down was a Friday. As was the day he had gone missing. Add to that the times he'd been having the dreams.

Elias remembered that the police had said that all the clocks in Leo's house had been stopped on 4:13 a.m.

His mind raced with the possibilities, both feasible and not so feasible, and his lips moved, but no words came out.

Paris was right. He *had* found something.

It was time.

It was happening.

And the piece of paper in his hand might be the only link to finding their friend alive.

Eight

AS SOON AS he was alone, Leo pressed his hands to the wall surrounding him, frantically running his palms over the supple leather surface. *Maybe I missed something,* he thought as he searched for a lever or some kind of hidden panel. He needed to get out of there. Now.

Before Alasdair came back to "dispose" of him.

Why the hell is this happening to me? He still didn't have that answer. One minute, he'd been at work, getting ready to launch the biggest project of his career, and now, there he was, trapped in a warped kind of nightmare, staring at all of his most sinful desires—

Oh no. No, no. He couldn't, and wouldn't, fantasize about someone who wanted him dead. No matter how sexy he was.

I need to get out of here. He's messing with my head.

As he moved his fingers over the curved wall, he shoved the image of the two males aside and instead started to think about his friends. What would they be thinking right now? Elias and Paris?

God only knows.

They'd known him his entire adult life, and he'd never just…disappeared.

If I were in their position, what would I be thinking?

He had no idea. It wouldn't be anything good though. That was for damn sure.

Resting his forehead against the surface, he cupped the back of his neck, frustrated at his hopeless situation.

It was all so strange. Surreal, even. And none of it made any sense. Then again, his world now involved vampires, so *sense* seemed to be a pretty big fucking leap of sanity in an otherwise insane reality.

And why is Alasdair hell-bent on thinking I'm hiding things from him?

There wasn't anything exceptional about him, unless it was his expertise in his chosen occupation they were after.

That has to be it, right?

Both men had spoken Greek, a language he was fluent in due to his upbringing and his studies. And the coins on the wall… Leo assessed the one right in front of him again and ran his finger over it.

Yes, they are definitely from the Archaic period.

For the last two years, he, Elias, and Paris had been working around the clock on their exhibit. What would they want with him in correlation to that? It still didn't make any sense.

When he came up with nothing, he let out an annoyed sigh. He wasn't hiding shit, and no matter what he told Alasdair, he wouldn't believe him.

Hell, at this point, he wished he *could* think of something convincing to get this over with. But then he'd be dead, and he wasn't quite ready for that yet.

"See? I knew you'd be a fighter."

Leo's spine stiffened at Alasdair's voice.

"Turn around."

"Fuck off," Leo retorted, sick and tired of being toyed with. Having expected harsh retaliation, he was dumbfounded when a deep laugh filled the room.

"Turn around, Leonidas," Alasdair instructed again, and then, inside his mind, he added, *Or would you like me to make you?*

Clenching his fists by his sides, Leo reluctantly did as he was told. Alasdair stood before him, his hands behind his back. He was sexy as sin, and the smug expression on his face told Leo that he knew it.

"Have you come to get rid of me?" Leo asked, unable to stop himself. What did he think he was doing, provoking the guy? But there was an anger radiating inside him that hadn't been there before. It was making him brave.

Stupid, but brave.

Alasdair brought his hands out from behind his back, and Leo immediately stepped away, unsure of his intentions.

"No need to run. I already told you I am not going to kill you…"

As his voice trailed off, Leo could practically hear the word *yet* begging to be tacked onto the end of that statement.

"Give me your left wrist."

Leo dropped his gaze to the object Alasdair was holding and shook his head. "You've got to be kidding."

"Do I strike you as the jovial sort?" he asked, taking another step forward. "Now, let's try this again. Give me your left wrist."

"Why?"

Instead of answering, Alasdair snatched Leo's wrist up between cool fingers and shackled it with the iron manacle. As the unyielding metal locked into place, Leo reached for it with his free hand, trying to pry it loose.

"Don't bother," Alasdair said and then tugged on the chain attached to the cuff. "There's no way to break free until I release you."

"And when will that be?" Leo asked, raising his eyes.

Alasdair shrugged, and the move was so…human that he almost seemed normal. That was until his lip curled up at the side and the razor point of one of his canines became visible, which sent a shudder through Leo's confused body.

"Whenever I decide."

"I don't get it," Leo muttered, still running his fingers over the metal in a futile attempt to extricate himself. "What do you even want from me?"

Alasdair wound the chain around his hand, and Leo was forced to move with it or stumble. When he was only inches from the vampire, Alasdair whispered, "I'm not quite sure yet. However, as soon as I decide, I will either tell you or you will be dead. For now, you're coming with me."

ALASDAIR STRODE ACROSS the room towards the pulley on the opposite wall, dragging Leo behind him. "Pick up the pace, Leonidas. Trust me when I say you won't like the alternative to walking on your own."

He glanced over his shoulder in time to see Leo straighten up and start to walk at a normal speed.

"Very good," he said when they both came to a stop. "You and I are going to go on a little field trip."

"What?"

"We're going back to your apartment. I want to know what it is you're not telling me."

"I'm not hiding anything. I don't know how many times I have to say it."

"You can say it a million times and I still won't believe you. Stay here," he instructed, looping one of the chain links over a hook attached to the wall.

On his way to the en suite to change his shirt, Alasdair paused when Leo muttered something under his breath. He then pivoted back around and faded out—only to fade back in directly opposite his human companion.

"What did you just say?" he asked as Leo's mouth fell open and he backed up to hit the wall.

"N-nothing."

Alasdair stroked his thumb over Leo's jugular. "That's twice now. Let's not make it three times."

He thought Leo would cower, but as he looked into his eyes, he saw the pupils...dilate. Vasilios had been right. Although he didn't want to be, Leo was very much attracted to him. The flushed cheeks, the rush of blood he could hear traveling south, and those heavy, lust-laden eyes. They all gave the human away—and made Alasdair want to fuck him until he could no longer stand.

Yes. He could use this to his advantage

"What's twice?"

Alasdair flicked his gaze down to the lips asking the question, and when the vein under his thumb throbbed in response, so did Alasdair's cock.

"That's *twice* you have lied to me. Don't do it a third time. Now. What. Did. You. Say?"

"I-I said," Leo said, slightly breathless.

Alasdair stroked him again. "You said what?"

"You're having…I don't know…some issues when it comes to me. So I said why don't you ask the suit guy, the one you called Vasilios, to read my mind?"

Disgusted that Leo was right and he *was* having issues with him, Alasdair abruptly spun away. He'd never come across someone who could best him, and he was more than a little irritated that Leo seemed to have worked that out.

"I am not having issues trusting you. I am having issues with believing for one second you are who you say you are. And do not speak his name. Not ever."

"You asked—"

"Stop talking," he thundered and turned back to see that Leo had indeed stopped talking. "You are very brave all of a sudden."

Leo raised his arm, the chain rattling. "What have I got to lose? That hook up there isn't for fun and games, I assume."

Despite himself, Alasdair wanted to smile for the first time in a long while. "Certainly not fun for you, no. Perhaps, for me." He pointed to the chain and stated, "*That* is going to attach to me. Not the hook on the ceiling."

"To you?"

"Yes. As in, I will be holding it."

"Like…like a leash?"

Alasdair thought about that for a second and then inclined his head in a slight nod. "Yes, if you want to think of it that way."

He studied the disgust that twisted Leo's mouth, but that didn't stop him from talking again.

"You lead people…us…I mean, humans, around on a leash? Like what? A pet? A slave? Some kinky fetish deal where you suck our blood dry and then kill us?"

Alasdair stalked forward until Leo's ass hit the wall. Then he brushed his lips over the neatly cut hair around the man's ear.

"I assure you, Leonidas. If I get kinky with anyone, they are more than happy to be chained up, hooked up, or fucked up by me. And if I decide to kill them afterwards, they are so high that they beg me for that release."

Alasdair flicked his tongue over Leo's cheek, and when he felt him shiver, he didn't have to be inside his head to know that it hadn't been from fear.

"Your kind," Leo asked, and Alasdair heard his pulse skip. "You kill *during* sex?"

The question was pitched low, Leo's voice raspy, and when he replied, "Sometimes…" Leo shifted his head so they were practically nose to nose.

This human was curious in the most unusual ways. Asking questions Alasdair would think would horrify him. But the telltale signs of arousal told him otherwise and had Alasdair fighting every instinct he had to keep his teeth off of him.

He'd always been a master at controlling his inner savage, until now. Of course, when it was of the utmost

importance, he was finding the challenge difficult. He
needed to move.

Now.

"But—" Leo said, stopping when Alasdair shifted
away so fast that the breeze from his departure ruffled his
blond hair.

"But?" he prodded when he was several feet away.

Leo blinked and then started again. "But the chain. It
can attach to the hook on the roof if you want it to. Can't it?"

Alasdair backed away from the brave and ever-
inquisitive human. "Oh yes, *file mou.* It most certainly can.
And that would be a fun game indeed."

THAT DOESN'T TELL me much, Leo thought as Alasdair
disappeared into the en suite, which left him to stare at the
ceiling.

He yanked at the cuff on his wrist again and cursed.
His heart was working double time as it tried to pump his
blood frenetically through his veins while also racing it
down to the rock-solid erection straining against his thin
pants.

When Alasdair's breath had swept over him and
he'd started talking about death and sex, God help him, his
cock had gotten harder with every fucked-up scenario he'd
imagined. Then add in the tongue along his cheek and Leo

was left contemplating his own sanity if he thought that sex with this guy, thing—*vampire*—was worth his life.

He was not going to get out of there alive, and as images of what that hook might be used for crashed into his head, he berated his lust-hazed mind.

This is where I'm going to die, he thought, and any desire he'd been feeling disappeared as a fresh wave of nausea tightened his gut.

What if Alasdair decided on a whim to hang him up and feed on him until he was drained? Or what if he hung him up and cut him open chest to sternum like they used to back in England…

"Hung, drawn, and quartered?" that silky voice asked as it sliced through the air.

Leo looked over and saw that Alasdair had come out of the en suite in a black, buttoned shirt.

"That's so messy. Especially the drawn-and-quartering part."

Leo studied the cocksure walk of the male coming his way and heard himself saying, "You get a perverse kind of pleasure out of this, don't you?"

"Out of?"

"My confusion. My fear. It turns you on, right? What kind of sick fuck are you?"

"Is that a trick question?" Alasdair asked, unhooking the chain. "I'm not a person, Leonidas. I'm vampire. That's the kind of sick fuck I am."

Leo struggled to pull away. "I don't want to be led from here like a dog. Or beamed up out of here," he rushed out, thinking they were about to do the vanishing act.

"Unfortunately for you, the last option is the only way out of this room. You're in luck, though, because that's not how you'll be leaving the lair itself." A grimace cross Alasdair's features. "We're leaving via the Walk."

"The Walk?"

"Yes. And you're going to shut your mouth and do as I say."

Leo's eyes narrowed as he asked, "Or you'll kill me?" He didn't dare look away from Alasdair.

He grinned manically. "Now you're starting to get it." Then he clamped a hand around his wrist, and before Leo could pull it free, they faded out of his prison cell.

Nine

IN LESS THAN a second, Alasdair and Leo appeared outside the room they'd just been in. The corridor was empty, as Alasdair had known it would be, and when Leo slumped forward into his arms, he moved them to the sidewall, propping him against the jagged bricks.

It was the night of the Walk, and everyone would be in the designated wing, lining the sides of the passageway, awaiting the showing. This was the one night of the month where they publicly presented their latest yielding, or piece of property, for the rest of the brood to see. It was a place to show off—to one-up each other.

Alasdair inspected Leo, who was still out cold, and realized he didn't loathe the thought of making an appearance. Usually, he avoided it like the plague, never caring to participate or see what others were indulging in.

He much preferred keeping his property to himself. But Leo had to be presented tonight, especially after Isadora had brought him to Vasilios's attention. No human was to be kept a secret from the brood, and if he didn't show his hand, many would question why.

He ran his eyes over the light hair covering Leo's chest, down his toned arm, and to the cuff surrounding his wrist. Fierce hunger growled to life inside him like an animal. He needed to feed, but ever since Leo had appeared, he hadn't had a taste for anything other than him.

Wanting a better look at the man who'd captured his attention, Alasdair moved in closer. His hair was the same color as Thanos's. But where Thanos wore his longer, Leo's was short, and right now, even though it was a mess, the top of his hair sat off to the right of a determined side part.

Alasdair licked his lips as his inspection continued down a slightly crooked nose that led to a thin top lip and fuller bottom. Though he'd once viewed Leo as nothing more than a meal, he was now entertaining *all* the sinful possibilities of the flesh—ones that would alarm the human but also appeal to his more carnal side.

He wanted answers about this man.

He needed to know about the secrets that coursed through his veins—the ones that could incapacitate him with one taste.

Force, however, was not getting him anywhere. He didn't think that would be necessary much longer though.

He remembered the way Leo had watched him with Vasilios. And now, when he'd had him against the wall.

No...force most certainly won't be necessary in convincing this man. Not when I can use other *means of coercion.*

Having decided on his new course of action, Alasdair placed his lips by Leo's ear and softly instructed, "Open your eyes." When Leo's eyelids flickered and opened, he added, "We have someplace to be."

LEO'S HEAD WAS pounding as his eyes opened and adjusted to the shadows. When Alasdair's face came into sharp focus, he grimaced. The vampire had done exactly what he'd asked him not to—the vanishing act.

"Does your kind not believe in doors?"

Alasdair looked away from him, studying the empty hallway. "Not in a room where the object is to keep the detainee from escaping."

"Detainee?" Leo asked, straightening his posture against the wall. "Don't you mean prisoner?"

When Alasdair returned his attention to him, his lips tipped up at the corners, and Leo could've sworn he was smiling at him. Not a sneer or a smug smirk, but a genuine smile.

"It's the same thing. Isn't it?"

Somewhat put off by the underlying humor and the curve of his lips, Leo averted his gaze to also glance down the hall. "Where are we?"

"Why, we're standing in a corridor, Leonidas."

Leo turned his face back to Alasdair's, and before he could ask that he be more specific, he said instead, "Why are you being so nice all of a sudden?"

"Nice," Alasdair said as if the word was completely foreign to him. Then he took a step towards him, and Leo had to suck in a breath to keep their bodies from touching. "I haven't even begun to be *nice* to you."

Leo refused to drop his eyes when Alasdair traced the pad of his index finger along the line of his jaw.

"But you'll know when I do."

Leo didn't trust or understand the sudden change in Alasdair's demeanor for a second. *He's likely getting ready to snap my neck.*

I promise you I am not. However, the idea of biting it is very appealing for several reasons.

The breath Leo had been holding rushed out at the thought of Alasdair putting his mouth on him that way. Then he admonished himself. He should be angry. Enraged, even. Not fucking turned on.

"Get out of my head," he snapped.

One of Alasdair's black eyebrows rose, and he lowered his hand. "Consider me gone. Though it should be noted, I know you enjoyed having me in you."

His choice of words had been deliberate, they had to have been, and Leo refused to acknowledge them as Alasdair backed away.

"Where are we?" he asked again.

"We're in the east corridor of my lair."

Leo opened his mouth to ask another question, but before he could speak, he was flattened against the wall, with Alasdair up against him. The finger that had just been tracing his jawline was now pressed to his lips, and Alasdair hissed, *"Shh.* Someone is coming.*"*

The eyes pinning him to the wall demanded his obedience, and the finger against his lips started to trace a line back and forth until Leo's mouth automatically parted and his tongue touched the tip of it. At the simple contact, Alasdair's eyes seemed to light from within. The green glistened back at him, and when his top lip pulled taut and those wicked fangs of his appeared, Leo's breath hitched in his throat.

Never had he felt this kind of heat. That fire that scorches skin from another's touch. Yet as he stood there now, he felt as though his entire body was about to go up in flames.

This man was all the things he shouldn't want, but as Alasdair continued to stroke his lip, all Leo could think about was him replacing that finger with his mouth.

What would it be like to kiss him? he thought as his eyes moved to the teeth that both fascinated and terrified him. *Would he graze them along my skin?*

"Be cautious, *file mou*."

At the warning, Leo's eyes flew up to Alasdair's as he dipped his finger deeper into his mouth. Leo sucked on it, unable to help himself, and his eyes slid shut as a low, moan emerged from his throat. He felt as if he were hypnotized.

"You might get more than you bargain for, with thoughts like that."

Ahh. That voice made Leo's dick harder than a goddamned rock, and he jutted his hips out, searching for relief. When Alasdair wedged his leg between his thighs, he couldn't stop himself from rubbing his aching length over the hard muscle there.

He reached for Alasdair's arm, something to anchor him to reality, and the rattle of the chain had his eyes dropping to the cuff on his wrist. *Fuck,* he'd forgotten about that, and though it should've snapped him the fuck out of whatever daze he was in, the sight of that shackle had the opposite effect. His head fell back against the bricks and he rolled his hips harder against Alasdair.

"Fuck," Leo groaned, and when the long length of Alasdair's cock aligned with his, Leo wanted to feel it naked against his skin. Fuck, he was close to reaching down and undoing his pants to get it.

"*Se thelo,*" Alasdair rasped.

Leo's fingers dug into the arm caging him against the wall. He was out of his fucking mind, *but God,* he wanted the vampire too. And when his eyes opened and caught Alasdair's, he nodded.

An arrogant as fuck smile stretched across Alasdair's lips, and he went from sexy to downright fucking dangerous in seconds. Then he swooped in and captured Leo's lips in a savage kiss.

Leo moaned into his mouth, not caring what would happen next, and when Alasdair's hands grabbed his ass, a blinding flash of light exploded before Leo's eyes. Suddenly, he was seeing—he had no idea what.

LEO BLINKED SEVERAL times, the scene playing out like a scripted show, startling in its familiarity. This was where he'd first seen Alasdair, back when he'd chased him down through the bathhouse.

What the…?

There, in front of him but not really there at all, was Alasdair.

Not the Alasdair who was currently kissing him though.

No, there, he had long, shoulder-length hair. In a white toga, he was running through an empty hall with a massive pool and thick, white columns surrounding it. His face was flushed, and as he stopped behind one of the pillars, his eyes slid shut and he tried to catch his breath.

Leo watched, fascinated, thinking it was another trick of the mind. Then Alasdair lowered a hand to stroke himself as he demanded to someone Leo couldn't see, "Show yourself" —

"LEONIDAS."

LEO SQUEEZED his eyes shut, and then he heard his name again.

"Leonidas?"

When he opened his eyes, he focused on the Alasdair who'd lifted his head. The one whose eyes were narrow and full of suspicion.

"What just happened? Your eyes—the color, it… What was that?"

Good question, Leo thought. He was about to tell him that he had no idea, but Alasdair shook his head and indicated behind him.

Three figures were walking by. Each was dressed in casual clothes: jeans, shirts, and jackets. They could've been anyone on the street—except for the three trailing behind them, one man and two women, each bound by chains like his own.

The man had a collar around his neck instead of a cuff at his wrist, and his gaze was on the ground as if he were studying where and how to put his feet with every step he took. He was dressed in loose, black pants that hung off his hipbones, and if it weren't for the drawstring tie, Leo was positive they would've fallen off. The man was thin— not grotesquely so, but enough that Leo could see his ribs.

The women were a different story altogether.

Voluptuous, plump, and confident in their steps, they glided by him and Alasdair. They were both wearing outfits of the same billowing, black material as the man's pants. It crisscrossed in narrow strips over their bare breasts, barely concealing them, and then met at the low waist below their navel, where a skirt flowed off their hips to the floor.

Around each of their wrists was a cuff much like his own, and Leo wondered if there was a difference between being collared or cuffed. He almost laughed at the thought. Never had he *ever* entertained the thought of anything remotely BDSM, so he really had no point of reference.

Is that what these vampires are into?

When the other occupants in the hall disappeared around the corner, Alasdair said quietly, "Come. I want answers, and so, apparently, do you. I'll show you the difference between a cuff and a collar, and you are going to tell me what the fuck happened back there."

ALASDAIR WAITED FOR the usual denial. That had been Leo's standard response. But as they walked in silence, he had a feeling this time might be different, judging by Leo's confused expression.

This was not good. When several adolescents made their way down the hall, Alasdair decided there was no better time than right then to mark Leo. He needed his scent on the human before they hit the actual Walk. He'd been so close too.

One minute more and Leo would've been on his knees with his cock in his mouth and his come down his throat. Except something had happened. The color of Leo's eyes had spread like ink across a body of water, encompassing the entire surface...

But what *was happening beyond the surface?*

"Where are we going?" Leo asked, finally breaking the silence.

"I already told you. We need to leave via the Walk."

Leo made a frustrated sound. "That doesn't tell me anything. What is the *Walk*?"

Alasdair stopped so abruptly that Leo almost ran into him. "I am not telling you anything more until you explain what you did back there."

Leo swallowed.

Alasdair raised an eyebrow. "Nothing?"

"I didn't *do* anything. It just happened."

"*What* happened?" Alasdair fired back, and instead of waiting for a response, he delved inside Leo's mind. He hunted around, searching for any kind of clue as to what had happened. But all he got was, *Get out of my head.*

Frustrated at the anomaly that Leo was, he demanded, "Tell me what you did."

"I. Don't. Know," Leo stressed and shook his head. "This is fucking ridiculous. If you don't believe me and think I'm some huge threat, why am I still here?"

Alasdair couldn't agree more. For some irritating reason he didn't understand, he couldn't bring himself to get rid of him. He had no idea what was going on with this man, but the deeper h got, the more...intrigued he became.

"The Walk happens each month," he said.

Leo's mouth parted in surprise, as if he'd expected death, not an answer to his original question.

"It's where we take our new yieldings and show them off amongst our kind."

"But I heard you tell the suit guy that I wasn't your—"

"I told you not to speak of him," Alasdair interrupted, yanking on the chain so Leo practically tripped up to his side.

"Why can't I speak of him? Because he's your lover? Big deal."

Alasdair found the question odd. What did he care who knew that particular fact? "You are not to speak of him because he is of much importance, unlike yourself. And yes, among the many things he is to me, my lover is one of them."

"So, you're gay?" Leo asked.

Alasdair cocked his head to the side at the thought Leo had but didn't voice: *Like me.*

"I'm vampire. We fuck whomever we want. We don't differentiate sex by gender. More so by species. Vampire, human, and so on," he told him. Then he slowly drew his fangs over his lower lip, causing Leo's eyes to fall to them.

"And how long have you *been* a vampire? I read that you were created by the gods. Apollo, Artemis, and what was the other one…" Leo mused.

Alasdair watched him cautiously, wondering how much the human knew—or thought he knew.

Then Leo snapped his fingers. "Oh and Hades. Scary god of death. Though that would make sense given your penchant for threats of murder and all."

"You have read wrong," Alasdair told him. "I was not created by the gods—"

"But by Vasilios?" Leo guessed.

Alasdair neither agreed nor disagreed, deciding that not saying a word was his best course of action. His silence, however, led to Leo's continued line of questioning.

"Well…every story usually begins with a thread of truth, right?"

"So it does," Alasdair said before he thought better of it.

"So I *am* right?" Leo asked again, a grin splitting his lips for the first time since he'd woken up—and Alasdair couldn't look away from him. Leo was enjoying himself, and when Alasdair intruded on his thoughts, he heard, *This is what I love about history. Discovering truths, and hell, I've never had a live relic to discuss things with.*

Alasdair started to walk again, choosing to ignore that he was *not* excited to be viewed as a relic by this particular man.

They were nearly at the end of the hall when Leo said, "You never told me how long it's been, you know, since you were changed."

"A long time." Then Alasdair thought about the questions he was being asked, and his suspicions of Leo rose again.

"How long?"

"You ask too many questions. Are you aware of that fact?"

"I don't care. This is the first time you've been talkative since you locked me up."

"I have no clue who or *what* you are, Leonidas. And what makes you think I'm telling you the truth?"

Leo didn't seem to have an answer for that. So Alasdair asked a question of his own. "Why do you want to know, anyway? You're the all-knowing historian. I would hardly think you need me to answer these questions for you."

Leo gave a false smile and shrugged. "Well, nothing like being able to ask the real thing. Plus, it's in my job description to be curious. You're likely older than anything I've ever dug up and dusted."

As they rounded the end of the hall, a mix of lustful groans and raunchy laughter met their ears, and Leo's sarcastic diatribe came to an abrupt end. There, lining the sides of the long, elaborate walkway, stood well over a hundred vampires.

Each of them was engaged in the usual activities that took place at this particular congregation. In varying degrees of undress, some were in the throes of a hallway fuck, while others were delighting in the pleasures of eating and being eaten.

As the debauchery took center stage, Alasdair ran his eyes over his brood until he spotted Isadora and Thanos towards the middle of the crowd.

Thanos had a young man pinned to the wall. One hand was down the front of his pants, pumping and pulling at what Alasdair suspected was a painfully engorged shaft. His teeth were deep in the man's carotid, and if the human was lucky, when Thanos was done he would get on his knees and finish the poor bastard in his mouth.

Isadora, on the other hand, had a redheaded woman kneeling by her side. The woman had her hand resting high on Isadora's thigh, and she appeared extremely satisfied.

With her dark hair pinned up in an elaborate updo Isadora looked regal as ever while she surveyed their congregation. Her eyes finally came to a stop when they reached him.

As she stood, Alasdair heard her address him, and so did every other vampire in the hall.

They all ceased what they were doing to look upon *who* had just stepped into the Walk. Silence filled the corridor, and not two seconds after it was confirmed, they bowed their heads.

Alasdair then turned to see that Leo's eyes had widened and his mouth had fallen open.

"*This* is where you're taking me?" he asked. Then, as if it were an afterthought, he muttered, "What is it? Some sort of orgy? And why have they all stopped talking?"

Alasdair looked back to the males and females of his lair and answered the simplest question first. "They have stopped talking because I have arrived."

LEO FIGURED THAT the arrogance those words had been delivered with was warranted. Especially if the way everyone within eyesight had stopped what they were doing to pay their respects.

He, on the other hand, couldn't believe what he was seeing. It was like some massive orgy or buffet. Or a mix of the two, because as far as he could see, there was a whole lot of fucking *and* eating going on.

As he continued to stare, dumbfounded, he sidled up a little closer to the one male who, ironically, felt like the safest option in the room. When Alasdair glanced at him, Leo's breath caught at the heat in his eyes, and he wondered if he was about to become a meal or a sex performer in the next few minutes.

Alasdair's voice slipped into his mind. *Which would you prefer?*

There was no way he was going to answer that, and
when Alasdair faced those waiting on him, Leo thought,
Who the hell is he to them?

"I don't generally attend these menial assemblies,"
Alasdair told him. "They're shocked to see me. They'll get
over that soon enough, and then you will become the object
of their attention."

"Me?"

"Yes, Leonidas. You."

Leo reluctantly pulled his eyes from everyone spread
out in front of them and turned. Not having realized how
close that would put his face to Alasdair's, he staggered
back.

"Why would they care about me?"

"Because you are here with me."

"And that's—"

"Unheard of," Alasdair finished for him.

Before Leo could ask what he meant, Alasdair's voice
was in his head again.

I don't parade my conquests about.

Leo glared at him. "Can you please stop doing that?
And I'm not your conquest."

*I can always speak aloud if you would prefer. However,
our kind have exceptional hearing, and if I say anything here, they
will expect you to get down and kneel by my side. Do you want
that, Leonidas? To kneel at my feet?*

Leo ignored the provocative question and asked one from earlier. "Why do some have collars and some have cuffs?"

He flinched when Alasdair reached for his wrist and brought it up under his nose. Then Alasdair closed his eyes and took a breath, as if inhaling his scent. Leo couldn't stop himself from looking at the beautiful, thick lashes resting on Alasdair's skin as his jaw bunched and ticked, and when his eyes flew back open, the hunger in them floored him.

"The collars signify a food source. The cuffs..." Alasdair whispered, and his breath floated across Leo's lips in a sensual caress, "signify a sexual one."

Then Alasdair walked away, pulling on the chain that bound them together, leaving him with no other choice but to follow.

Ten

KEEP YOUR EYES down and stay three paces behind me,
Alasdair instructed. *Remember, they are able to read your*
thoughts, Leonidas.

When Leo said nothing and his mind went blank, an
odd sense of...pride rose within him. He then dismissed it as
utter ridiculousness, because what did he care if this human
could erase his thoughts on command? It really was of no
consequence to him. Even if it was most unusual.

His eyes roved over the members of his brood as
they slowly began to raise their heads and look upon their
afentikó. They didn't have to utter a word for him to know
what they were all thinking. The astonishment plastered on
their ashen faces said it all.

Why is Alasdair here tonight?
And who is that with him?

Perhaps the most important question on their minds, however, was: *Has he claimed the one he presents?*

More questions would no doubt arise over the appearance of both him and the human, but right now Alasdair needed this horde to believe that the man following ever so reluctantly behind him was spending the days *and* the nights in his bed. Otherwise, things would get messy real fast as others battled for his leftovers.

While they weaved through the crowd of curious onlookers, Alasdair kept his chin held high. The last time several of these vampires had seen him, he'd been on his knees, being tortured in a most atrocious way by Vasilios. It was imperative that they realized he was back in full health and, as always, his position within the brood was at the top.

His age and lineage put him above everyone who stood in the walkway—and they knew it. With Vasilios as his sire, he was one of the most powerful vampires to exist. There weren't many who matched his power, years, or wisdom, except for—

"Thanos, Isa," he said as he came to a stop before his cousins. "I had a feeling I'd see you both here this evening."

Isadora, elegant as ever in a black cocktail dress, slipped a hand through the crook of Thanos's arm. Around her neck was a black ribbon choker with a gold rose hanging from it.

"You didn't think we'd miss this, did you?" Her blue eyes shifted to glance behind him. "You could've at least given the poor thing a shirt, Alasdair, really."

"Oh, I don't know, Isa. I rather like this unfettered glimpse we're getting of what Alasdair has deemed worthy of his attention. I have to say, I can certainly see why."

Alasdair gave Thanos, whose lips were stained with the blood of the human he'd been consuming, a pointed look. "I'm surprised you managed to pull yourself away from your *own* yielding. Is he the one who has kept you so distracted this week that we haven't seen hide nor hair from you?"

A villainous grin full of sparkling, white teeth crossed Thanos's boyishly handsome face. He might not have appeared older than his early twenties, but he had several more years on Isadora and a few less than Alasdair. Which made this charming, vampire *lethal*.

"He and several others," Thanos replied. "We've been testing the resilience of the new bed Eton had delivered. It's hardly my fault I was ordered to stay in it. But…even I wouldn't have missed this for all the distractions in the world. It's gratifying to know that someone can still make your cock hard. I, for one, know how well you can use it—when you choose to," he said with a mocking bow.

"Stop flirting, Thanos," Isadora said. "Like you said, his is hard for someone else. How often does he bring a human to the Walk? I think this is very interesting indeed." Her glossy, scarlet lips curved with amusement as she sized Leo up.

"You're right," Thanos agreed, turning her way. "But some things never change, and I can't help myself with him." Then he returned his attention to Alasdair, and his eyes practically twinkled with mischief. "This one must be *very* special. I figured I'd come down and see if you'd offer up a sample. I promise I'd be gentle."

With the eyes of many still on them, Alasdair walked forward until his cousin backed up into the shadows. He gave Thanos a look that required no words—it was as clear as the scowl on his face that the answer was not going to be in his favor.

Thanos let out a rumbling laugh and winked. "I'm just teasing, Alasdair. But all's good. I suppose you have good reason to worry. You do know me *better* than most. Afraid I'd break him, huh?" The light in his eyes changed from mischievous to licentious in a flash as they flicked over his shoulder to Leo. "I probably would. He looks extremely fuckable. I wouldn't want to go easy on him."

LEO FELT AS though he were rooted to the spot. He glanced at the vampire eyeing him like a slice of prime beef, but before their eyes could meet, he averted his gaze.

The male was tall, taller than Alasdair, but younger, maybe twenty-two or twenty-three at most. He was dressed in black jeans and a tight, black shirt that clung to muscles upon muscles, and his hair was the same color as his—light and blond. Where Leo wore his short, though, the vampire had his knotted in a low tail at the back of his head.

Do not look him in the eye, Leonidas.

The warning was so unexpected that Leo jerked his head up and stared at the back of Alasdair's head.

Thanos is arrogant enough to think that, if you are looking at him, you are inviting him to play.

And you aren't that arrogant? Leo thought, unable to help himself.

I never said that. The difference is you want me in your head…among other places.

"Are you quite done, Thanos?" Alasdair asked, transitioning smoothly back to speech.

"I suppose so. Though it seems selfish that you'd keep him all to yourself. Apparently you're still in a foul mood after your punishment."

"My decision not to share *my* yielding has nothing to do with a foul mood and everything to do with your lack of self-control. But now that you mention it, I'm glad you were concerned enough after my punishment to see if I was still alive."

Thanos shrugged. "There is no way Vasilios would eliminate you. I wasn't concerned. However, when I heard about this one…" he drawled, licking his lips.

"Thanos, no," Alasdair repeated, as if he were scolding a determined child. He then shifted to the left, blocking the vampires' direct path to where he was standing.

"But you never bring your humans out to play. What is it about this one, Alasdair? Let me see."

"What's special about him is my business. Unless I choose to share him with you," Alasdair grit out between his teeth.

"And will you?" Thanos asked, his voice dropping to a seductive timbre. "Share him with me?"

The thought of being between the two vampires should've appalled Leo. Except physically, he was more than aware he was amongst the most prime male specimens he'd ever seen in his life. And even if they acted as though his existence was a mere blip on their radar, apparently, the idea of them touching him had his stupid dick raring to go.

Fuck, I didn't think I was that goddamn lonely.

"You know, Thanos...I would," Alasdair finally said. "If you could promise not to be the greedy fuck you usually are in bed."

"Well, where's the fun in that? And *he* just admitted to being lonely. Not doing your job, huh?" Thanos asked, flashing an unrepentant grin at Alasdair. "Plus, what better place to be greedy than when one is sampling the pleasures of the flesh? I don't remember you being so concerned with my appetite when I was in *your* bed."

Leo wanted to disappear from sight as embarrassment brought a flush to his cheeks. He looked between the two men, and then the last part of *what* the male had said penetrated his brain.

These two have...have fucked. He wasn't sure why, but that irritated him enough to think as loudly as he possibly could, *Don't even think about offering me to him.*

Leonidas, he can —

"Oh, he's quite spirited, isn't he?" Thanos chuckled.

Fuck, Leo had forgotten that everyone could hear and only Alasdair could respond.

That's right. And you'd best remember it if you want to leave here alive. I told you, down here, humans are the weakest link. You are the lowest denominator. Consider yourself my property. I pick and choose who touches you, fucks you, and feeds from you.

"Well, that's fucked up. We aren't living in the Middle Ages," Leo said, not even realizing he'd spoken aloud.

"The Middle Ages?" Isadora laughed. "Whatever are you saying to him, Alasdair?"

Leo had the insane image of Alasdair rolling his eyes in exasperation. Not that he'd likely ever do something as undignified as that.

You are going to get yourself killed if you don't pay more attention. To shed some light on your disgust and horror, however, most of us come from the Middle Ages. So that's the way our society is structured, Mr. Archaeologist. Now, keep your eyes on your feet and your thoughts silent.

Leo reluctantly did as he had been told, thinking back to the images he'd once studied in Elias's class of the feudal pyramids of the Middle Ages. He remembered that the weakest and lowest segment of the diagram was always the peasants or slaves, and then he shut his eyes.

Well, when put that way, it made sense. Because that was exactly what he was at the moment, wasn't it? Alasdair's slave. But then he had another thought—

If I'm your property, who are you *in your community's pyramid?*

"Pyramids?" Thanos asked, rudely intruding on his thoughts again. "You have the wrong country, *agóri.* We hail from Greece, not Egypt. What is he babbling about, Alasdair?"

Leo kept silent and waited to hear what Alasdair would say. Instead of answering the male directly, he turned to face him and the crowd behind them. Then, in a tone that brooked no question or argument, he announced, "I would be Lord to all of them. And, going forth, master to you."

ALASDAIR HAD NO idea what had provoked him to make such an announcement. But as the words had left his lips, and a flurry of whispers swept through the corridor, a satisfying sense of possession had overwhelmed him.

This was a first. He'd brought humans, although
rarely, to the Walk. But never had he publicly claimed
another. And even though Vasilios had encouraged the act,
Alasdair wondered how he would feel when word of it
reached him.

"Now, isn't *that* fascinating…" Isadora purred
behind him. "Only a couple of hours earlier, you were
adamant he was not yours."

Alasdair studied Leo's face for a reaction, but instead
of surprise or indignation, his eyes glazed over and he
started to sway.

"I think he's going to pass out." Isadora laughed, and
the sound grated on Alasdair's nerves. "Looks like I'm not
the only one who finds the idea of an orgasm from you
horrifying."

Alasdair tuned his cousin out and took a step
towards Leo, well aware that everyone in the hall was
watching them. "What is wrong with you?"

"Nothing," Leo muttered and pitched forward on his
toes.

Alasdair put a hand on his shoulder, steadying him.
"Again, you lie to me. Tell me. What is wrong with you?"

Leo brought a hand up to his forehead, and then he
stumbled.

"Can you walk?"

Leo's head snapped up, and he aimed a fierce,
annoyed look at him. *Yes, I can walk. Don't touch me…master.*

Instead of heeding the request, Alasdair gripped Leo's shoulders and pulled him up so he could place his lips by his ear. "I'm trying to prevent you from becoming a buffet to a ravenous horde of carnivores. But if that's what you want…"

"No," Leo rasped.

"Then what kind of game are you playing?"

Leo shifted and their lips were so close Alasdair had to restrain himself from sweeping his tongue across Leo's lower one.

"No game. I'm so tired all of a sudden," he whispered, and his eyelids fluttered shut. "I can't…I can't keep my eyes open."

Magic, Alasdair thought. *It has to be.* And the only one of them who had ever dabbled in it…

Alasdair spun around to glare accusingly at Thanos, who had a self-satisfied smirk across his lips. "You did this," he hissed out.

"I did," his cousin replied as he crossed his arms over his chest.

"Why?" Alasdair demanded as Leo went limp and he had to hold him upright.

Thanos strolled over without a care in the world, now that Alasdair's hands were occupied, and stroked a finger down Leo's temple, cheek, and jaw.

"Because, cousin, he's had your full attention for the last month. So much so you've been slacking on your duties and endured one fucked-up punishment. Eton wanted me to see the human up close, and you were not about to allow it."

When a deep growl emerged from him, Thanos had the good sense to pull his hand away.

"If you want to keep him," Thanos suggested, lowering his voice so only the two of them could hear, "you better do more than rub your scent over him and 'say' he's yours. These cretins won't believe it unless they can smell you on him *and* in him. You know better than that. I'm merely giving you a friendly reminder, cousin."

"I don't need a reminder," Alasdair snapped.

"Don't you?" Thanos asked. "You're so wrapped up in this golden-haired *agóri* that you didn't even notice Vasilios at the other end of the hall just now."

Alasdair's eyes flew to the far end of the corridor.

Thanos tsked him. "It's too late. He's long gone, and I'm assuming he hid himself from you, wanting to see this display as much as the rest of us. The Ancients are curious too, Alasdair. So, again, I ask you: Who is it that's captured your attention, cousin?"

When Thanos made a move to touch Leo a second time, Alasdair bared his teeth like a cornered animal. Then, without answering, he closed his eyes and did something he'd told Leo he wouldn't. He faded both of them from the lair.

Eleven

LEO WOKE TO the muffled sound of voices chatting nearby. His eyelids were heavy as he forced them open and took in his surroundings, and then the familiarity of his own bedroom bombarded him.

The tallboy he'd stuffed several seasons' worth of clothes in sat at a diagonal angle in the far left corner, and the rickety secondhand desk he'd bought at the old antique store off Parnell and Rotham was nestled in beside it. On the opposite wall, his four-level bookshelf was jam-packed with textbooks and history journals, which caused it to lean to one side even though he'd crammed it in next to the wall for extra support.

Everything was exactly how it should have been—except for the voices.

Once he'd sat up in his bed, he grabbed the white T-shirt on the end of it and pulled it over his head. Then he picked up his comfy, grey cardigan from the back of his desk chair.

God, what he wouldn't do for a shower.

He'd taken advantage of the en suite when he'd been locked up, using the soap and water to keep as clean as he could. But he hadn't trusted his surroundings long enough to fully strip and get under the warm spray of the shower.

This was the first time in two weeks he'd been fully clothed, so he felt he finally had some sort of defense in place. He swung his legs over the edge of the mattress and pressed his fingers to the bridge of his nose, squeezing his eyes shut. His head was killing him, and that could only mean one thing.

Alasdair and his vanishing act.

He scanned his bedroom, and when he saw no one else, he frowned. *Maybe Alasdair was some sort of nightmare.* But it was the thought that followed which was truly perplexing. *Then who the hell is in my apartment?*

With that in mind, Leo stood and cursed as something sharp dug into the bottom of his foot. His mouth fell open when he saw a metal chain attached to an open cuff lying on his bedroom floor.

Oh shit. So nix it all being a nightmare. Crouching down, he picked the cuff up. Clearly he hadn't imagined all of it.

"Oh, listen. I think I hear him now."

Leo froze as that silky voice drifted into his room.

No...it couldn't be.

But as a chair dragged across the kitchen tiles, Leo ordered himself to move, not wanting to be trapped in his bedroom with the vampire who'd taken him hostage, if that was who was coming for him.

He dropped the cuff to the floor with a loud clang and kicked it under the frame. He then scanned the room, desperately trying to find some kind of weapon or deterrent to use against Alasdair when he finally opened the—

"Leo, it's about time you woke up."

Leo rubbed his eyes to make sure he wasn't hallucinating, and when the figure remained the same, his head began to spin as if he were about to pass out again.

Instead, he managed, "Elias?"

ALASDAIR SAT IN the tiny kitchen of Leo's apartment and stared at the man seated opposite him. He was irritable and hungry as hell.

Fuck, it'd been way too long since he'd fed, and sitting in a house full of potential meals wasn't helping him overlook the issue. Add in the tiny detail of all the curtains he'd shut and that there'd be no chance of a witness and the idea of feeding became extra appealing.

No...now isn't the time.

The human across from him had introduced himself as Paris when Alasdair had first opened Leo's front door. And where the other man, Elias, had seemed impolite and skeptical of who he was, this Paris guy had merely given him a friendly smile—much like the one he was now aiming his way.

"So, you said you met Leo at The Dirty Dog."

"That's right," Alasdair said, as he kept an ear on what was happening down the hall.

Leo had just opened the bedroom door and whispered his friend's name like a prayer—a prayer he'd imagined the past two weeks, no doubt. Pity he was shit out of luck on that front.

"And you two hooked up and decided to take off into the sunset? Without telling anyone?"

This guy needed to stop with all the questions. Alasdair had let the two men inside begrudgingly, wanting to see if they were...odd like Leo.

Who did he associate with? And did they possess the same kind of abilities he did? It was something he was in the process of discovering for himself.

Focusing all of his attention on Paris, Alasdair leaned in to place his arms on the table. Then he lowered his voice, letting the timbre of it stroke over the other man's senses.

"That's right. Haven't you ever done anything...impulsive?"

Paris nodded and shifted in his seat. Then he reached up to push a loose strand of hair that had escaped his hair tie behind his ears.

"Hmm, Paris?" Alasdair practically purred, willing the compulsion to take over the glassy-eyed man.

Paris's mouth opened, but a voice down the hall captured Alasdair's attention and he held a hand up, indicating silence—and he got it.

"Leo, we've been so worried about you. Where the hell have you been? And who is this Alasdair guy making us coffee?"

Speaking of coffee, Alasdair reached for his mug and brought it to his lips, curious as to how Leo would respond to his friend's questions. He wasn't particularly worried about him spilling his secret. After all, even if he did say he'd been taken by vampires, who in their right mind would believe him?

"I... He's..."

"Yes?" the Elias guy demanded, and Alasdair decided right then—he didn't like the guy. "He's what? Please don't tell me you did all this because the guy's hot. I get it. He's pretty wow, Leo. But to disappear with him? We thought you were dead, for fuck's sake."

Alasdair dropped the compulsion and peered over his mug at Paris, who was now leaning back in his chair with a relaxed expression on his face. More than happy he was unlike Leo, in that he was none the wiser to what had just been done to him, Alasdair placed his mug on the table and got to his feet. While he made his way down the hall, Elias spoke again.

"I can't believe you of all people pulled this shit this week. You knew how important this was to us. We've been working on it for years. *Years.* And you were going to throw it away for a good fuck? Awesome."

"Elias, listen to me," Leo finally said. "I'm not fucking him. He's...he's..."

"Why bother lying now? He already told us you gave him a key to your place."

Alasdair stopped by the corner, out of sight, and waited for—

"He said *what?*"

Despite his hunger practically gnawing a hole through his stomach lining, and that he'd no doubt pissed Vasilios off tonight, Alasdair found a wicked grin stretching his mouth at Leo's rage. *That sure woke the human up.*

"Where the hell is he?"

Not one to ever hide from a demand, Alasdair stepped into view and when Leo saw him, he pushed a simple thought inside his mind: *Miss me?*

LIKE A TOOTHACHE, Leo thought as he brushed by Elias and marched over to the infuriating vampire. *So I didn't dream him up. Good to know I'm not delusional at least.*

The menacing male currently leaning against his wall was very real, and he looked as sinful as he did deadly. With his long legs crossed at the ankles and his arms mirroring the pose over his chest, he appeared as normal as the rest of them. *Except for the small fact that he could kill us all in the blink of an eye.*

Choose your next words very carefully, file mou. I wouldn't want anything to happen to your friends.

Coming to a stop opposite Alasdair, Leo crossed his arms and held his ground. He was in his apartment now, damn it. On his turf. And he wouldn't be—

What? Intimidated? Don't forget what I am, Leonidas. Just because I haven't killed your friends yet doesn't mean I am not imagining them as my next meal. Now, turn around and tell the stubborn one over there that you fell madly in love with me two weeks ago and lost your head. Well, not literally. But there's always time for that later.

Leo glowered at him, and as Alasdair's eyes creased around the edges, he was amazed by the way his lips tipped up into a sexy curve. Add one more weapon to Alasdair's arsenal—that seductive smile was killer.

"Did you think I'd left? I was waiting until you woke up. I thought you needed the extra sleep. You know, especially after the last two weeks we spent together."

When Alasdair added a flirty wink to accompany the outrageous words flying from his mouth, Leo clenched his teeth together so hard he was surprised they didn't crack.

"That's *nice* of you," he forced from between tight lips.

Alasdair pushed away from the wall and took a step towards him. "Your friends here were telling me how worried they've been about you."

He remained rigid as Alasdair placed his hands on his shoulders.

"I thought you called them. You told me before we left that you had contacted everyone you'd needed to."

Shut up, Leo stressed inside his head so only Alasdair would hear.

"Leo?" That time, his name was said behind him— from Elias.

Alasdair released him, and Leo pivoted back around to face his longtime friend and employer. The man who'd made him fall in love with history back when he'd been in college.

"Why didn't you call me?"

Leo didn't know what to say. No matter *what* he said, nothing would excuse what Elias thought he'd done.

"Because you knew I'd say no to taking time off at the moment. Correct?"

Leo remained silent as Elias stormed over to where they stood.

When he stopped, he cast a suspicious eye over at Alasdair. "We already contacted the police to tell them you're home safe and sound. Not that I know what the fuck to think about your mental state." He sighed in disappointment and ran his fingers through his short, black hair. "I expect your ass to be in my office tomorrow morning no later than seven thirty a.m. *Which* is when I'll decide if you still have a job or not."

Leo swallowed as Elias aimed a steely glare at Alasdair.

"I would like to say it's nice to meet you, but I don't trust you. So let's say this has been interesting. If he doesn't show up tomorrow, expect to see your face plastered all over the news by noon. Got it?"

Leo tensed, expecting to see Alasdair's fingers wrapped around his boss's arm and his fangs sinking into his neck. Instead, Alasdair was offering his hand. When Elias took it, Alasdair nodded once and said quite seriously, "I will make sure Leonidas is at work on time tomorrow morning."

Elias looked his way one last time and muttered, "See that you do," before he strode back into the kitchen. "Come on, Paris. We found who we were looking for. Not that he seems to care too much."

Leo winced at that, and then a chair scraped across the tile floor. As his friends left his apartment, he realized, with something bordering on murderous rage, that even though Alasdair hadn't killed him, he'd still managed to effectively fuck his entire life up.

Twelve

LEO QUIETLY WALKED over to the kitchen sink and braced his hands on the counter. They were shaking he was so livid. His back was still facing Alasdair, and for the last several minutes, tense silence had filled the small space.

He wasn't sure what had happened between now and when he'd been standing amongst the crowd of hungry vampires back at the Walk. But he knew one thing: He'd be damned if he would go back there without a fight.

"Who said I was going to take you back?"

Alasdair's voice closing in had Leo rounding on him with a glare.

"Why won't you just leave me alone?" he finally asked as Alasdair came to a standstill by the kitchen table. "First, you terrorize me, then you kidnap me, and now, you're hell-bent on destroying my life. If this is your version of playing with your food, I think you've taken it far enough."

Alasdair's brow rose as he studied him. "Haven't you awoken in a particularly spirited mood? Thanos was right. I like it," he said, his tone dropping a few octaves. "It's more fitting of you."

"You know nothing about me. And I'm positive you care even less," he grit out, his anger rising inside him now as he bravely stepped closer. "Why haven't you killed me? I don't get what your deal is. Are you bored? Defective? Or something else I haven't thought of?"

The words fell off his tongue and hovered in the air between them like a provocative dare. He wasn't sure how Alasdair would react, but before he could continue, he was crushed back against the sink. His hands were trapped behind his back, and the counter dug into his hips as Alasdair held him in place.

"I assure you I am certainly not defective. And you should stop talking. Your words, they will get you—"

"What, killed? You said you liked my newfound spirit. Now, all of a sudden, you don't?"

"We vampires, we're fickle creatures. We change our minds every split second," Alasdair said. "And right now, I'd prefer you to shut your mouth. Or I'll do it for you. Permanently."

Leo narrowed his eyes, refusing to back down. "You keep issuing deadly threats, yet here I am, alive and standing in my apartment. Right back where I started."

Straining against the hand holding him captive, he pushed his face in closer to Alasdair's. "The only difference this time? I know you can't feed from me or something happens to you. You get all locked up, don't you? So. You going to snap my neck instead?"

The fingers around his wrists constricted, making it clear Alasdair could do whatever he wanted with him right then, but...

"I don't think so. I also think you have no idea what happened the night you tried to kill me. And that pisses you off because you think you know everything. But you don't, do you? You're a little bit scared."

"Stop talking. *Now*."

The smart thing to do would've been to heed the warning, but Leo was on too much of a roll to stop now. "I think it's even more than that though. You find me..." His voice trailed off as Alasdair's top lip retracted.

"Oh, don't stop now. I find you *what*, Leonidas?"

Just like the previous times Alasdair had threatened him, Leo's body reacted. His breath came in rapid bursts, and a warm flush hit his cheeks. He was aroused by this side of Alasdair.

This intimidating I-can-kill-you-with-my-bare-hands side.

For some reason, it got him off and gave a whole new meaning to wanting the bad boy.

When Alasdair pulled him close, Leo's heart began to trip all over itself, and his cock made it crystal clear he was undeniably attracted to the male snarling at him. That was when he was struck with another truly baffling thought—he wanted Alasdair to crush his lips against his and kiss him.

"I asked you a question. Now answer me. I find you *what?*"

Leo's eyes fell to the lips issuing the demand, and he replied, "You want me. I can tell. You find me as fascinating as I find you."

"And what makes you think that?"

Leo raised his eyes, and his breath caught at the light in Alasdair's. "Your eyes. They were glowing that time you were with the other male, Vasilios. When he was kissing you and sucking you. They're glowing now. They do that because you're turned on, am I right?"

Alasdair lowered those eyes down his body, and Leo's erection ached under the inspection.

"You also said as much," he continued, not to be dissuaded. "You never attend that thing we went to tonight. But then, when we arrived, you told everyone I was yours. And what about that cuff lying on the floor in my bedroom? You know, the one you used to parade me around like I was your latest—"

Alasdair shifted and leaned in the distance separating them to whisper, "Fuck?"

"Yes." Leo barely breathed as the tips of those frightening as fuck teeth grazed across the curve of his lower lip. And when Alasdair stroked the back of his fingers down his cheek, a shiver of pure lust snaked through Leo's veins.

He was sure he was about to remember how to speak when Alasdair moved his mouth to the corner of his and asked, "Is that what you want, Leonidas? To lie on your back, spread your legs, and let me inside you whenever I desire? Or how about we skip the bed altogether and I take you against whatever is near? Hmm? Are you sure your cock isn't speaking for your head, *file mou*? Because, yes. *Se thelo*. And if I have you, I will not let you go until I am done."

Leo let out the shaky breath he'd been holding, and against all common sense, he daringly pressed his tongue to the tip of one of Alasdair's fangs. And that's when a deep rumbling growl left Alasdair.

A dangerous thrill coursed through him, pumping his fevered blood directly to his cock as his own actions and Alasdair's wild response affected him.

Fuck, he's sexy. The glowing eyes, those killer teeth, and the way he fell in and out of his native tongue when he was aroused. Sexy was an understatement. Alasdair was every wicked thought and fantasy Leo could have imagined.

He could kill him any time he wanted. *But God help me, I don't care,* Leo thought as he said, "Yes."

THIS WAS ABOUT to get complicated as hell. When Leo had tongued his left canine, Alasdair's cock stiffened like an iron poker. *Ballsy human,* taking liberties that made Alasdair want to fuck him until he got him out of his system.

But he had to think…or at least try to.

Fucking your prey was never a good idea. It always ended badly. Either they became clingy and needy, never wanting to leave your side, or they became the messy by-product of a feed-and-fuck frenzy—something he'd learned to avoid after the first time it'd happened to him well over a thousand years ago. But when Leo whimpered into his mouth and bucked forward against him, Alasdair's opinion on the subject took on an entirely different view.

He spun them around and, with a flash of thought, shoved Leo on top of the kitchen table so hard the legs scraped against the tile floor as it slid under their combined weight. With his hands now freed, Leo clutched at his shirtfront, and Alasdair maneuvered his way between his legs, placing his hands on the surface and pinning the human in.

"So you think you want that, do you? To be my yielding? To submit to my every demand, my every whim?"

When sensual need swirled inside Leo's eyes, Alasdair's own arousal ramped up to the ragged edge. Leo's erection strained through his thin pants, and Alasdair couldn't help himself from driving his hips up and connecting their rigid lengths.

I'd be inside your body. Your mind. Sometimes both.

The red stain on Leo's cheeks made Alasdair want the man underneath him begging for it, dying for the control he could ultimately give. He wanted to sink his teeth, *and* his cock, inside the man laid out under him. But knowing what happened the last time, Alasdair didn't dare risk it.

He took Leo's hands from his shirt and stretched them above his head, holding them trapped against the table.

You have no idea what you are inviting, Leonidas Chapel.

When Leo spread his legs farther apart, Alasdair narrowed his eyes at the thought the man let echo through his mind.

I know exactly what I'm inviting. Maybe you're just too scared to touch me.

Alasdair revealed his teeth in a feral smile and growled. The control he usually held so tight finally snapped in half.

THE SOUND THAT came from Alasdair would've been a warning to most, a threat of imminent danger. But the deep cadence had Leo twisting up to get closer to the body pressing him down on the table. He found it difficult to breathe as a warm tongue licked over the pulse at the base of his throat, but he managed to take a shaky breath.

Who's scared now? You, Leonidas?

He heard the question inside his mind, and even though the answer was a definite yes, he forced himself to say, "No."

Cool lips pressed against the skin under his ear, and in his mind, Alasdair whispered, *Again, you lie to me.*

He was ready to deny it, when Alasdair raised his head and crushed their mouths together. Leo writhed under the hard frame sliding over the top of his, and when Alasdair slipped his tongue out to sample his lower lip, everything flashed to white.

No, no, no.

It was happening again. That same odd kind of flashback. One minute, he was in the present with Alasdair, and the next—

"HMM... IT'S HARD to believe I found you before you promised yourself to another, agóri?"

I'm somewhere else entirely. Fuck, again? What is this? Wake up.

Wake. Up. Chapel.

He didn't wake, but his vision cleared, and he saw Alasdair lounging on the steps of the large pool in the bathhouse. The crystal-clear water lapped at his chest, and half of his long hair was pulled up and tied away from his handsome face. Between his legs stood the other vampire, Vasilios. His muscular back appeared smooth as stone, and the look on Alasdair's face as he gazed at the one before him was full of adoration—and Leo knew that what he was seeing had happened many years ago.

"Who said I am not promised?"

"Ahh yes, I suppose she counts, even if it was orchestrated by your fathers. Well, won't they be disappointed when you do not return from this evening's excursion."

"Perhaps. But I cannot find it in myself to care."

Witnessing moments like this was fucked up. It gave Leo a sense of unease in the pit of his stomach. This was an invasion of privacy, a glimpse of Alasdair's past, and it felt wrong to be witnessing all that he was. He wasn't sure why it was happening, but when Alasdair shifted off the step of the pool and moved closer to Vasilios, Leo wanted it to end.

He wanted to be away from the scene unfolding before his eyes and back in the kitchen where —

"Ahh…" *Yes, right back here,* where cool fingers had snaked between his legs and encircled his cock.

"It happened again, didn't it?" Alasdair asked.

Leo panted and closed his eyes, hoping to hide whatever had just happened from the curious male hovering above him.

"What goes on when your eyes do that? When they cloud over that way?"

When Alasdair's fingers stroked up the length of his erection and he leaned to the side to suck on his lobe, Leo groaned. He'd never wanted someone as much as he wanted the male currently working him over. He was close to begging when Alasdair nipped the shell of his ear and pushed into his mind.

You still won't say? Then let me show you what's going on in my mind.

And just like that, Leo saw an image of them as they were now—but not.

He was stripped naked, and bent down over him was Alasdair.

He had him pinned to the table, and when he raised his head and glanced Leo's way, a drop of blood slid down the corner of his mouth.

Fuck…fuck, that's hot.

Where Leo had once thought he would be disgusted by Alasdair feeding from him—suddenly, he was not. Every beat of his heart was like a warning, telling him this was madness. But as it kept time with his throbbing dick, he realized he'd never wanted to come so hard in his life as he did while watching *that*. The twisted image had turned him on even more.

Twisted is right. But you want it anyway, don't you?

Brought back to reality by that tempting voice, Leo grunted and flexed under the grip still holding him to the table.

Alasdair was spot on. Sexual arousal had overtaken his sanity and he *wanted* to be fucked by Alasdair. Even if it meant his very possible death.

One day soon, it will happen. I have promised myself that. But not tonight, Leonidas. Not tonight.

As the words drifted inside his dazed mind, Leo tried to make sense of everything that had happened, but before he could, it all stopped.

Alasdair was gone.

Not only had he vanished from Leo's mind, but he'd also faded from his kitchen, leaving him alone for the first time in two weeks.

Thirteen

ISADORA PACED BACK and forth outside Alasdair's bedroom. He'd returned alone an hour earlier from wherever he'd disappeared to with his human. Since then, he'd sequestered himself inside his chambers and had not come out.

Ugh, she hated when he got all broody and irritable. It usually meant he needed to fucking eat. But, being the arrogant ass he was, Alasdair always pushed his control to the breaking point. It was also evident from the fact he hadn't fully claimed his yielding that the imbecile was waiting until he was ravenous. And with the way he was stalking that human male, she knew he wouldn't have taken a meal elsewhere.

She knocked twice, waiting for him to grant her access. However, when nothing came from behind the locked door, she decided she'd had enough waiting.

She faded inside and scanned the large quarters for him. When she spotted him walking out of the bathroom, he had only a towel around his waist and his hair was sticking up in wet strands.

Ahh. It appears someone is trying to wash away his evening's activities.

"Were you planning to let me in or ignore me all evening, cousin?"

"Does it matter?" he asked as he walked by her, dropping the towel to the floor.

"No. Not particularly. I have need for you in the Adjudication Room. I know I've been dealing with things for the most part, but I would like you to step in on this particular hearing."

She watched unashamedly as he shrugged into a black shirt and pants. Then she thought about what a truly handsome male he was by any standards. It was almost distracting. When he raised a bored eyebrow, she shook herself out of her study of him and continued.

"Stratos has been brought to me. One of the guards patrolling the streets picked him up earlier this evening."

"Picked him up for doing what?" Alasdair asked as he buttoned his shirt. "Stratos hardly strikes me as the sort to be causing trouble. He's always towed the line."

"Yes, I know, which is why it's so odd. He appears different tonight. Almost possessed in a way."

Alasdair frowned at her and then shrugged as if it weren't his problem.

"Do you really think I would come to you if I didn't need your help? He's hiding something, and nothing I have done has worked."

"What do you think he's hiding?" he asked, this last piece of information obviously piquing his interest.

"I don't know, but every time I think he's about to say, he shuts down."

Alasdair crossed his arms as he mulled her words over. "Did you contact the Ancients? What did they say?"

"They seem to be…away right now."

"All three of them?"

"Yes, all three."

When a flash of disbelief crossed Alasdair's features, she knew what he was thinking. It was odd that all three would leave the main lair at the same time. However, if they had been taught anything over the years, it was to never doubt their Ancient's judgment. If they needed to be somewhere, it was for a good reason.

"Well," Alasdair finally said. "What are we waiting around for? I suppose we need to pay Stratos a visit and get to the bottom of this."

"ALASDAIR, HAVE YOU heard a word I've said to you in the last five minutes?" Isadora asked, as she tapped her polished fingernail on the arm of her chair. They'd been sitting in tense silence while Alasdair assessed the situation hanging from the center of the Adjudication Room. "If we leave him up there much longer, having him present for a trial will prove difficult. Due to his being dead and all."

The hard lines of Alasdair's face were as set as stone as he stared at the male in front of them. "What do I care if he's dead? He's not telling me anything useful now, and all I've heard so far are lies. Stratos, we know you were consorting with a messenger. You haven't yet denied it, but on the same hand, you haven't told us why you would be so stupid. So Isa," Alasdair said with an air of congeniality about him that was at odds with the situation, "I'm not sure why he would be *given* a trial, all things considered."

Isadora let her eyes drift to the vampire who was currently attached to the large metallic hook in the center of the ceiling by ankle cuffs. "Because it's the fair thing to do?" she ventured, knowing she somehow had to pull her cousin from his volatile mood.

He glanced over at her, looking skeptical. "Have you ever known me to be concerned by what is fair and what is not?"

"Well, no."

"Then what makes you think I would start now?"

She leaned over until their shoulders touched and lowered her voice. "Because in situations like these, our job is to ask questions, not terminate."

Alasdair looked back to the male squirming around from where he dangled helplessly. He then faced her again. "Is that supposed to mean something to me? Yes, my job is to ask questions. If answers are not given, I am afforded the power to make life-or-death decisions. It is a job both you and Thanos refused due to…weak stomachs, I presume. You came to me," he stated, and Isadora was beginning to think that had been a mistake, given Alasdair's current temper. "So, if you don't mind, I will handle this as I have always handled such cases."

"But cousin, we have known Stratos most of our lives. And he's…"

"What, Isa? What is he, other than a traitor? Messengers are forbidden consorts. Stratos is well aware of this law. If you break it, you pay. It's no different for an elder than for a newling."

She sighed—she was not about to win this. Alasdair had not been his usual self for quite some time, and tonight, ever since he'd returned, he had been in a right foul mood.

"Really, Alasdair, you need to snap out of whatever this is. Thanos is having far too much fun trying to think of new ways to annoy you, and I don't even want to imagine what Vasilios has in store after last time. It's clear that dealing with that human is the cause of this odious mood, so why bother with him?"

As she peered into her cousin's mind to understand what was going on, the irritated emotions in his head showed her how conflicted he was. He was remembering his evening and where he'd been with the male. In some sort of kitchen, where they were—

"You kissed him?" Isadora asked, interrupting his train of thought.

"Get the fuck out of my head, Isa."

"I would if I thought for one second you were using it."

"Get out, unless you want me to hurt *you* instead of him," he barked at her, standing to make his way over to the vampire awaiting his punishment. Or death.

When Alasdair stopped, he was eye level with Stratos, whose pallid skin looked more so than the norm. His cobalt-colored eyes were dark and full of rebellion, save for the flicker of fear as the two wounds through his jugular veins seeped blood, draining him in a most painful way.

"Stratos, you know why you're here, do you not?"

The vampire's eyes creased at the sides as they narrowed, but he offered no response.

"It was reported that you were found with a messenger."

Again, the vampire remained mute.

"I know you are aware that this is forbidden," Alasdair said, staring at the strung-up male. "Why would you involve yourself with one of these creatures, Stratos?"

"I…" he sputtered. "She…"

Considering Alasdair's current disposition and the events of recent weeks, she didn't think Stratos stood much chance of survival if he didn't start talking. He knew the consequences of what happened if one was discovered fraternizing with a messenger. They were tortured for the information they knew or had given up and then eliminated.

A messenger was nothing but a tool used between realms. A race of beings who could travel through all portals, all time divides, and come out unscathed and unaged. They held allegiance to no one, but they were quite happy to deliver information at a price.

A price that could be outbid by an enemy should they offer the messenger something more tempting.

Only three were permitted to *ever* approach such beings: Diomêdês, Eton, and Vasilios. They were the only ones who had any loyalty from those creatures, and even they rarely sought them out.

"Let's get one thing straight, she is not a *she*," Isadora stressed as she walked over to the two males. "*It* is a being of no gender. You know this."

"But she… *It* looked like—"

"It doesn't matter," she snapped. "Involving yourself with one of their kind leads to nothing but questions and problems for everyone. Which is why it is strictly forbidden. You aren't a newling, so again, we have to ask: Why?"

Alasdair clasped his hands behind his back and turned away from the both of them. She wondered how this would end, but knew it would only be a matter of time until she'd find out.

"What did it tell you?" Isadora demanded, and as she'd expected, Stratos lied.

"Nothing."

"Try. Again." Her tone was icy enough to make the air in the room frigid. She grasped the vampire's hair and hauled him up to place her lips by his temple. "If you tell me, I'll make sure Alasdair ends this quickly. If you don't, well, you know how it went with him and your cousin. The smell of burnt flesh takes weeks to dissipate, and I'm not in the mood for a spring clean. So let's try this again. What did it tell you?"

As she waited for a response, she wondered what could've tempted the vampire to risk his immortality.

"She...she wasn't like the others..."

Baring her teeth, she growled in his ear, "What do you mean?"

When he didn't answer, Isadora twisted her fingers in his hair and arched his neck back, widening the gashes on his throat. The pained cry that ricocheted off the leather-padded walls pierced the air, but it wouldn't be heard beyond the room they were in.

"Start talking. This will be much easier for you if you do."

"She was sent from our creators..."

"The Ancients would never—" Isadora started.

"No—not the Ancients."

With that new piece of information, Alasdair turned back and leaned down until his face hovered only inches from the other vampire's. Stratos *definitely* had their attention now.

"Who else is there?" Alasdair asked.

"The ones who created *them*…" he hissed up at him.

Alasdair clamped his fingers into the jagged wounds on either side of Stratos's windpipe, and when he flashed his fangs at him, he stated as calmly as if he were conversing over drinks and not torture, "Ambrogio created the Ancients. This we already know. Tell me something new, I'm growing bored."

Stratos gurgled and blood trickled out of the corner of his mouth as his eyes rolled to the back of his head. "I know nothing more…"

Alasdair looked across at her, the skepticism evident in his eyes. He didn't believe that for a second. "Tell me why, Stratos."

The male focused on Alasdair, and a crazed smile spread across his mouth, revealing blood-stained teeth. After a hysterical sound resembling a laugh bubbled up from his ravaged throat, he whispered, "You don't even know."

Fed up with the fucked-up mind games, Alasdair jerked him up, close to ripping his esophagus free, and the strangled scream that came to an abrupt halt told Isadora that Stratos was now beyond vocal communication.

"I *will* find out," Alasdair vowed in a low, menacing tone.

Just before his windpipe was torn free of his body, taking his head with it, Stratos thought loud enough so they both heard, *You don't even know...*

LEO SQUINTED INTO the still darkness of his bedroom. His blood rushed around his head, loud in his ears, as he ordered himself across the threshold and into the room that was once his safe haven. With a trembling hand, he checked the lock on his window. Not that it would stop Alasdair, but it made him feel better anyway. Then he walked back to his bed, where he pulled the covers down and crawled inside.

For the last two weeks, he'd been living a nightmare. One that had revolved around the alluring vampire who'd left him flat on his back on his kitchen table. Yet here he was now, staring up at the ceiling, unable to get him out of his head.

Three hours had passed since Alasdair had vanished without a word, and still, he couldn't decide how he really felt about the events of the past couple of weeks.

The bedroom he'd once been so comfortable in suddenly felt vast and empty as he lay there wondering if... *What? He's going to come back? Christ, Chapel. Wake up. You're lucky to be alive. He's gone. You wanted him gone, so be happy.*

Happy was the last thing he was, though. He was restless and confused. His body had responded to Alasdair's as it would any *human* man that extraordinarily sexy. His cock hardened, his pulse raced, but whenever they'd kissed he was brought back to reality real fucking quick.

This was *not* a human he was attracted to, and every time things got heated between them, Leo got a flash of memory, or sight, or somefuckingthing. He'd seen Alasdair as he'd been… in the past.

But how can that be?

He was probably projecting. Wishing to see someone who wasn't really there and imagining Alasdair as a human to eliminate the sense of danger.

But as he clutched the covers in his hands and his knuckles turned white, his eyes landed on a book on his nightstand. The same one he'd been reading the night Alasdair had taken him.

No matter how hard he tried, his mind kept imagining Alasdair in the white toga and leather sandals.

That has to be it. His work project.

It was spilling over into his sleep, so he willed himself to forget the vampire. Alasdair had destroyed all semblance of a normal reality for him. Maybe, if he could get some uninterrupted shut-eye, he'd wake in the morning and his life would return to the way it used to be.

As the security of alertness faded and he drifted off into wary slumber, though, Leo heard that familiar and hypnotic voice inside his mind, promising, *You're not rid of me yet, file mou. I'll be seeing you tomorrow night, Leonidas Chapel.*

Fourteen

LEO STOOD IN the center of Elias's office and waited. The fact that he'd been waiting for over twenty minutes was a fairly good indication he was in deep shit.

He remembered a time when he'd been a student in one of Elias's classes. He'd been caught mouthing off to a friend about how their "teacher" always showed up late on Wednesdays, so he didn't see the need to show up on time.

Yeah, Elias had him wait in his office after *that* particular class for forty-five minutes. He'd missed a date he'd had later that night, and Leo would never forget the smug look on his teacher's face when he'd walked in the office, told him not to have such a big mouth, then let him go.

Forty-five minutes for ten damn seconds. Asshole.

But that's what made Elias Elias. He was a total hard-ass when need be, but Leo was also extremely lucky to have him in his life. He'd been a guiding hand to both him and Paris when they'd taken an extra interest in his courses. What had started as an academic relationship had eventually turned into a friendship that now spanned years.

Whoever said history was for geeks and old men hadn't meant Elias Fontana. He was quite possibly the most intelligent person Leo knew, and he didn't take shit from anyone.

Leo unbuttoned his navy-blue cardigan and took his bag off, placing it on one of the elaborate, wooden chairs in the room. Elias sure did like his collectables. The two chairs in his office were likely worth more than Leo could imagine, with the stunning silver engrained in the arms and legs. He always meant to ask him what year they were from but inevitably forgot.

It felt like years instead of weeks since he'd stepped foot inside the museum. Even then, he usually took the elevator down to where his office was located in the basement—or, as they called it, "his dungeon." He rarely came up to the main offices.

He scratched the back of his head and thought about what he was going to say when his friend, and boss, finally did show up.

Maybe it would be best to go with the lie Alasdair had already told. *At least then Elias will just be pissed, not reaching for the phone to have me admitted to the psych ward.*

He sat down in the chair opposite the desk and tipped his head back, closing his eyes. As much as he wasn't looking forward to this meeting, he was dreading the evening more. He still wasn't sure whether or not he'd imagined Alasdair's voice as he'd drifted off to sleep last night. If he *had* heard it, though, when and where the vampire would show up, he had no idea.

His eyes moved to the window on the left side of Elias's office, and the sunrise got him thinking.

Can Alasdair move about in the daylight? Or is the myth about burning in the sun just a myth?

It would explain why he wouldn't be around until tonight. So Leo pulled out the notebook he'd stuffed in his pocket earlier and removed the pen attached to the side binding. He always worked better when he had his questions written down. As if, when they were out of his brain, he had more room for other important things.

Last night, he'd started a list of questions he wanted answered if Alasdair happened to reappear in his life. Questions like: *Can they eat normal food?* It was a valid one, especially considering *his* blood was likely the desired meal of choice. He jotted down his question about sunlight, and when he was putting the notebook away, the door behind him finally opened.

Leo stood as Elias walked through the door. He dumped his briefcase on the ground, unbuttoned his black, woolen coat, and then came across the room and around the end of his desk. His dark hair was windblown, and the stubble on his face looked a day or so old. He pulled his desk chair out, but before he sat down, he raised his head to pin Leo with eerie, silver eyes.

Suddenly, Leo's palms began to sweat as if he were seventeen all over again. He remembered the first time he'd really looked at Elias back then, and like now, his eyes almost shined at him. They were unreal. Everyone always said so.

"Are you early? Or am I late?" he asked as he shrugged out of his coat.

"You're late."

Elias threw the heavy material across the corner of his desk and sat in his chair. "Good."

Leo grimaced as he took his seat and crossed his leg so his ankle rested on his knee. He bounced his leg as he waited for Elias to say more, and when he didn't, Leo thought it might be best to get a head start.

"Elias, look. I'm so sorry—"

"Sorry? You're *sorry*?"

Leo winced at the disgruntled question. *So much for a head start.*

"Do you know how fucking worried we've been these past two weeks? Sorry isn't going to cut it here. So I sure as shit hope you have a better explanation than that."

He opened his mouth, about to feed him the lie Alasdair had started, when Elias leaned across the desk and shook his head.

"And don't you dare try to tell me you fell in love and disappeared for thirteen days, Leonidas. I've known you for nearly eleven years, and you've never been so stupid or thoughtless."

Leo stared tongue-tied at the man he'd grown to admire and respect over the years. As Elias waited for him to tell the truth, Leo wasn't quite sure what to say.

"Start talking, Leo. Give me something so I believe you still give a shit about this job you have worked your ass off for. Are you really going to throw your life away for someone you just met?"

"No," Leo murmured.

"No? Then help me understand. Where the fuck have you been? Are you caught up in something you can't get out of?"

Leo brought his head up and frowned. "Such as?"

"I don't know. You tell me. Drugs? Does that guy have you doing things you don't want to do? He looked the type."

He didn't mean to, but Leo couldn't stop himself from laughing at the absurd thought of Alasdair as a drug dealer. He supposed, from an outside perspective, he did come off as arrogant and somewhat scary in the way nothing seemed to intimidate him.

But a drug dealer? No.

"I'm glad you find this amusing," Elias grit out, his patience running thin. "Because if that's what's going on here, drugs, we can go down and report him."

"No. No," Leo denied adamantly, pulling himself together. He uncrossed his legs and sat forward, putting his elbows on his knees so he could rest his face in his palms. "He's not a drug dealer. For God's sake, Elias, give me some credit."

"I'm giving you no fucking credit right now," he thundered. "You don't deserve it. You just took off. No note for your friends, no call to your *boss*—"

"I didn't have a choice," Leo finally said, getting to his feet. He ran his hand through his hair and then gripped the back of his neck as he stared at Elias. "I couldn't call you."

Elias tilted his head to the side, carefully contemplating his next words. "Why not?"

Leo dropped his hand and shook his head. "I can't tell you."

Elias sighed. "Try again, Leo."

"I. Can't. Tell. You," he said, enunciating each word. "Look at me. Do I look like I'm enjoying myself here?"

The silence was strained as Elias looked him over, and all Leo could hear was the anxious beat of his heart. It was funny—Elias, in his own way, commanded a room as effectively as Alasdair did. The only difference was there was no immediate threat of death with this man.

Until today, maybe.

"Do you still want to work here, Leo?"

"Of course," he answered immediately. "It was never about that—Jesus. I feel like my whole fucking life has turned on its head."

Elias nodded and got to his feet. Leo watched him make his way over to him, reminded why he'd once had a crush on his university teacher. Elias was tall, his suit outlined his broad shoulders, and when he stopped so they were face-to-face, Leo noted, not for the first time, how handsome his friend was. It really was a shame he was straight.

"Paris found this yesterday," he told him as he reached into his pocket and pulled out a folded piece of paper.

Leo took it from him.

"Tell me where you've been, Leo," Elias said in a low voice.

When the paper was released, Leo raised his eyes to meet Elias's silver ones and thought he saw... *No, it can't be.* However, Leo could've sworn he had seen a flash of knowledge in them. *What is he waiting for me to say?*

"I can't."

"Why not? We've told each other everything for years."

Leo dropped his eyes and busied himself unfolding the paper. When he saw the notes he'd made of his recurrent dreams, he touched his finger to the words.

How the hell... "Where did you get this?"

"I told you. Paris found it in your office last night."

Leo looked at the date of the final entry and then took a cautious step away from Elias.

"What's wrong?" he asked, but Leo didn't answer, his mind instead whirling as he tried to remember bringing that piece of paper to his office. But...

I didn't. I left it at home, in the drawer of my desk.

"Leo?"

Leo grabbed his bag and stuffed the paper inside. "I've gotta go."

"Hang on one damn minute," Elias demanded, grabbing his arm. "I hope you mean you have to go downstairs, because we only have a couple of days and then the exhibit opens."

Leo glanced at the hand Elias had on his arm. What was going on? *How did he get that piece of paper?*

"So, I still have a job?"

Elias frowned and released his hold. "Yes. Unless you keep this bizarre behavior up. Then, friend or no friend, I'll have to reassess your job duties."

"Okay," Leo agreed, hastily backing out of the office. "I'll...I'll be downstairs if you need me."

Then he left, not giving Elias another chance to speak.

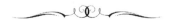

ELIAS WAITED UNTIL Leo had disappeared before shutting the door and walking back over to his desk. He sat down and reached for the clock on the corner of it. Gently, he unlatched and opened the small door at the back that hid the mechanisms inside. Then he removed the small key resting on the wooden base.

After closing the clock, he moved it aside so he wouldn't knock it over and then inserted the key into the center drawer of his desk. Upon rolling it open, he took out the leather-bound journal and untied the binding knotted across the center.

It'd been years since he'd looked at the entries, but right there, written neatly down the first page, were several of them, each of them having occurred nearly ten years ago exactly. He'd marked the date, the time, and the strange blinding light that had been in each of the dreams. But the one journal entry he kept coming back to was the first one, the one that was different than all the others.

Different than the ones Leo had *also* documented.

9/16/05, 3:13 a.m. - Yesterday was my first day teaching. Nerves finally caught up to me, I think, which might explain why I had such an odd dream tonight. It was about two of my students. Not anything creepy. But they were definitely in it. Leonidas Chapel and Paris Antoniou. Two boys whose names could be straight out of the history books I'm teaching from. But the odd thing about the dream was we weren't in class. We were standing in some sort of hall. It was massive in size, and there was a marble altar in front of us. Seated behind the altar were three figures (I think they were men.) The light that was shining on the three of us was so bright I could barely see at all. I was in the middle, Leonidas was to my left, and Paris to the right. Then a voice so commanding I felt the weight of the order down to my bones said, "Born of us, you are the three. When the time comes, they shall find you." Then I woke.

Fifteen

LEO'S MIND WAS a mess as he walked to the two elevators at the far end of the corporate floor. He pressed the down button and fiddled with the strap of his bag while he waited for the elevator to arrive.

Since he'd left Elias's office, he'd gone over their conversation several times. But no matter how it played out, the piece of paper, the one Elias had lied about, might as well have been burning a hole in his bag.

His foot tapped as the light indicated the elevator had stopped on the ground floor. It still had five floors to climb until it reached him, and his agitation rose with each level.

Why did Elias have his journal entry? *And why not admit to snooping around my place while I was gone instead of lying?* It made no sense at all.

He ran his fingers down the strap of his bag and then flipped the top flap open to pull the paper out. Staring at the words, he ran his fingers over them again, reading them back in his mind.

I was standing in a huge room, at an altar or something, and there was a light. A bright, blinding light—

DING.

When the elevator announced its arrival, Leo looked up from the paper and watched the metallic doors slide open.

There, standing inside, was Alasdair. Wearing all black, from his boots to his coat, and with his beautifully sculptured face, he resembled some sort of fallen angel. One who had frozen Leo.

As the doors began to slide shut, Alasdair causally pushed off the wall and jabbed one of the buttons. Once they'd whooshed back open, Leo heard in his head, *Won't you come inside, Leonidas?*

Leo licked his lips, and when Alasdair's eyes dropped to them, he clutched the paper in his hand.

I told you I would be back.

"You said tonight," Leo said out loud, and then he thought, *What difference does it make what time he showed up?*

"I changed my mind," Alasdair said as he raised an arm to hold the elevator open.

An office door opened and shut behind Leo, and then footsteps made their way towards them.

"Better hurry. I haven't eaten this morning, and after the night I've had, I'm a little testy."

Shit. He really had no other choice as he entered the small confines of the elevator and again thought, *How do I get myself into these situations?*

AS LEO WALKED by, Alasdair closed his eyes and inhaled, taking in his fresh scent. It was all he could do to stop himself from taking Leo's arm and sinking his teeth into him. The only thing preventing him from acting on the urge was the knowledge of what would happen should he give in to his hunger.

Fuck, I need to find someone to feed on and soon.

The doors to the elevator closed, locking him inside with Leo, who was now flattening himself against the far wall. Alasdair couldn't stop himself from moving towards him.

After he'd finished with Stratos and cleaned himself up, he'd gotten to thinking about what the vampire had said before his demise.

She was different... You don't even know.

Stratos was, ironically, dead on. He didn't have a goddamned clue what he'd been talking about, and neither did Isadora. Not that she seemed to care too much. She'd told him quite plainly that she wouldn't bother trying to decipher the words of a deranged mind when she could be out pursuing other, more enjoyable pastimes. Such as her redhead.

It was a selfish deed to disregard the dead and what they'd died for so blithely, but that's who they were at the core. Selfish, narcissistic creatures. And as he placed his hands on the wall on either side of Leo's head, his cousin's words echoed through his mind.

"Go and feed, Alasdair. Find a warm body to fuck. Forget about that human you've been obsessing over, and forget Stratos. Let it go."

But he couldn't. Something felt…off. Stratos hadn't been the type to do what he had done, and *that* was still bothering him. So was the fact that the one person he wanted to fuck was also harboring a most dangerous weapon.

"So you *can* walk outside when it's daylight?"

The question from Leo was so unexpected Alasdair lost his train of thought and dropped his hands, crossing them over his chest. He eyed the human and wondered when this man had decided he was no longer a threat.

Maybe it's time to remedy that. "That's the first question you ask when trapped in an elevator with a hungry carnivore?"

"Hey, look," Leo said, trying to appear casual. "I'm hungry too and could do with some eggs and bacon. But you don't have to worry about me attacking you. I expect the same courtesy."

Alasdair resumed his previous position with his hands by either side of Leo's head, pleased when the man clamped his mouth shut. "And why would you expect that?"

Leo's throat contracted as he swallowed, and Alasdair lowered his eyes to his pulse.

"Because you want something from me."

The words could've been taken several ways. Alasdair knew Leo was referring to information, yet he couldn't seem to help himself from lowering his lips to the corner of Leo's mouth.

"And what is that? The pleasure I denied myself last night? Is that what you think I want, Leonidas?"

Leo's breath brushed over his lips as he dared to ask, "Why *did* you deny yourself?"

He was surprised to discover how much he liked this bolder side of Leo, and he nipped his lower lip then said, "I like how it feels to hunt you down. To toy with you. To tease you until you're begging for it. It's in my nature."

Several seconds passed, and the air became thick with the same sexual tension from the previous night. The desire that had been ignited was still hovering between them, unfulfilled and most definitely unsatisfied.

"So you want me to be scared of you. And I was, *am*, terrified. You're really fucking scary. But I can't help but wonder why something as destructive as you is so…"

"So?" Alasdair pressed.

Leo's breath faltered when Alasdair moved his mouth down to his neck and licked a path along the vein pulsating there. "So...so attractive."

Alasdair chuckled at the reluctant compliment. "While it's incredibly flattering that you think my looks were designed this way due to what I am, it's just not so." He then grazed his teeth along the line of Leo's jaw and told him, "We appear as we were when turned. Minus, of course, anything cosmetic, such as a haircut. The vampire gene merely adds an eternal...shine of sorts. An immortality elixir, some might say."

When Leo arched his head away without even realizing, exposing the column of his throat to him like a final meal to a dying man, Alasdair's stomach knotted.

I must be fucking insane to torment myself this way. I know what his blood can do to me. And yet...I still want it.

"So you've always been this...this..." Leo trailed off on a sigh, not finishing his thought.

Alasdair raised his head, not quite certain his control could be counted on.

"Come on. You must know how hot you are," Leo said, straightening back up and shaking his head as if to clear it.

"Hot?" he asked, the word breaking through his thought as one he wasn't familiar with.

The elevator came to a halt, and when the doors opened, Leo slid past, keeping a wary eye on him, and walked out into the corridor.

Alasdair followed down the dimly lit hall. "This place reminds me of home."

Leo glanced over his shoulder and rolled his eyes at him. "Of course it does. We're in a basement."

"Your boss makes you work in a basement? Hardly seems like a job worth getting upset over losing."

When Leo stopped and spun to face him, Alasdair slid his hands into the pockets of his pants.

"I'm lucky I still have a job, no thanks to you. And I wouldn't be so judgmental. Like you said, you live in the equivalent of this basement."

He gave a slight nod. "You could look at it that way, I suppose. *Or* that you're lucky to be alive and able to come back to said job *because* of me."

Leo scoffed. "Why? Because when you tried to kill me you got paralyzed? That's not luck because of your goodwill. That's luck due to my own body's kickass defense system."

Alasdair faded in and out so quickly he had their bodies pressed intimately together before Leo could react. "A defense you claim to know nothing about."

"Ye...yeah. That's right," Leo stuttered.

Alasdair stared him down as he reached for the piece of paper. But Leo's fist tightened stubbornly, refusing to let it go.

"Give it to me, Leo."

"No. It's none of your business."

"I don't care. I want to know what's on it."

"There's nothing on it."

"Why do you insist on lying to me when you know I can find out the truth?"

Leo locked his jaw, refusing to say any more, and glared at him.

"Fine. Let's do this the hard way."

As what was about to happen seemed to dawn on Leo, he shook his head, but it was too late. He was already inside his mind.

GIVE ME THE paper, Leonidas.

Yeah, he hated when Alasdair delved inside his head. It felt so intimate and invasive. But when he did that weird body-*and*-mind-control thing, Leo wanted to scream at him to fuck off and leave him alone. Being at someone's mercy was not pleasant. At least, when it was physical, he had some recourse. This was so…one sided.

His arm rose, and he handed Alasdair the journal entry. Then he watched in a daze as he unfolded and read what was on it. When Alasdair was done, he looked at him with a fierce scowl. Alasdair had gone from sexy to scary as fucking hell.

Who told you about this?

"Told me about what?"

About the Assembly Hall? How do you know of it?

Leo's mind scrambled through his memories and thoughts for something about an Assembly Hall but came up with nothing. "I don't know what the Assembly Hall is."

Alasdair grabbed him by the wrist and yanked him forward, thrusting the paper in his face. *You wrote about it here, several times. It's dated before we met. If you don't know what it is, how did you know to write it?*

Compelled to answer with only the truth, Leo opened his mouth and replied, "I don't know."

I don't believe you. At each turn there's more tricks, more deception. You can even fight this *somehow.*

Leo couldn't fight the mind game Alasdair was playing. Every word shoved into his head was heavy and authoritative, and he couldn't do anything other than stand there. So, when Alasdair faded them out of the hall, he expected to find himself back in the strange room with the leather walls and metal hooks. Once he'd come to, though, he was stunned to be on the worn couch against the brick wall of his office.

ALASDAIR PACED THE length of Leo's office, staring at the chaotic mess of photographs, posters, and timelines pinned all over the wall. He'd dumped Leo on the couch when he'd faded them inside—and that's when he'd spotted it. An entire wall filled with hundreds of images from days long past.

The temples, the arenas, the…

No, it can't be.

He pulled one of the photographs off the wall. As he studied the familiar crumbling columns, and the large, rectangular pool that sank deep into the earth, a jolt of sensation struck his otherwise lifeless heart.

It was *his* bathhouse.

The one where Vasilios had turned him.

The same one he'd projected Leo to that first night.

This was *not* a coincidence. Something bigger was at work, and when he rounded back and saw Leo pushing himself up into a seated position, he knew this human was somehow involved.

Reacting purely on instinct, he was across the room and pinning Leo to the couch with no other thought than to extract the truth from him. With his fingers wrapped around Leo's throat, he watched him with distrustful eyes, concerned for his own safety for the first time ever.

When Leo coughed and reached for his hand, Alasdair glared down at him, wanting nothing more than to end this new emotion of uncertainty by snapping the man's neck. But he knew that he wouldn't.

He was angry. He felt oddly…betrayed.

When their eyes locked and Leo's mouth opened, Alasdair shoved the photo in his face and demanded, "What is this?"

Leo clawed at his grip, trying desperately to break free, but he was relentless in his pursuit for the truth. He wasn't going to free him until he knew what the fuck was going on.

"I...I... It's research."

"Research?" Alasdair hissed, his face close enough to Leo's that he could taste the other man's breath when he gasped. "You said you didn't know who, or what, I was."

"I don't."

"Don't *lie* to me," he thundered, his fangs piercing through his gums.

Leo's eyes flicked to them, and his heart pounded. "I'm...not," he said, his voice faltering as he pushed the words through squashed vocal cords.

"Then how do you know of this place? No one knows where I was turned. Yet you have a photo of it taped to your fucking wall."

The legs trapped between Alasdair's scissored apart as Leo tried to shift out from under him. But he widened his own and trapped Leo's between them. Then he pushed him deeper into the tattered couch cushions.

"It's for the exhibit," Leo rushed out. "A place we were researching for our exhibit. That's all. I didn't, *don't*, know anything more."

The words rang of truth, but the coincidence was too much for him to accept. He didn't believe that, out of all the destinations, *all* the ancient ruins, the one place Leonidas was studying happened to be—

"That's where you were changed…turned into a vampire, isn't it? That's what you meant a minute ago?"

Alasdair focused on the man trapped under him, and found that he *wanted* to tell this stranger everything about himself. But he didn't dare.

This, what he was doing right now, was dangerous. No matter how many times he told himself that, though, he couldn't bring himself to leave. He felt drawn to Leo in a way he'd only ever felt once in his life, and *that* realization solidified what he'd been thinking all along.

Leonidas Chapel wasn't merely a mortal. A mortal couldn't, and wouldn't, capture the sole attention of his kind without some kind of…power. Whatever he was, Alasdair had never seen the likes of him, and for that reason alone, Leo was perhaps the biggest danger of all.

LEO KNEW THE smart thing to do was to shut his mouth. But, as he looked up into the fierce face hovering over his own, he wanted to know more.

Alasdair was unlike anybody, or any*thing*, he'd ever come across, and every part of him demanded he learn as much as he could before he vanished—or, worse, decided to kill him after all.

With a tentative hand, he touched one of Alasdair's high cheekbones, and when he flinched, Leo yanked his hand back.

"How old are you?" he asked, finally voicing the one question he'd been wanting to ask since he'd realized exactly what he was. "You have to be close to—"

"I'm old," Alasdair said.

"Well, you look no older than your mid thirties."

The sound Alasdair made was derisive as he shifted his body over the top of his, and it was all Leo could do not to pant. *Yeah*, he had a vampire practically strangling him, but the weight of Alasdair's lower body brushing over his cock counteracted the fear coursing through him.

"You're the one who has been studying me. Why don't *you* tell me how old I am?"

Leo stared up at the serious face and the luminescent eyes looking down at him. Alasdair's emotions were riding him, and he was reacting based solely on his instincts. Instincts that were telling him that, for some reason, little old him was a danger. Alasdair felt threatened and was flexing his power. Something that both terrified and, oddly enough, turned Leo on.

"I'm not studying you. I… *We* have been working on an exhibit for the museum. That's just one of the locations we were recreating as a place people used to socialize. For meetings and…well, you know. You were there—can you please let go of my throat?"

Alasdair released his grip and placed his hands on either side of Leo's head. Then he cocked his head to the side, much the way an animal does when it's watching its prey try to squirm away, and Leo began to do just that. He tried to move under the body holding him down, but when Alasdair's brow rose as if his attempt was ridiculous, he quit moving altogether.

"Then you don't need me to tell you how old I am. You already know."

Leo glanced at the photo in Alasdair's fist, now a scrunched-up remnant of its former self, and thought about the date of the image. *Ancient Athens 47 BC, and it's now 2015. So that makes him—*

"You're over two thousand years old."

"And you know too much." Then Alasdair vanished.

Leo angled his head and saw him standing in front of his research wall again, his back to him.

"Do you not find this odd?"

Leo stood and pressed his fingers to his forehead. Ever since he'd met Alasdair, his entire *world* had become a little odd. *As in fucked up beyond all things sane.*

"Yes. But I never knew your kind existed. So, I mean, is this… Do *you* find this odd?"

Alasdair turned and regarded him carefully—as if seeing him for the first time. Then he answered, "I do."

Leo waited, figuring there had to be more than that. Then, realizing what Alasdair was about to do, he sprinted across the room and reached out to grip the vampire's wrist as he faded, with him in tow, right out of his office.

Sixteen

NO HE FUCKING didn't.

When Alasdair appeared at the foot of Vasilios's bed and Leo fell at his feet in a heap, he looked down at the human, completely perplexed.

What does he think he's doing? And how did he know to grab me at that precise moment? With those and at least ten other questions running through his mind, Alasdair nearly forgot where he'd ended up until the male whose bedroom they were in spoke up.

"Well, well. This is a pleasant surprise."

Alasdair tore his eyes from Leo long enough to look at the male he'd come in search of. Vasilios was lounging in the center of his monstrous bed, and as usual, clothed or naked, as he currently was, he commanded the room like a king on a throne. When Alasdair took in his bronzed torso and the black silk sheet draped across his waist, his cock stiffened, and his feet wanted to move him in his sire's direction. It was the same reaction he'd been having for centuries.

"I was not expecting to see you today, Alasdair, though we do need to talk. What brings you to my bedchambers?"

It was obvious from the tenting of the sheets that, although Vasilios hadn't expected him, he certainly wasn't opposed to his being there. As the familiar surge of lust ran through him, Alasdair was about to answer, but Leo moaned, recapturing his attention.

"I see, you brought your yielding with you."

Vasilios's biting tone brought his eyes back to him. He'd removed the covers now, and Alasdair watched him closely as he climbed out of bed.

"I have to admit, this is the first time I have ever felt cheated of your attention. I don't much enjoy the feeling."

Alasdair kept his eyes on the male headed his way, but as he got closer, he couldn't help himself from looking down to the thick cock that proudly jutted out from its owner. The same one that had pleasured him so many times over the years.

"Should I be concerned?"

"Concerned?" Alasdair asked, even though he knew exactly what he meant.

Vasilios trailed his eyes over him, and as he stood there under the other vampire's inspection, Alasdair was torn between the desire to go to him and another, more complex one—the desire to crouch down over Leo and protect him.

Protect him? From what? Vasilios?

The idea was preposterous. He would never defy him in such a way. But as the Ancient got closer, the urge intensified.

Vasilios shifted his gaze to where Leo lay and said, "Yes. Concerned that your obsession here will make me have to hurt you. Is that what you want? For me to hurt you?"

Alasdair didn't know what he wanted. His mind was all over the fucking place. He wanted answers—he knew that much.

Back in Leo's office, he'd thought the smartest thing to do was to come here to get them. He'd thought to explain all that happened with Leo to his sire and see if he knew anything of it. Perhaps Vasilios had knowledge of what Leo was or why he had the ability to do what he could do.

What he hadn't counted on was the human latching on to his arm and coming with him.

Now, there they were, in the presence of the oldest and most powerful vampire in this realm, and he could only hope Leo remained unconscious. The mood radiating off Vasilios was ferocious, and the idea of telling him anything other than what he wanted to hear was quickly dissipating.

Stepping around Leo, Alasdair ran a hand through his hair and walked towards his sire. When he stopped opposite him, he wrapped his fingers around Vasilios's stiff erection and said, "I'm still recovering from the last time you hurt me. I'm not quite sure my body could handle another of your punishments."

Full of confidence, as always, Vasilios fucked his cock through the tight fist surrounding it. "You look fully recovered to me. Though it is hard to tell through all of your clothing, *agóri*. Time to lose them, *nai*?"

Before he could answer, Alasdair's clothes were gone. One thought and they were a mere memory on the floor. Hunger flared in Vasilios's eyes as he devoured the sight of his naked body, and the flame that ignited their green depths excited him. It always did.

Hundreds—no, thousands—had wanted to be owned by this male over the years of his existence, and only one ever truly had been—him.

"Flawless as always," Vasilios praised, bringing a hand up to trace his fingers down the center of his chest. "Do not fret. I left no scars. You are still the most exquisite thing I own."

Those words normally wouldn't bother him. Alasdair knew whom he belonged to. This time, however, he thought of the expression on Leo's face when he'd explained on the night of the Walk that his brood now saw him as his property.

"Alasdair?"

Alasdair groaned as familiar fingers curled around his shaft. He closed his eyes, letting his head fall back while he ordered his mind clear of the human who, for right now, was passed out cold on the floor.

"Ah, and there your mind goes. Wandering back to *him*."

They stood as close as they could possibly get without being inside one another, and when Vasilios stroked his fist up to the head of his length and twisted his wrist, Alasdair grunted and returned the gesture.

"*Mhmm*. Thinking of your golden-haired boy. The one you have yet to claim with this magnificent cock of yours."

Alasdair ran his tongue over his top lip, the words and Vasilios's touch making his gums tingle. He hadn't come here for this, but when Vasilios bent his head and grazed his teeth along his collarbone, Alasdair knew he was only minutes away from being fucked.

"You make me *hungry*, Alasdair. Standing here so hard and aroused. And though I should be offended you're busy thinking of another while I have you in my hand, I'll forgo that to feed from you."

Alasdair's breath caught and his hand stopped moving when Vasilios cupped the back of his neck with his free hand.

"After all, why should I be jealous of such an inferior being? It seems so petty for someone such as myself when there is no comparison between us two."

The lips talking could be so cruel at times. Yet, at others, like now, they could deliver the most erotic experience imagined.

"Wake him, *omorfo mou agóri*. I want him to see whom you belong to before you use *this* to lay claim to him."

Alasdair did as he had been told, reaching out to Leo's mind and waking him. Then he positioned himself on the bed and waited to be of service.

LEO'S MIND WAS a hazy mass of confusion when he finally came to. He wasn't sure what had possessed him to grab Alasdair back in his office, but a certain look had flashed in the vampire's eyes, and he'd known he was about to bolt, *or vanish.*

Now…where the hell am I?

Wherever he was, he'd never been there before. He was sprawled across a hardwood surface, and the sooner he got up and moving, the better. He needed to find Alasdair. He wasn't ready to be done with their previous conversation, and if he was willing to continue having it after his life had been threatened, then the least the vampire could do was stick around long enough to explain why he'd thought all of this was *odd.*

As his eyes adjusted to the light of the room, the massive claw foot of a wooden bed frame came into focus, and he froze.

A bedroom, he thought. *I'm in a bedroom…but whose?*

He was about to sit up and look around for the mercurial male, when a deep, throaty growl of satisfaction rang through the room. The sound was so erotic that the sensual cadence of it enveloped him and seemed to stroke its way down between his legs. Leo's cock throbbed in response, and he palmed the erection swelling inside his pants.

Fuck. Where the hell did that come from?

He closed his eyes, squeezing his fingers around himself as he willed his dick to behave. But right when he thought he had control over it, he heard that growl again, followed by a voice.

"*Parta.* You know how you want it."

Jesus, that's hot. Take it? Take what? Leo thought, scrambling up to his knees. *And…that voice.* He'd know that coaxing, powerful voice anywhere.

He slowly raised his eyes over the elaborately carved footboard, and when he saw long, white fingers curled over the top of it, his mouth fell open in astonishment.

What was happening only a few feet away from him was something he had only ever imagined in his dirtiest, horniest dreams. Alasdair was—*Christ…fuck.* He was completely naked, and Leo blinked a couple times, trying to decide if he was hallucinating. But when a harsh curse echoed throughout the room, and the fingers on the wood flexed, Leo knew he wasn't. His eyes flicked up to watch Alasdair toss his head back and snarl.

I definitely did not *dream this up,* he thought, transfixed by what was going on. He wasn't sure his brain had the capacity to conceive such an animalistic vision.

A large hand smoothed over the back of Alasdair's dark hair, and as it gripped the back of his neck and held him in place, Alasdair's eyes collided with his. The glow in Alasdair's seemed to ignite a fire inside Leo, and his cock went from under control to a pulsating reminder that, *God…*he really loved men.

He then looked at the second occupant of the bed, but there was really no need. He already knew who he'd see—and he was right. There, situated on his knees, with his cock balls-deep inside Alasdair, was Vasilios. And the sight of him naked and fucking Alasdair had Leo's dick weeping in response.

Mhmm. The low hum of gratification vibrated through his mind as Alasdair braced his arms against the wood to hold himself in place. *Come here, file mou. You know you want to.*

Of course he fucking wanted to, and Alasdair knew that. But, as the invitation penetrated his brain, Leo shuffled away. When his back hit a wall, Alasdair's fangs, those razor-edged fangs of his, slid down into place. Vasilios cursed violently as he gripped Alasdair's hair and then twisted his head to the side.

Like a beast being brought to heel, Alasdair growled, and Leo winced at the force being used. But Alasdair bucked back against the other vampire, clearly enjoying it. Vasilios aligned his chest with Alasdair's back, and when he caught Leo watching them, his eyes flashed bright.

Oh, mother of God. If he'd thought Alasdair could hold his attention, *this guy must be a fucking hypnotist.*

A conceited smirk crossed Vasilios's mouth, reminding Leo he could hear his every thought. Then *his* fangs punched out of his gums, and Leo couldn't stop himself from cupping his erection through his pants.

He knew what the vampire was about to do. Knew it as if he'd announced his intention out loud. Then he did it.

Vasilios parted his lips and struck, sinking his teeth deep into Alasdair's neck, and the roar that ripped out of Alasdair was one of sublime ecstasy.

Leo frantically unbuttoned his pants and pulled the zipper down. He needed to get his hand on his dick, and he needed it right fucking now.

As he wrapped his fingers around the painful hard-on, he spread his legs and jerked up through his fist. His own groan of pleasure escaped his mouth as he masturbated to the unrestrained mating taking place on the bed, his heart pounding like a fucking jackhammer.

What does it feel like, he wondered. *What does it feel like when they bite one another?*

Come here, Alasdair's voice invited inside his mind, and the command for his body to do what it had been told took over.

After getting to his feet, Leo walked over to the side of the bed where the two were entwined. His eyes roved over the naked tangle of arms and legs, and then a firm hand clamped onto Alasdair's shoulder to haul him up to his knees.

When both males were kneeling back to front, Leo couldn't help from looking down to Alasdair's stiff cock.

Get on the bed, Alasdair commanded, and Leo's eyes flew to the vampire Vasilios. He wasn't sure why he bothered, though, because the next thing Leo knew, he was climbing on the mattress and lying flat on his back through no will of his own.

Once he was situated with his legs spread wide, Leo thought his heart might fly out of his chest as Vasilios ran his tongue up the side of Alasdair's neck, licking the blood trickling down his skin.

Leo's cock pounded at the visual they made, and he wanted nothing more than to be able to get himself off to them. But he couldn't. He was trapped in his body, save for the movement of his eyes. So he lay there and waited for whatever would happen next.

God, let them touch me, he thought, staring up at the feral-looking vampire getting ready to... *What did Alasdair call it?*

*Fuck and feed. He's going to fuck me while he feeds,
Leonidas. And you are going to watch.*

Leo couldn't stop the ragged sound that left him
then, when Alasdair moved down over him and planted his
hands on either side of his head. His face was so close that
Leo wanted to crane up and take his lips with his own, but
when he tried, he realized he was still under Alasdair's will.

"He really is *poli omorfos, agóri.* I see the allure. It
won't be a hardship to watch him come when we do. Until
then, keep your yielding still."

Alasdair grunted in response as Vasilios sank his
teeth back into his neck and then delivered a hard thrust to
his body. Leo's eyes widened at the disturbing display but
couldn't stop himself from watching.

He wanted to touch the man whose muscles were
shaking as he held himself in place for the one who groaned
and sucked from his vein. Or better yet, he wanted to touch
himself where his pants were open and his shaft throbbed
against his thigh.

This is insane, Leo thought. *Totally fucking insane.* But
when Vasilios raised his head and his teeth left Alasdair's
throat, Alasdair lowered his body a fraction farther and
dragged it over his.

When the long, hard length of Alasdair's cock grazed
his own, Leo's eyes squeezed shut from the eroticism of it.

Mhmm.

Alasdair's raspy groan of sexual gratification pushed
into Leo's mind right before a hoarse shout left his lips. Leo

opened his eyes at the cry, and he didn't have to be behind him to know that Vasilios had just re-entered Alasdair.

The hands by his head clenched the covers, and Alasdair's nostrils flared at the brutal force of the thrust. Then his eyes found Leo's and he licked those lush lips. There was no doubt Alasdair lived for this kind of possession.

Still trapped as he was, Leo could do nothing more than lie there. Every time the vampire shoved his cock in and out of Alasdair, Alasdair would grind his erection hard against Leo's, causing one hell of a mess as sticky pre-come dripped from its tip.

He might not have voluntarily come to this bed, but now that he was there, watching the hedonistic smorgasbord unfold, all he could hope for was some kind of completion before it ended. Because, if not, he might die from the amount of frustration he was enduring.

VASILIOS'S FINGERS DUG into Alasdair's neck as his cock tunneled into his body. He could tell by the way his sire's hips had picked up pace that he was about to strike again, and when Vasilios halted both their movements and his teeth once again fastened to his carotid, Alasdair felt as though his eyes would roll to the back of his head.

The pleasure was sublime. There was none other like it. It was both brutal and beautiful, and the feeling was a fucking rush.

When he'd first invited Leo over, it'd been with the intention of distracting Vasilios from whatever slight he'd been feeling. However, the second Leo had stopped by the bed, his sire's fingers had grasped his shoulder and Alasdair was certain he'd miscalculated.

But when he'd gotten Leo up on the mattress and under them, Vasilios had sunk his teeth into his throat, along with his conditions—*You can have him join, but he doesn't touch you. Not while I feed*—and the vicious fucking he was now receiving was the result.

Underneath him, Leo lay with his legs open and his pants undone. His cock was flushed and engorged, and Alasdair knew exactly what Leo wanted right then: to fuck his fist until he came.

But he couldn't risk it. Not until Vasilios was ready.

When his shoulder was released, and he was pushed down over Leo, Alasdair started to really grind his cock against the man.

This was Vasilios's way of allowing him to get off now that his climax was near, so Alasdair took advantage and began to chase his own orgasm. He knew the quickest way to get it would be to release Leo's body back to him, so he closed his eyes and did just that.

THE MINUTE ALASDAIR'S eyes shut, Leo's body came
back under his control. He reached down and shoved his
pants below his hips as Alasdair rolled his over the top of
him. *Fucking yes...that feels amazing*, Leo thought and arched
up in response, wanting to feel that beautiful bare cock
along his.

He kept his eyes open, determined not to become
overwhelmed, but it was difficult because this was the
hottest fucking thing he'd ever been a part of—even though,
subconsciously, he knew he hadn't had a choice at all.

Their erections lined up perfectly, and the weight of
Alasdair's body on top of his was deliciously insistent as the
third male in this hell of a mindfuck beared down over them
both.

Leo bowed up again into the solid body rub he was
receiving, and when his eyes moved beyond Alasdair's face
to the striking one of his lover, his mind almost shut down
on him. Lust and fever shone in Vasilios's eyes, and
Alasdair's blood stained his lips as he licked them and his
teeth retracted.

"Oh shit," Leo whispered, awed by what he was
seeing. Then Alasdair bent his head and dragged his tongue
up along his neck.

The pulse thudding at the base of his throat must've
been like a red flag to these two, but Leo couldn't help the

erratic beating of his heart. He was too aroused, too caught up in the moment being created by the perverse vampires looming over him, to care.

All he wanted was to come. He wanted Alasdair to bite him, and then he wanted to come all over the both of them. *Hell, all over the three of us. Wait a second. What the fuck am I thinking?*

Exactly what I am. Alasdair's thought hit his mind the second his lips crushed down onto his.

As his tongue slid inside, Leo moaned into the kiss and sucked on the sensual intruder. He propelled his hips up, desperately trying to find some relief for his aching balls, and then Alasdair jerked his head back and bared his fangs as hot, sticky fluid hit Leo's stomach.

The sight was so fucking brutish and carnal that Leo's own climax raced down his spine wanting release, and just when he was about to explode—it happened.

That fucking bright shard of light that had him squeezing his eyes shut—and suddenly, his vision changed.

NO LONGER LYING underneath Alasdair, Leo froze. He was on his stomach as a breeze drifted across his skin. His erection was still pounding, and he was about to push up and look around when a strong body crowded down behind him, pressing him to the pallet that lay on the hard ground beneath him.

"Uh ah. Do not move. It is time."

As that familiar, lyrical tone met his ears, Leo became motionless. The man behind him was...

Oh shit, this can't be happening. Not now.

But when he was flipped over onto his back with no effort at all, he knew that it was. There, hovering over him, was Vasilios, and he was gloriously naked and very aroused.

Leo's eyes shifted frantically to take in his surroundings, and that's when he realized they were no longer in the bedroom from earlier. No longer where Alasdair was on the bed with the two of them.

He was back in the bathhouse.

Back in time.

Where Alasdair was nowhere in sight.

Leo was about to speak, but the male's fangs appeared as he reverently brushed aside a piece of his long hair.

Finally, Leo understood what was going on. He wasn't seeing Alasdair in the vision because, this time, he was —

"Alasdair, son of Lapidos. You do not know how long I have waited for you."

Then those sharp points sank into his neck and Leo lost consciousness.

Seventeen

"DO YOU CARE to explain what just happened here, Alasdair?"

Alasdair heard the question linger in the air as he closed his eyes and collapsed onto the mattress. His body was listless after being so well used. He'd been drained of his blood, his energy, and the will to speak at all.

He rolled onto his back and placed his hands behind his head. Vasilios was at the other end, leaning against the solid headboard, his legs stretched out, crossed at the ankles. He was studying him with intense focus.

"Alasdair," Vasilios said again, nudging his naked hip with his toes.

He looked over at where Leo was passed out beside them. He wanted to explain what had happened in those last few seconds, when Leo's eyes had snapped wide open and he'd seemed to leave their plane of existence. But the problem was he didn't have any answers that would satisfy his sire.

I don't even have any that satisfy me.

He had a strange sensation of unease. It was as if his confidence had somehow disappeared because Leo, *a human*, had him all twisted up inside. Usually, he'd have no problem discussing anything with Vasilios. But he'd left things too long, and now, he was so caught up in his misplaced pride and arrogance of being defeated that he'd let his fixation with unraveling the hows turn into something more.

At least, that's what he was telling himself.

There was no other logical explanation as to why he was so consumed by the man.

He stared at Vasilios, who was watching him while stroking a lazy finger up and down Alasdair's leg. Then he narrowed his eyes on him.

"You missed a very important meeting this past month. I'm surprised you haven't bothered to ask me about it. Or have you been so preoccupied that you forgot it even took place?"

The meeting. *Fuck*, it *had* slipped his mind. After the night he'd been punished and the days he'd spent healing, Alasdair had been hell-bent on getting back to Leo. Any thoughts of meetings or brood business had gone by the wayside, and as the realization of how he'd been acting hit him, Alasdair discovered his behavior really had changed.

Then Vasilios spoke, bringing him back to the present. "Several weeks back, the other Ancients and I received some information—"

"From who?" Alasdair interrupted, and then he caught himself and fell silent.

"*Ypomoní*. It was left in the Chamber, up on the podium, a place no one can enter unless extremely powerful. A scroll with ancient writings on it, a message sent to us. It stated that our time walking the Earth was coming to a close. That the end was near. The threat resembled many we've received in the past. One full of false posturing and annihilation. That's when we knew we were dealing with something unlike anything any of us have seen."

"What do you mean unlike anything you have seen?" Alasdair asked, keeping his eyes locked with Vasilios's.

"The message made a direct reference to our *true* beginnings. Whoever sent that correspondence knows far more than anyone we've faced in the past." Vasilios seemed to think over his next words as he sat up and studied him carefully. "We sent Stratos to seek out a messenger. To learn if they had heard anything or knew anything that we did not. The plan was to get the information from him and then tell you and your cousins what we had learned. But now, thanks to you, we have a problem. I've recently been informed that Stratos met with a rather horrid ending last night. So any information he may have had died with him."

Oh fuck. Fuck, Alasdair thought as he slowly crossed his legs and reached for the sheet. He couldn't tell what was going on behind Vasilios's sharp gaze, but he wanted to be covered as much as possible—all things considered.

"I apologize," he started, not knowing what else to say. How was he to have known that Stratos had been gathering information for them? *Why didn't the damn vampire say so?*

"Apologies are a little too late now. I don't know what to do with you anymore, Alasdair. First, it was your lack of obedience with me, and now, this? Your usual stringent control snapping and leaving a destructive path in its wake?" Vasilios sighed. "We were keeping this quiet until we knew more. Stratos was under strict instructions—"

"Compulsion," Alasdair muttered, *finally* understanding the male's willingness to die. "He was under compulsion."

"Yes. He'd been compelled to keep his mouth shut about his assignment."

"Even if it meant his death?"

Vasilios's eyes flared at his judgmental tone. "Why are you so surprised? He isn't the first. The males know what they sign up for as one of the guard. His use to us was to extract information. He was happy to do so. Maybe not so happy to die, however. Alasdair, our number-one priority is to keep you and your cousins safe. But it's also vital that we keep the lair calm. If we were to mention there was a threat to our very existence, you know the reaction that would follow. We aren't the most...rational of creatures. We didn't want to alert anyone of danger on a mere hunch. We wanted facts."

Alasdair stared at Vasilios as he tried to understand what his Ancient was telling him—but he wasn't close to being finished yet.

"It seems, however, we are no longer going to be afforded those since *you* tore Stratos's head off. That temper of yours makes you act impulsively. There was a reason all those years ago that you learned to curb it. I wish you would remember that." Vasilios paused, his inspection making Alasdair uneasy. "Not only have you disappointed me, but you've put your cousin in a most unpleasant situation. Diomêdês is dealing with her as we speak. The two of you made a thoughtless decision last night. And due to it, we have no advantage."

Alasdair tried to feel bad about what he'd done, but he was finding it difficult when he felt he'd been acting blind. Isadora had taken him to the Adjudication Room and presented a traitor, and he'd dealt with him accordingly. Stratos's taunting him was his own bad luck.

Along with being compelled, that is.

The thought had barely entered his mind when Vasilios had him flat on his back beside Leo and his hands restrained by his head.

"You see? This is what I mean. You are preoccupied. This human has you acting *defiant* and *rash*," he bit out by his ear, enunciating each word. "And while I admit to liking that while I'm inside you, out there, you are fucking things up for us, Alasdair."

The way Vasilios's eyes darkened to black conveyed his fury. He was enraged, and Alasdair kept quiet—now wasn't the time to speak. He swallowed, more a reflex than anything else, as he stared into the irate face hovering over his own. This was the second time in only weeks he'd seen anger, disappointment, and confusion on his sire's face. He wished he could *unsee* it.

When Vasilios's lips parted and his fangs extended in a snarl, Alasdair realized his misstep.

"I did not mean that how it sounded," he rushed out.

"Is that so? Because I have *never* heard you think it before."

Alasdair pushed himself up off the bed, wondering if Vasilios would relent. He had his answer when the other vampire rolled to his back, allowing him on top.

"I was merely reflecting on my wrongdoings. You know that. Don't make this what it is not due to a mood."

"A mood? What am I, an irritable housewife? Forgive me, *agóri*, but your actions hardly convince me of what you're trying to make me believe."

Alasdair stretched out over the top of him, and then he laid his head on his shoulder. He wasn't sure why, but he felt guilty—yet another emotion he'd not experienced since becoming immortal. The only thing was, he wasn't sure if the guilt was towards the one underneath him or the one on the bed beside them.

As he lay there, he realized how imperative it was that things went back to the way they had always been. He had an obligation, a duty to his brood, and his very existence was entwined with the one whose body his was currently molded to. He couldn't afford any more fuck-ups, and it was time to let his obsession go.

"I never would have done what I did last night had I known," he admitted quietly. "How can I fix this?"

Vasilios stroked a hand down his back, and Alasdair was curious whether or not he would tell him. Perhaps he would make him wait if he doubted his loyalty, but then he started to talk.

"Unless you can bring back the dead, Alasdair, nothing will fix what you did."

"I have yet to master that particular power."

"Hmm. Nor have I."

"But surely you could send me or someone else to speak with this messenger—"

"No," Vasilios said, the word sharp and final. "This threat, it is different. It has us…"

Alasdair lifted his head and waited. He'd never seen Vasilios hesitate for anything.

"It has you what?"

His Ancient's eyes connected with his, now back to their usual green, and Alasdair was surprised to see an edge of fear in them.

"It has us concerned. You and your cousins are *not* to go after the messenger. Do I make myself clear?"

"No, you do not." Alasdair shifted to the side of him and stroked his fingers down his sire's cheek. "You know that Isa, Thanos, and I can each be trusted, so let us help. Or is there another reason I am missing? What aren't you telling me?"

Vasilios reached for the finger now tracing his jaw and brought it to his lips. He reverently kissed the end of it and then gave a grim smile. "Diomêdês, Eton, and I—we were all named in the initial message that was sent."

"That's not so unusual, is it? The Ancients are always named in threats to our kind."

"Yes, we are. But this is the first time *you* have been threatened to achieve our destruction. That means they know how our bloodlines work, Alasdair. They know that, to dispose of you three, they will effectively be cutting the heart from the body."

Alasdair grimaced. Vasilios was right. It was not safe to go after the messenger himself, and that frustrated the hell out of him. His instinct was to protect Vasilios, but his Ancient's instinct to protect *him* was much stronger.

"You will *not* go after them, Alasdair."

"I know," he said. Deciding to focus on something else, he asked, "They? You keep saying they. Do you know who's sending these scrolls?"

A frown of consternation formed between Vasilios's eyebrows. "We have some suspicions. The only ones who would be powerful enough to enter the Chamber would be the gods themselves. But, as of now, we can't be certain."

Alasdair ran a hand down Vasilios's arm, and when he got to his fingers, he brought them up and placed them over his chest—over the heart Vasilios had once stopped to give him life eternal.

"But surely you don't suspect them? *Gods*?" Alasdair scoffed. "What would they want with us? And why now, when they've never shown their faces before?"

Vasilios laughed, but the sound was not one of joy. "Oh, I do not suspect the deities themselves. They would never deem this task worthy of them. They would send someone in their place…"

Alasdair remained silent, trying to absorb all that he'd learned to decide how to proceed.

Our lineage.

Back where it all began.

My death.

Our destruction.

Myths…Greek gods.

As all the words jumbled through his mind, Alasdair's eyes shifted to the motionless man beside them.

The one who could paralyze him with his blood.

Who could somehow remember what happens during a compulsion.

And the *same* one who was a walking, talking encylofuckingpedia on everything Greek—gods included.

The coincidence was too much for him to overlook, and the confusion inside him turned to blinding rage.

He'd known betrayal in his life. He'd lived through too many generations not to know the bitter taste of it. But as it finally fell into place, ending Leo's life seemed like the easier task.

He ordered his mind blank, not wanting Vasilios to see what he was thinking.

Not yet.

"Don't overly worry yourself, Vasilios. Nothing has managed to kill me yet," he said in an effort for them to move on or end the conversation so he could find Isadora and Thanos. He desperately needed an opinion that wasn't his own.

He expected the usual smirk or perhaps a slap at his own arrogance, but instead, Vasilios said, "They created us, Alasdair. They know our strengths *and* weaknesses because they're the ones who gave them. Do not be fooled. They do have the capability to end us. And to do that, they know they must start with you. "

Eighteen

ISADORA SAT ACROSS from Thanos and watched him pour another finger of bourbon.

It was his third in under thirty minutes, and she envied his constitution. If she had his fortitude when it came to alcohol, she'd be joining him. As it was, she was forced to sit there with an excruciating ache in her right shoulder joint courtesy of Diomêdês, who had dislocated it.

He'd instructed her, not a second after it was done, to leave it as it was until Alasdair returned. Maybe then she'd be less willing to play the faithful right hand to an impulsive fool. If she did not, he'd been more than clear that he would think up something more atrocious to remind her that his word was her law.

That'd been over two and a half hours ago, and she was getting to the point that, when Alasdair did show up, she might just willingly rip her own arm off and beat him with it.

She couldn't believe the colossal fuck-up they'd made, but at the same time, it was hardly their fault. The three of them had been kept in the dark. She understood that the Ancients had been trying to protect them, but in the process, they'd hidden important information. Information about their very existence.

When she'd emerged from her sire's chambers after an hour-long lecture, she'd immediately gone in search of Thanos. Since Alasdair was out—*no doubt chasing around that fool human*—she figured the sooner she tracked her other cousin down, the quicker she could find out what he'd been told. She soon discovered he knew nothing more than she did.

"Maybe you should let up on those," she suggested, looking pointedly at the half-full glass in Thanos's hand.

They were sitting in the Adjudication Room, awaiting Alasdair's arrival. The copious amounts of alcohol Thanos was downing and the way she was twisting the rose charm on her choker were both clear indications of their nerves.

But who can blame us? Threats of your impending death and the entire race's termination will do that to you.

"Don't concern yourself with me. I'm fine. I'm bored…but I'm fine." Thanos stood, holding the bottle of bourbon. Then he paced back and forth across the plush rug she was stretched out on. "Maybe you should *start* drinking, Isa. Especially if what we were told tonight is true."

Cradling her lame arm across her waist, she pursed her lips, contemplating the idea. Then she shook her head. "No. I want to be coherent when Alasdair gets here. Not so drunk I'm passed out on the floor."

Thanos raised the glass and took a swig of the amber-colored liquid. "Well, you're already lying on it. Why not make this more fun for me? Tell me, Isa. What's it like to be the only vampire who can still become inebriated?"

She glared over at his smirking face. "Painful, because I have to lie here one hundred percent sober and listen to you."

"Aww, don't be bitter. I'm not even a little bit drunk."

"I'm not. It's just one of the many unfortunate by-products of my human genetics. Nothing I can do about it."

"No, I don't suppose there is. But come on. Just one glass while we wait."

She rolled her eyes. "Stop it, Thanos."

He winked at her, and as she was about to say more, Alasdair appeared inside the room, dressed in all black, his human draped over his shoulder.

He looked like the devil himself—and the scowl he wore spoke of bloody murder. He let the male in his hands fall at his feet with a thump, and as Isadora looked over at the human, Alasdair asked, "Did you know?"

She brought her eyes up to his and indicated her damaged arm. "Do I look as though I knew?"

His eyes swept over her, and once he'd registered the loose limb, he inspected Thanos. "Of course you are in one piece, as always."

Thanos shrugged and slid his free hand into his pocket. "Well, Eton is away at the moment, and I didn't partake in the beheading of an informant."

Isadora sat up then, and snapped around to face him. "We didn't *know* he was an informant."

"Yes. Well, apparently, your sires don't really care about that little fact." Thanos sighed. "I have to say, Alasdair, I'm surprised you are still able to walk."

"As am I," Alasdair muttered.

"Why's he here?" she asked, nodding beside her.

"He took ahold of me when I faded from his workplace," Alasdair said, but Isadora had a feeling there was a lot more to it than that.

"And you let him?" she asked, incredulity in her tone.

Alasdair's dark expression told her that he certainly had *not*, and then Thanos's laugh echoed around the room. They both looked at him, and the smile on his mouth was full of devilry.

"No, I did not *let* him," Alasdair said. "He seemed to know I was going to do it before I did it."

"And he just *grabbed* on to you?" Thanos laughed again.

Alasdair growled. "What the fuck is so amusing about this to you?"

Thanos finished the drink in his hand and gave him a pearly white grin fit for a toothpaste commercial. "I just saw where you both ended up in your mind, cousin. Gotta say— brave for a human, isn't he? How *did* Vasilios react to his unexpected guest?"

Alasdair glared so hard at their cousin that Isadora thought she was going to have to get between the two males.

"He was fine."

Thanos chewed on a piece of ice and then wagged his eyebrows. "Yes, I see. He looks *very* fine kneeling behind you."

"Get out of my fucking head, Thanos," Alasdair warned.

"Or else what? Your threat on my life is not the first tonight. So please take a number. There is a line."

Isadora got to her feet. Thanos could be frustrating at times, so she stood in front of Alasdair and looked him over. When it appeared he was in perfectly good health, she pouted.

"I assume by that expression and your arm that you received the same dress down I did?" Alasdair said.

"Apparently not exactly the same. *You* are in one piece."

Thanos scoffed. "As far as we can see. Any bite marks under those clothes we should know about, Alasdair?"

"Ignore him," Isadora advised when Alasdair's jaw bunched. "I was told by Diomêdês that I wasn't to heal myself until you arrived."

Alasdair winced, and then he did something he very rarely did—he rolled his sleeve up and offered her his vein. "Feed."

"But—"

He took a step towards her and clasped her left shoulder in his strong hand. Then he raised his arm until it hovered in front of her lips and said softly, "Let us say I am returning the favor."

She shifted her eyes to his, and her fangs descended. Feeding from Alasdair was as much a privilege as it was pleasure. Because, while each of them was the first sired of an Ancient, Alasdair was sired to Vasilios, the most powerful of them all. It was Vasilios's blood that made Alasdair's all the more sweet.

Her top lip pulled taut across her teeth, and then she took his arm with her left hand. Lowering her head, she licked the spot where she could see his vein, and then she slowly sank her teeth into his flesh. When the intoxicating blend of his blood entered her mouth, she closed her eyes, and as it flowed through her veins to her wounded shoulder, she caught glimpses of Alasdair's mind.

The human, standing with him in a room full of photographs. Then again appearing at his feet in Vasilios's room. And then the human…watching the two of them as they fucked.

Alasdair's mind was a mass of confusion, tangled between his reality and his obsession. When Isadora withdrew her teeth from his wrist, she licked the wound so it would heal and whispered, "It's time to end this."

Alasdair pulled his arm free of her but said nothing. She knew he understood, just as she knew he would rebel against any voice of reason. Once Alasdair's mind was set, it took something monumental to dissuade him.

"So, there's something I don't quite understand," Thanos spoke up, reminding her he was still in the room with them. "If you were told what we were, dear cousin, why are you still toting the human around? There are much more important things to focus on now besides your cock."

"I agree," Alasdair said as he rolled his shirtsleeve down and walked over to where Thanos had sat back in the chair. "Which is exactly why he *is* still here. I think he has something to do with it."

Isadora's mouth fell open, and then, without warning, she laughed, much like Thanos had earlier. But while his had been mocking and full of sarcasm, hers sounded oddly crazed even to her own ears.

"You think *he* has something to do with it? Look at him, Alasdair. We could kill him right now and he'd be none the wiser. How could someone as small as he, be involved in the destruction of something as large as us?"

"Think about it," Alasdair suggested. "That night I tried to feed from him, his blood dropped me to the floor like poison. It paralyzed me to the point that, if he had known how, he could have ended me. He can also remember what happens during a full compulsion."

As that little tidbit was revealed, Isadora thought Thanos's eyes would pop out of his head.

"What? And you still have him around? *Alive?* What the fuck is the matter with you?"

"That's the whole point, Thanos. I don't know. I don't *know* why I'm drawn to him the way I am—or why he can do what he does. But now, something else has started." Alasdair paused as if daring either of them to interrupt. When neither of them did, he continued. "Something happens whenever we kiss."

Thanos's lips twitched. "Like what? Did the Earth move?"

"You're such a fucking comedian, Thanos. Aren't you paying attention? He is a threat. A threat I've never come across, and he's one I haven't been able to stay away from."

The two of them looked at Alasdair, their mouths parted in shock. Then Thanos stepped towards their cousin and said, "I assume you have a plan? You always do. A way to test your theory?"

Alasdair grimaced as though he'd swallowed a razor blade, and as the *plan* entered his mind, they all saw what he thought would work.

Thanos laughed. "Oh, Alasdair, I thought you'd never ask."

Nineteen

VOICES.

ONE, TWO...no, three voices.

That's what Leo heard when he cracked his eyes open. A shooting pain splintered inside his skull as he tried to move his arms—he wanted to rub at his temple. But he couldn't move them. His wrists stung, and as he tugged on one of them, the rough abrasion of rope scratched his skin.

Disoriented, he shifted, trying to sit up so he could get a better look at his surroundings, but from the awkward position he was in—*Lying flat on my damn stomach*—it was difficult to push himself up.

Squeezing his eyes shut, he took a deep breath. There was a stabbing sensation in his temple coming from a transport that had to have happened—recently.

The last thing he remembered was... *Alasdair, the other vampire, and then...oh fuck.*

Then he'd woken up in the middle of a flashback. Under that Vasilios guy, who'd been about to bite him. He remembered the way his body had reacted as the powerful male had loomed over him.

As Alasdair, Leo had wanted Vasilios with every fiber of his being. His cock had been harder than it had ever been, his flesh hot to the touch, and when the vampire had told him it was time, Leo had felt the pride and desire swirl through Alasdair's blood.

He'd *wanted* to be owned by that male. More than he'd wanted to live.

Shaking his head, hoping to free his mind of memories that weren't his, Leo rolled to his side and used his shoulder to shove himself up. The voices in the room increased in volume.

"I'm not sure that would be the smartest thing to do in this case, Thanos, are you?"

The question ended abruptly, and it seemed to echo around... *My office,* Leo realized, as he finally got himself upright and seated. He was back in his office, on the couch.

"Your human," a low voice noted, "is awake."

Leo's eyes skidded to a stop on the three figures across the room. They had their backs to him, and when they turned, he realized he recognized them all.

Alasdair was standing between the male and female from the Walk. The same male who'd wanted... *Yeah... best*

not to think about that while they're within mind-invading
distance.

"Huh," the male vampire pondered, his eyes roving over Leo. "His thoughts are rather amusing, aren't they? No wonder you kept him around, Alasdair. But he doesn't seem to fear us much, does he?"

Leo's eyes darted to Alasdair for... *What? Reassurance?* Why did he think he would protect him? If the stony expression on his face was any indication, he could quickly dispel any hope of that happening. Alasdair's frown made him look homicidal, and just like that, the other male in the room got the reaction he wanted. Suddenly, Leo feared them *very* much.

Alasdair prowled over to him, his eyes never wavering from his face, and when they were toe-to-toe, he looked down at him and stated in a tone so bone-chilling that Leo's heart almost gave out, "Stand up."

The command was issued verbally, and Leo could still feel the choice was his. He wondered at that for a brief second, but then he glanced at the other two vampires in the room and knew why he wasn't being compelled to act. He had nowhere to go. He was like an animal of prey surrounded by a pack of hungry lions. If he made one wrong move, they would pounce, attack, and kill.

Ever so slowly, Leo scooted to the edge of the couch and then stood until he was level with Alasdair. He raised his head, and when their eyes connected, he sucked in a swift breath. He'd only ever seen this look in Alasdair's eyes once—when he'd thrown him across the room that first night they'd talked.

The intensity in his eyes had the hairs on Leo's arms standing tall. He then dropped his gaze to the lips that had kissed his twice now and watched them pull into a tight line as if Alasdair had read his thought and was displeased with it.

"I'm going to ask you a question, human."

Ahh, so we're no longer on a first-name basis. Something had really pissed Alasdair off. Those furious eyes turned to slits, but he merely continued with his thought as though he hadn't heard Leo's at all.

"You are going to answer me. If you answer wrong, I *will* kill you this time."

Leo's mouth fell open, and an unintelligible sound came from him as he looked over Alasdair's shoulder to the two flanking his office door.

"Do you understand?"

The curt question brought his eyes back to Alasdair's, and Leo shook his head. "No," he managed. "I don't understand."

He thought he caught emotion flicker across those livid eyes, but he must've imagined it, because Alasdair reached out then and grasped the material of his shirt, yanking him forward. His tied hands were trapped between their bodies, and then Alasdair leaned in and whispered, "I warned you not to lie to me."

Leo bit down on his lip hard, trying to stop his protest, and sought out the eyes of the female across the room. He wasn't sure why he looked at her, but he thought maybe she would show some kind of compassion. Maybe she would come to his rescue.

But why should she? Because she's a woman?

She might have been female, but the cold way she was observing what was going on indicated she was as unforgiving as the vampire currently holding him.

Leo angled his head the best he could to look Alasdair in the eye. "I don't know what you're talking about. But I didn't lie to you. Not once."

Alasdair gave him a grim smile, and the laugh that came out of his mouth was anything but joyful. "No?"

"No," he stressed, his lips close to Alasdair's. So close he could— *What? Fucking stop this already! He's about to kill you, not kiss you.*

"See, now, that is where you're wrong."

Before Leo knew what was happening, Alasdair pulled him in the final distance and took his lips in a ruthless kiss.

IT WAS NEVER smart to act in anger. Alasdair was more than aware of that. But as he stood in front of Leo with his fingers curled into his shirt, he wanted nothing more than to shake him until the truth fell out of him like loose change. Just as he'd suspected, the human was stubbornly holding on to his story that he knew nothing.

After learning what he had in Vasilios's bedchambers, Alasdair had been on a mission. Somehow, he knew Leo was involved in the threats they'd received. It was far too much of a coincidence to think this man, this enigma, was enough to keep him twisted up inside without some kind of power. Then add in that his blood was practically a tranquilizer and something was happening when the two of them kissed and that brought him back to his plan.

As his mouth met Leo's, a gasp left him and drifted between Alasdair's lips. His fingers eased in their hold on Leo's shirt, and when he pushed his tongue between his lips, it happened.

The pale eyes, which had been wide with alarm, started to swirl and the color completely engulfed the surface. Leo's hands moved up to grip his, and Alasdair heard a growl rumble in his own throat. Even though there was a very obvious threat to Leo's life right then, the man was responding as if they were naked and on a bed, which brought his own response to the surface.

But Alasdair would be damned if he acted on it. He was doing this to acquire knowledge, and he needed his cousins to witness it.

He kept their mouths aligned, angling his head for a deeper connection as he dove in to really taste Leo for the first time. They'd kissed before, but they had been hurried, quick matings of their mouths, which he'd pulled away from whenever the incident had occurred.

But not this time.

This time, Alasdair made certain to really savor the lips moving under his own, to lick and flick every corner and crevice he could, as he rubbed his cock against Leo's bound hands. This would likely be his final chance to taste him, and with the safety net of Isadora and Thanos there in case anything should happen, Alasdair really let go.

He released Leo's shirt and slid his hands into the short strands of his hair. Leo's body vibrated against his, and the moan that emerged was blissful. No matter what was happening behind those filmed eyes, Leo was definitely feeling what he was.

Alasdair pushed his hips harder against Leo's restrained hands, and he grunted when several fingers stroked over him. His cock was pounding between them, and the flavor of Leo on his tongue was flooding his heightened senses. He wanted nothing more than to strip him naked and fuck him right there on the couch, not caring one bit that his cousins were there. But then Thanos was inside his head, urging him to pull back.

We cannot hear anything, Alasdair. His thoughts, they are blank, and usually, we would at least hear him thinking about his cock... like you are thinking about yours.

Alasdair pulled his fingers free of Leo's hair and lifted his head, grasping his bound arms as Leo swayed away from him. He couldn't help himself from looking one

final time at the glistening lips only inches from his, and
when Leo ran his tongue along them as if savoring the
lingering taste, Alasdair moved in, about to take more.

Don't, cousin. We know nothing of what he is. Isadora's
voice was a sharp warning inside his head, and though she
was right, he couldn't stop himself from baring his teeth as
he glared over his shoulder at her.

*You want to fuck something? Thanos is here and
salivating over your display. I daresay, in about two minutes, he'll
be more than willing. Until then, move aside. We are here to test
your theory, remember?*

Thanos sauntered towards him and Leo, and as he
got closer, Leo's mind came back into focus.

Why'd you stop?

Leo's eyes had returned to their usual shade.
Alasdair wanted to speak, to ask questions and demand
answers of him, but that route had proved unsuccessful in
the past, so testing his theory was the only other option.

When Thanos stepped up beside him, Leo's gaze
shifted to him. Alasdair could sense Leo's unease, and when
he looked over at Thanos, the expression in the vampire's
cerulean eyes was enough to have him issuing a warning.

*Once. You get to do this once, and then you stop. Do you
understand?*

Thanos faced him, and when one of his eyebrows
rose and his lips tipped up in a provocative smile, Alasdair
recalled the couple hundred times they'd shared a bed with,
and without, others. Thanos was an extremely greedy lover,

renowned for being insatiable. His appetites were unequaled. That alone would have been enough to cause concern, but add in that he was performing for an audience and they were about to get an eye-opening display.

Why, I understand perfectly, cousin.

LEO SHOOK HIS head as Alasdair stepped aside and the taller vampire took his place. *No!* he screamed in his head as he glared at Alasdair. *Why are you doing this?*

He backed up, and when the backs of his knees hit the edge of the couch, he fell, only to find himself trapped under the male who was now straddling his lap.

"This is a much more comfortable position," the vampire taunted and took his chin in a tight hold. Then he tilted Leo's face up, and as he gazed down at him with blazing, blue eyes, he grinned, exposing his fangs. "Thank you for being so thoughtful."

Leo tried to yank his head back, but when Alasdair's voice entered his mind, he froze. *Sit still and he won't hurt you. You might actually enjoy it.*

Too angry to keep his thoughts private, Leo fumed as he glowered at the one he'd foolishly started to trust and spat out, "What do you care?"

Before he could hope to get an answer, the male on top of him fused their mouths together.

WHEN HE'D FIRST thought up this plan, Alasdair had believed it to be a good one. He wanted to see if he was the only one causing a reaction in Leo or if it was all of their kind. But as he stood off to the side and watched Thanos kiss *his* yielding, any thought of discovery and revenge changed to possessive anger.

He moved forward to haul Thanos off Leo, but Isadora appeared at his side and clasped his wrist between her fingers.

Let him, Alasdair. You came to us for a reason. Now, see if you can hear anything.

Alasdair's gut churned as a groan came from Thanos, and he wanted to hit something—hard.

I came to you to test a theory. Thanos doesn't have to enjoy it so much.

Isadora's husky chuckle sounded as her thought was relayed inside his head. *He made no secret of wanting to taste your human. That should've clued you in. Perhaps it would've been better had I been the one to test the theory.*

Alasdair shook his head. *You are not his type, ómorfo korítsi. I need him to respond, not turn ice cold.*

He returned his attention to Thanos and ground his teeth together as he watched the back of Thanos's head. He tried to concentrate beyond the red blur of anger he felt at seeing him on top of Leo, but it was fucking difficult. He hadn't thought this far ahead, and he hadn't expected to want to kill anyone who touched the human. But that's what he wanted: to fucking kill Thanos for touching what was his.

Isadora's fingers tightened, and she warned under her breath, "Don't make me hurt you, Alasdair."

"I'd like to see you try."

"We both know I can't defeat you. But I would make you suffer. Look inside your human's mind. See what you can see."

Alasdair focused on the two over on the couch and then closed his eyes. If he couldn't actually see what was going on, his cousin had a better chance at survival. He shoved past Thanos's depraved thoughts, not wanting more of a reason to strangle him, and then delved into the human mind beyond.

Not sure what to expect, Alasdair was stunned when, *Why is Alasdair doing this?* Was Leo's primary thought.

He'd thought he would see lustful imaginings of Thanos naked and inside Leo. No one usually had the willpower to resist his cousin's seductive tongue, and that he wasn't in Leo's thoughts at all pleased Alasdair more than he cared to admit.

He quickly pushed that emotion the fuck out of his way, though, when he recalled what he was supposed to be doing, and continued to listen to Leo's thoughts.

Is it because of what happened between the three of us? Is he upset that I saw him and that Vasilios guy? It was his fault. He made me do it. Or maybe it's because of what happened after —

Before Leo could finish that thought, Alasdair was behind Thanos and tearing him away.

"Calm down, cousin. Your possessive streak is completely unnecessary. He thought of you the entire time."

Not the entire time. He reached for the rope around Leo's wrists and yanked him to his feet. "What do you mean what happened *after*?"

LEO'S HEART WAS thumping. It was thumping so hard he thought it might pound clear out of his chest. Alasdair's lips were so close Leo could taste his breath, and suddenly, he couldn't remember the question.

"Wh...what?"

"Don't play coy with me, *file mou*. Not now. What did you mean when you said *what happened after*?"

Leo glanced at the vampire who'd just been all over him, feeling nothing in the way of a response. He was surprised, because the guy was his usual type. But when he looked back at Alasdair, his erection seemed to have its own fucked-up idea about where it wanted to go.

"Tell me what you saw," Alasdair demanded. "What's happening when your eyes glaze over and *my* mouth is on yours? Because nothing happened when you touched Thanos."

He should've been frightened. Terrified, actually. But he'd had enough of being played with like a mouse before the cat's meal—so, instead, he smiled.

"I see *you*," Leo finally admitted, letting his eyes trail down Alasdair's frame. "I saw you before you were *this*. With long hair and flushed cheeks. I saw you the night he turned you *into* this."

As the words left his mouth, Leo wondered when he'd developed a fucking death wish. He figured it was around the time he'd woken up and discovered that a vampire was the master of his fate. But Alasdair had asked for answers, and if telling him what he wanted to know might save his life, he wasn't dumb enough to keep it a secret.

Alasdair's eyes darkened, and then he hissed. "You're lying."

Leo tried to yank his hands away, but the action was no use. Alasdair had too tight of a grip on them.

"Why would I, *omorfo mou agóri?*" Leo asked, using the Greek words he'd heard Vasilios whisper to him in his visions.

"That proves nothing. You continue to try to fool me. Vasilios said that the night in the Adjudication Room. You were there. Your deceptions are sorely lacking, Leonidas. I am disappointed."

Leo gave a slow nod and blinked once. Then he tilted his head up and whispered, "I'm sorry you find me lacking, *Alasdair, son of Lapidos. You do not know how long I have waited for you.*"

As *those* words registered with the vampire, Leo saw a flash of disbelief in his eyes. There was no way he could've known his full human name without it being the truth. But before anything more was said, Alasdair faded the two of them from the room.

Twenty

"WHERE THE FUCK did they just go?" Thanos demanded.

Isadora's blood boiled, and she clenched her fists by her sides.

"Isa?"

He hadn't just done what she thought he had... *Did he?* But as she stared at the empty space Alasdair had vacated, she knew he had.

"I can't believe he pulled this shit after what we discussed. He ordered me to—"

"Shut up," she snapped, trying to reach out to Alasdair's mind. *But, of course, he fucking blanked it out.* "He's shut me out."

"That fucking prick," Thanos growled. "If he's not already dead by the time we catch up to him, I'll kill him myself."

Isadora spun on her heel and reached for the door. "Not if I beat you to it."

She twisted the handle, hell-bent on tracking down her wayward cousin, and as she flung it open to see where the hell Alasdair had taken them, she came face-to-face with—

"Elias…"

ELIAS'S NAME WHISPERED from the lips of the woman standing in front of him had his arm halting in midair. He couldn't believe what he was seeing, but as he lowered his hand and looked into a face he'd never been able to forget, he managed only one word.

"Isadora?"

The wide eyes and slack-jawed expression on her flawless face revealed that she was as unnerved to see him as he was her.

"What are you doing here?" he got out, but when her mouth opened to answer, a man with a scary-as-fuck scowl on his face stepped out from behind the door.

As the man caught Elias's apprehension, he schooled his features to a more neutral expression and then spoke. "Good evening, sir."

Elias's eyes shifted to the man's blue ones, and when a slow, easy smile curved the stranger's lips, pinpricks of unease bristled under his skin.

Unease obtained by only one thing—ingrained knowledge.

Taking a wary step back, Elias slipped his hand into his pocket and ran his fingers over the silver letter opener he always kept there. He'd had it especially made on his twenty-eighth birthday, and his heart started a rapid tattoo in his chest as a rush of adrenaline hit it like an electric shock.

This can't be right, he thought as he studied the face of his past. *And certainly not like this. She can't be…*

But as he studied her porcelain complexion and ruby-red lips, his brain disagreed. Isadora hadn't aged at all. Her features were all achingly familiar, and as the hair on his arms stood on end, the pieces of this fucked up puzzle began to make sense.

"How strange to see you again, Elias," she said, drawing his attention back to her.

But there was no need.

This was the moment. The moment he'd been told of all those years ago. The one he'd been preparing for, and it was all wrapped up in a woman from his past. *One of life's ironies, no doubt. Yeah,* well, irony could fuck right off as far as he was concerned.

He'd dreamed many times over of a life with Isadora, and now, he'd come to find that it hadn't been a dream at all. She'd been drawn back to him because of this, and she didn't even realize it. His dream of one day being with her again—it was over before it had even begun.

She stared at him, waiting for an answer, and he knew he had to tread very carefully.

"Yes. It's very strange. Do you want to tell me why a woman I haven't seen in years is coming out of the private office of one of my employees?"

Her midnight-blue eyes flared as though she weren't used to being questioned, and then the intimidating guy placed a hand on her shoulder.

A calming gesture? Elias wondered. *Who is he? A boyfriend? A husband? A lover?*

"Well...we were just—"

"Leaving," the man stated, urging Isadora to take a step forward.

As she started to walk, Elias put his hand up and shook his head. "I don't think so. You two are trespassing."

"And now, we're finished doing so," the man said in a deceptively calm voice. "You're going to want to move."

The order was firm, and with the *get the fuck out of the way or I will do it for you* look aimed his way, Elias knew the wise thing to do was to move—but he had never claimed to be wise.

"You should let us go," Isadora said, and then she swallowed back anything else she'd been about to say.

"And you should start talking," he said. "I'm not letting you two leave without some kind of explanation and possible police involvement."

"Elias…"

His name sounded like a warning now, and his idiotic cock remembered a time when she'd issued that same warning but in a seductive let's-fuck kind of way.

"Don't even try, Isadora. Your threats won't work here."

"Let us leave," the guy said.

When Elias looked at him, he heard, *Step aside, human. We need to leave,* echo inside his head, and an arrogant smirk crossed his features. He was about to trump this asshole's card in the best way imaginable.

He took a step forward and replied, "You're not going anywhere."

ISADORA'S MOUTH FELL open as Elias Fontana did the impossible—replied to a full compulsion.

She was about to turn to Thanos and see what the hell he made of it all when a thin, silver blade whizzed past her face and pierced through the side of her cousin's neck. Thanos shouted out a pained curse and reached for the object as a firm hand wrapped around her wrist. Caught completely off guard, she gasped as she was pulled towards a man she'd once willingly gone to, and her feet froze when she spotted the shiny, silver film that had completely encompassed Elias's eyes. They were much the same as Alasdair's human's. However, where his had been a dull grey, Elias's shone like liquid silver.

This wasn't the easygoing, sexy-as-hell teacher she'd met years ago. This man was something else entirely. He was confident, arrogant, and somehow managing to hang on to her as she tried in vain to pull her arm free.

She didn't understand what was happening, or maybe, somewhere inside her, she did, because when she tried to fade out of Elias's grip, he laughed and shook his head.

"Oh, no, Isadora, first sired to Diomêdês. I've been waiting for you."

Twenty-One

SOMETHING WAS DIFFERENT.

The second they appeared in his kitchen, Leo expected to fall to the floor and pass out. But instead, he remained alert and on his feet. The usual ache in his skull, which always followed one of Alasdair's spectacular disappearing acts, was there, but it wasn't as harsh as it usually was.

Yes, something is definitely happening.

"You didn't pass out," Alasdair said with his back against the fridge. He was as far away from him as possible given the small confines, and when Leo took a step in his direction, the vampire spoke again. "Stay where you are. And start talking. No more bullshit, Leonidas."

Although the question had been asked of him before, this time, it was posed differently. With an air of…caution to it.

"I already told you everything I know."

"And you are lying!" Alasdair shouted so loudly Leo swore the walls of his apartment shook.

"I am *not* lying," he countered. "How many times do I have to tell you—"

"Until I believe you," Alasdair said.

Leo rubbed his temple and pulled one of his kitchen chairs out to sit.

"You've seen me," Alasdair said, his voice so low Leo had to strain to hear him. "Seen me when I was human. Before Vasilios. Before I was *this*. And now, now, you know what I am…*who* I am."

Leo frowned. "Yes. You told me."

"No. Before that," Alasdair accused. "You knew who I was *before* that. That's why you sought me out."

"Ah…no. You tracked me down. *You* bit me—"

"And then I almost died."

Leo crossed his arms over his chest, the irony of the conversation not lost on him in the slightest. "So, what? You're upset because you almost died that night instead of me? Excuse me if I'm not feeling too sympathetic."

Alasdair's top lip drew back, and as a snarl left his throat, his fangs came into view, gleaming and terrifying in their appearance. "You know things about me no one else knows. How is that possible?"

"We've already been over this."

"And we'll go over it again until either I am satisfied or…"

"Or…" Leo hedged. "If you're thinking it, the least you could do is say it."

Alasdair ignored him. "Start talking while you are still able to."

"I told you," he said as though he were sitting with a preschooler instead of an extremely powerful immortal. "I've been getting these…visions. I don't know what they are. Whenever you…we kiss."

Alasdair's eyes zeroed in on him. "Visions of me when I was a mortal?"

Leo licked his dry lips and nodded. "At first, yes. But the last one I had, when we were—" Leo stopped abruptly, not even sure what to call what they had done with the other vampire.

"When you watched Vasilios fuck me."

Okay, so he calls it like it is. Good to know, Leo thought as his body started to overheat from the reminder. He coughed and nodded. "Um, yes. Then."

Alasdair said nothing. Instead, he watched him in a way that had Leo squirming in his seat.

"In the last vision, you were in his bed. Well, I was there, actually. I don't know how that happened, but yeah, I was you, and *we* were in a bed—his bed, naked. And then he bit me. I mean you." Leo let out an irritable grumble and shook his head. "See? Would I be this fucking confused if I knew what the hell was going on? What *is* going on?"

Alasdair pushed away from the fridge and took a seat opposite him. The move was so normal, all things considered, that Leo laughed. The sound coming out of his mouth was slightly hysterical, and when Alasdair's frown hardened, his hilarity increased.

"You don't know, do you? All this weird shit is happening to me and you don't even know what it is."

"I didn't think so," Alasdair mused.

"You didn't think so? But what? Now, you suddenly do?" In the blink of an eye, his hilarity turned into his own brand of self-righteous anger. "Is it because you bit me? Is this your fucking fault? Did you infect me?"

Alasdair cocked his head to the side. "No."

"No? That's it?" Leo slapped his palms on the table and shot to his feet as though someone had pinched him on the ass. "You have totally fucked up my life, not to mention my head. Vampires, visions, and beaming me here and there. And now, you want to sit here and say nothing? Okay. Take a seat. Relax. Would you like a coffee?"

He glared down at the vampire who'd kidnapped him, threatened him, and, on several occasions, tried to kill him, and when their eyes connected, Leo couldn't do a fucking thing to pull his gaze away.

"I am drawn to you, Leonidas. I cannot seem to leave you be."

The anger that had been churning in his gut dispelled as the dangerously beautiful creature opposite him slowly rose to his feet.

"I have been drawn to you since the night I saw you coming out of that bar you used to frequent."

Unable to find his tongue, Leo tried to recall ever seeing Alasdair at The Dirty Dog. *But no*, he would never forget having seen him. He would never forget Alasdair's face as long as he lived. Which, right now, the time frame was totally up for debate.

"It was about two weeks before that night I came to your bed."

Wait, Leo thought, *that's when my dreams started to—*

"You stepped out into the street, and I followed you home. That was the first time I saw you. I wanted you then, and…*se thelo tora.*"

Leo sucked in a breath and stood up straight. Alasdair had been watching him? Following him for at least two weeks before he'd tried to… *Yeah, okay. Let's not dwell on the killing part. He'd been following me.* That part, for some reason, really turned him on.

"At first, I thought I was hunting my next meal. Nothing out of the ordinary," he explained. "You see, I like control, and I enjoy the chase. But even I found it strange that I continually ended up standing outside your window, waiting. Waiting for that perfect moment where I would finally feed from you. And I wanted it…"

Leo's pulse thrummed as Alasdair's hypnotic voice told the story.

"I wanted it more than I have ever wanted it before. It was all I thought about," he admitted as he walked around the table towards him.

Leo pivoted and then watched Alasdair, unable to move. When he stopped in front of him, Leo knew he should step away, but no matter how hard he ordered his feet to do so, they wouldn't fucking budge.

"I wanted to taste you on my tongue, *file mou*. Consume that which flows through your veins. It was an obsession. It still is."

Alasdair raised his hand, and Leo flinched at the move. He was so wired that he wasn't sure what he was feeling, but as his blood rushed around his head, his cock reacted to the male opposite him in the most primal way. He was hard and eager for release.

"Don't you see? I *couldn't* leave you alone. I didn't want to. And now…" Alasdair's hand cupped the back of his neck. He pulled him forward, and Leo stumbled and placed his hands on Alasdair's chest.

"Now?" he asked, barely able to breathe.

Alasdair's eyes drifted to his mouth. "Now, I know why."

Then he leaned in, and Leo prayed like the idiot he was for another kiss like the one back in his office. But at the last second, Alasdair angled his face away and pressed his lips to his throat. Leo let out the groan that had been building inside him and dug his fingers into the solid wall of muscle under his palms.

He had no idea what Alasdair had been talking about, but right then, he didn't give a shit. The lips moving along his throat were cool, but the tongue that flicked over his pulse point was blazing hot. He sucked in a ragged breath as it trailed directly up his vein to his ear, where Alasdair whispered, "You are not who you think you are, Leonidas Chapel."

Leo's eyes drifted shut, and his erection ached between his thighs. He was close to pleading with Alasdair to touch him—to demand that he finish what he kept starting—when the tip of a sharp fang grazed over his earlobe.

Fuck…that is such a rush. The danger packed into that tiny gesture had him close to coming. But then he remembered Alasdair's words and bravely asked, "Then who am I?"

Alasdair's lips hovered over his ear, and as his warm breath washed over his skin, he whispered, "I believe you may be the one…"

Leo pressed his palm flat against the chest he'd been clutching, pushing Alasdair back so he could look at him. "The one?"

Alasdair's eyes blazed with heated jade, and then he lifted him off his toes. "Yes. The one who has been sent here to kill me."

A TORTUROUS GROWL escaped Alasdair as he dug his fingers into Leo's arms. Every instinct he possessed was urging him to do it. To end this madness then and there with a quick, vicious snap to this human's neck.

But, while that emotion was formidable, he could sense another, more elusive one trying to surface. It was an emotion he hadn't felt in years. *Two millennia to be precise.* One he'd never thought he'd feel again. *Compassion.*

He cared about Leo. The thought of him not walking the Earth any longer…bothered him.

His eyes moved to the parted lips he'd finally gotten a full taste of, and that's when Leo said, "Look at me. How could *I* possibly kill *you*?"

It was a good question, one he still didn't have an answer for. But somehow, Alasdair knew that, as sure as the sun could kill him, so could Leonidas.

Their eyes connected, and once again, the pale grey of Leo's irises started to swirl.

It was happening again.

This time without anything more than touching.

Before Alasdair had a chance to speak, though, Leo's eyes fluttered shut and he fell limp in his arms.

Ancient Greece—47 BC

LEO RAISED A hand to shade his eyes, squinting against the brilliance of the sun. He struggled to sit from where he had landed flat on his back, and when he was finally upright, a warm breeze ruffled his hair. He blinked and then scanned the area, and as he started to comprehend what exactly he was seeing, he scrambled to his feet, panic setting in.

The low, raspy caw of a raven soaring overhead had him looking up into the clear, blue skies. His mind whirled as he pivoted around in a full circle, and then he did it once more, taking in his surroundings.

No…no. There's no way…

"Wake up. Wake up, wake up," he ordered himself. He always woke up almost immediately after he'd seen whatever he was seeing.

But not this time.

His palms began to sweat as the vast expanse of mountainous terrain threatened to swallow him whole.

Am I too young to die from a heart attack? *he wondered. Was this another flashback? Or a dream? He really needed to see someone about getting on medication when he woke. Clearly, he was losing his mind.*

But that's when he saw him. Through a crowd of men gathered at the top of several massive stone stairs.

Alasdair…

Twenty-Two

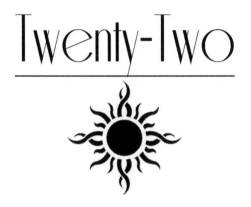

LEO EXAMINED THE *crowd milling about, and when no one seemed to notice him, he wove his way through the people chattering to one another in Greek. It was obvious they couldn't see him from their lack of reaction to a man dressed as he was, but that didn't stop him from trying to get one.*

He stepped up to a young woman dressed in a beige chiton with a brown strophion and waved his hand about. When she continued to talk as though he weren't there, Leo shook his head.

Unreal.

He couldn't believe what he was seeing. Then again, every time this had happened, he'd caught glimpses of Alasdair's life. But this was different. This wasn't a glimpse in a dream. This was a full-on show-and-tell session. Leo felt that he was actually there this time. There in the past.

Deciding to worry about that bit of what-the-fuck later, he continued up the winding path to the temple, the gravel crunching underfoot. He took in the way people were dressed, the dialect they were speaking, and the food being bartered for from the carts off to the side.

When he got to the wide steps, he craned his head back to take in the enormous structure as it stood towering over the people in all its majestic glory. He'd only ever seen the ancient temples in recreations, or photographs taken of the ruins, which remained today. But standing between the huge columns as he now found himself, he was awestruck.

He was about to go in search of Alasdair, when the deep, melodic laughter of a man caught his attention. He stopped when he spotted an all-too-familiar figure standing in the shadows— Vasilios.

Leo's eyes shifted to the man and woman he was addressing, but he didn't recognize them. Do they know what he is? *he wondered. But when Vasilios ran his finger down the woman's jaw, Leo figured they did not.*

He walked over closer, wanting to hear what was being said, and when he was near enough to detect their voices, he caught it. Vasilios was asking the woman if he had seen Lapidos that morning, and if her betrothed, Alasdair, would be present.

Huh, *Leo thought.* So this has to be before they met that night in the bathhouse. Before Alasdair was turned.

The proprietorial expression that flickered in the vampire's eyes made Leo feel sorry for the woman. He knew what Vasilios was doing: compelling her to find out where his quarry was. And it was clear by the monotone of her voice when she told him Alasdair was inside that she had no clue what was going on.

Poor woman. She doesn't even realize she just handed her fiancé over.

Leo didn't wait around to hear any more. He wanted to track down the man he'd originally followed up the stairs — and he was, at this moment, still a man.

He had a sudden urge to see what Alasdair had been like before Vasilios had gotten to him.

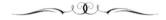

Present Day — Elias's Office

ISADORA KEPT A careful eye on Elias while he paced back and forth in front of her. Moments earlier, he'd practically dragged her into an office—his, she presumed—locked the door, and shoved her into a wooden chair that had ornate *silver* filigree engrained into it. Her wrists were tied to the arms, her ankles to the legs, and she couldn't move.

Even if she hadn't been restrained, she didn't have the strength to raise her limbs, and the pain from the poisonous toxins was making her survival instincts claw to the surface and demand that she kill her enemy.

Which brought her back to Elias.

He sat down behind a bulky desk, his calculating eyes fixated on her. His lips were pulled tight in a grim way that screamed of anger and annoyance, but she was unmoved.

Too fucking bad for him, she thought and futilely tugged at her arms.

"Did you know?"

The question was so unexpected in the otherwise silent room that she jumped at the bite to it, though she managed to keep her features impassive.

"Did I know...what, Elias? That you're a maniac? No. I didn't know that."

"Don't fuck around with me, Isadora. You know what I'm talking about."

Deciding to play ignorant, she shook her head. She didn't *really* know what he was talking about. Not all of it, anyway.

"I really don't. All I know is that you stabbed my"— she stopped herself from saying *cousin* and instead went with—"friend in the neck."

Elias sat forward and rested his forearms on the desk. Then he narrowed his eyes on her, and she felt exposed under the inspection.

When they'd been together all those years ago, this man had been sexy, attentive, and flirtatious, and she'd considered taking him as her yielding. Not that he'd ever known that.

What, exactly is *he?* There'd been a few vampire hunters over the years who'd tried to take them down, but none who had ever gotten the best of her and Thanos. *What if... No, it couldn't be that.* But then Alasdair's human, who he suspected, worked for Elias...

So maybe? Maybe he is one of those who Diomêdês was warning me of.

No.

Not Elias. It wasn't possible.

"Your friend, is he?" Elias's voice cut through her thoughts, and when she nodded, a scornful laugh left him. "Stop lying, Isadora. I know."

Refusing to admit anything unless he said it first, she remained silent.

"Don't want to say what you are? Is that what's going on here?" he asked as he stood and walked around the desk.

She tracked his movements, looking for any weakness he might possess. *Is he favoring a leg? Does one foot drag behind the other, even a little?* But there was nothing. From all outward appearances, her adversary, her potential victim, seemed to be in peak fighting ability. Which was better shape than she could say for herself in her present condition.

He crossed the space between them, then he leaned down and placed his hands over hers, pressing her flesh harder against the silver. She hissed at him, the pain running up her arms almost unbearable, and when satisfaction flashed in his eyes, he brought his face in close to hers and whispered, "I know what you are, Isadora. I can feel it now. So let me see. You owe me that."

She knew her eyes had to be glowing a fierce, bright blue. He was so near that she could smell the familiar woodsy scent wafting off his skin, and as his lips arrogantly quirked on the side, she wanted to wipe that look off his face with the back of her hand.

Her fangs pierced through her gums and her top lip pulled back when he taunted, "Bare your teeth for me."

Unable to stop herself, she lurched forward with a frustrated snarl and revealed her deadliest weapon at her opponent, finally confirming his suspicions.

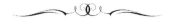

Ancient Greece—47 BC

LEO STEPPED INSIDE the temple, surprised at the eerie silence that greeted him. He shouldn't have been, considering the thickness of the stone walls. They would block out any kind of commotion beyond them, and it amazed Leo to think that anything could have brought them to the ground.

As he walked farther inside the place of worship, hushed whispers met his ears. Groups of men and women were gathered in small clusters, and when Leo searched the area for Alasdair, he spotted him standing a few feet away with several young men.

He wandered down the center aisle, unease swirling in his gut.

He wasn't sure why he was being shown all of this. When it had first occurred, he'd figured it was some strange power Alasdair was giving off, but even he wasn't aware of what Leo knew of his past. He'd said as much in the kitchen before he'd ended up here.

So why am I having these dreams? These invasive flashbacks into Alasdair's life? *He didn't understand at all.*

As he continued, he noted how strange it was walking past people only to have them ignore him because he wasn't there. Yet, at the same time, it would've been even more unusual for them to see a man who was attired in completely different clothes.

He came to a stop a short distance from Alasdair and took a moment to really look at him. He was wearing a similar outfit to the one he had on the first time Leo had had one of these visions —a white toga with the same brown sandals. He was so attractive that he could've been a movie star in a Greek or Roman classic. Instead of his long hair being tied back from his face as Leo had seen it before, it was left loose today and had a golden laurel wreath sitting on top of it. He was laughing at the man beside him, and the expression was so foreign that it made him look like another man. Leo had a sudden desire to have him laugh with him *like that.*

Unable to help himself, he moved towards the group of four and stood on the outskirts, listening to them talk. He was so caught up in witnessing this snapshot of Alasdair's humanity that it wasn't until Vasilios was standing directly behind Alasdair that Leo noticed him at all.

Leo's eyes were glued to Vasilios, as he leaned in to smell the ends of Alasdair's hair. Leo had seen Alasdair do the same to him several times, so he knew exactly what Vasilios was doing — catching his scent. But then the vampire looked up, their eyes caught, and a wickedly depraved smile hit his lips as he ran his tongue along his top lip.

Oh fuck.

Vasilios could see him.

November — Leo's apartment

ALASDAIR STARED DOWN at Leo, whose eyes currently resembled smoky marbles. He'd laid him on his couch after he'd collapsed in his arms, and the lingering effects of hunger and desire were draining from him.

Where does he go when this happens?

Leo had said that he had flashbacks. Flashbacks to when *he* was a human. But never before had he been out for this long.

So, was this the same?

Alasdair wasn't sure how he felt about Leo seeing him as he'd once been. But he knew one thing: It was bringing back feelings he'd long since believed were dormant. He found himself wanting to push Leo for more. More information on what he'd seen and if he *liked* what he'd seen. But in the end, Alasdair decided it didn't matter what Leo thought one way or another. His feelings were of no consequence to him.

Alasdair tried to reach out to his mind with a thought, to push his way in as he had before. But, as he searched for the usual opening, it was no longer there. Any access he'd had to his yielding was gone. *Your yielding, is he now?*

Annoyed at himself for giving a shit, he made himself leave and check Leo's small apartment in case there was something he'd missed. When he got to his bedroom, he saw the book he'd thrown off him all those weeks ago on the nightstand.

Heroes, Gods, and Monsters of the Greek Myths.

He picked it up and flicked through the pages. Images of the Greek gods were littered throughout the text, and photos of the land he'd left a long time ago called to him. But when the page stopped on an image of Apollo, Alasdair put his hand on it, tracing a finger over the man.

He examined the sketch of the god and took in his features. The strong jawline, the crooked nose, and the fable of his light-blond hair and grey eyes. Then Alasdair pictured Leonidas's face.

Motherfucker. How could he have missed it? *He's almost a perfect replica.*

Alasdair slammed the book shut and opened his mind to his cousins. He couldn't believe that it had taken him this long to put two and two together.

Too busy thinking with your cock. That's why. Fuck.

When Thanos connected with him and rasped out, *Hurry. Isa—she's been taken. And I've got a slight problem on my hands*, Alasdair's gut tightened.

It had started.

The war. The fight. Or whatever the fuck was coming for them had been triggered. And he had a feeling Leo had been the key.

His anger rose. He'd been deceived.

Leo was not who he claimed to be.

And once he woke and told him what he wanted to hear, he *would* find a way to end this obsession once and for all.

Twenty-Three

Ancient Greece—47 BC

LEO'S HEART WAS going to give out. He was positive. With as many jolts as it had been getting, it was going to give the fuck out. He stood as still as he possibly could as the stunning vampire behind Alasdair held his gaze.

Maybe he's not looking at me, *he thought, and then he looked over his shoulder. But there was no one behind him. So he turned back, wondering if he was about to be maimed right there in his vision, but when he glanced beyond Alasdair's shoulder, Vasilios was gone.*

Where the…

Leo spun around to see if he'd missed him or if he was going to appear somewhere to ravage his throat, but instead of finding Alasdair and Vasilios, he was somewhere else entirely.

ALASDAIR PICKED LEO up and slung him over his shoulder. He really didn't want to do this. Not now, and not with Thanos. But he didn't have a choice. He couldn't leave Leo behind, and he had to go to his cousin's aid.

Holding on to the backs of Leo's thighs, he faded back to the office where he'd left Isadora and Thanos, and what he saw when he appeared made his knees want to buckle. Thanos was on his ass, his back against the wall, clutching his neck. Blood oozed between his fingers and trailed down his arm in rivers of crimson liquid, and when his blue eyes found his, they appeared lackluster compared to the usual twinkle the vampire sported.

What the fuck is the matter with him?

Alasdair crouched by his cousin's side and put Leo on the ground. Then he looked at Thanos's disturbingly sallow complexion. He was in trouble.

"Show me," Alasdair demanded, gesturing to the wound his cousin was covering with his hand. When he refused to let go, Alasdair repeated himself. "Show me."

"I can't," Thanos managed to say between grim lips.

"Why not? Just take your hand away. I'll heal you."

Thanos grimaced. "My hand. It's fused to the silver."

Alasdair shifted closer and saw exactly what Thanos meant. His left arm was across his chest, and his palm was flat against the side of his neck as though he'd reached to remove the weapon that'd been used. But it appeared that, when he'd taken hold of it, the metal had melted into his fingers and his hand, melding it with the wound and making it impossible to directly heal.

The silver was pressed between Thanos's neck and hand, and tiny little bubbles boiled there. The pain must've been excruciating, not only from the poison, but also from the burn. Silver only melted when it reached 1763.2° F, a little factoid Alasdair had picked up through many years manning the torture chair of the Adjudication Room. So it was a fucking miracle Thanos could still speak.

The ghastly grey veins traveling up his neck to his ear were straining out against his skin, which was paper thin where the poison was coursing through him.

"Who did this?"

Thanos tried to straighten up but hissed and slumped back down. "Some fucker Isa knows—"

"What do you mean Isa knows?"

"Some tall bastard in a preppy-ass suit and tie. Gotta say, cousin. Didn't think this is how I'd die."

"You are not going to die," Alasdair swore as he tried to find a way to stop the toxic liquid from spreading.

"There's no way to heal this shit without direct contact, and you know it. It's too deep in the blood. I'd figured a dagger would be it for me, or maybe you ripping my head off in annoyance, but not a fucking letter opener by some goddamn human."

So that's what was now nothing more than an adhesive between his neck and his palm.

"You need to go find Isa."

"If you think I'm leaving here—"

"Go!" Thanos roared.

Alasdair reached for the hand lying limp by his cousin's side. "No. Now, shut the fuck up and give me your hand."

Thanos opened his mouth to protest but must've thought better of it and decided to do as he'd been told. Instead of his palm being cool to the touch, it was close to scorching.

Like all cold-blooded creatures, their variable body temperature adjusted to their surroundings—or emotions. In this case, Thanos's skin was heating due to severe pain. But Alasdair tightened his fingers around his cousin's limp ones and gnashed his back teeth together to fight the pain off.

Mine is nothing compared to his.

He clamped his other hand around Leo's wrist, and as he was about to fade them all from the room, a photograph fell from the wall and landed by them.

When Alasdair glanced at it, the bathhouses were staring back at him. The ones that had set him on his quest for answers when he'd last been in this room alone with Leo.

That was when the world he had always known began to fall apart. And that made him wonder as his eyes shifted to the human who was still eerily unconscious, *Is that where he is now?*

Ancient Athens — 47 BC

IT WAS AS if someone had changed the channel on the TV.

Leo scrubbed his eyes, and when he reopened them, he recognized his new location.

He was back at the bathhouse.

It was nighttime.

And there was a definite tension in the air — of the sexual kind.

Then he heard it. A shout of uninhibited ecstasy.

Leo's pulse thumped and his cock twitched. Then, as if he couldn't stop his feet from moving, he started walking in the direction of the sound. Gooseflesh covered his skin, but it wasn't borne out of fear.

It was anticipation.

A cool breeze whipped through the open roof of the house and swirled down around his feet, brushing his pants against his thighs.

"*You really should not walk alone in the night, omorfo mou agóri.*"

Leo recognized the voice. *Vasilios.*

Oh God. God…

He stopped walking and curled his fingers into his palms. Did he really want to keep going? He knew exactly who that groan belonged to, and he wasn't sure if he wanted to see Alasdair with his vampire again.

And why is that, *he asked himself. Probably because* he *was always interrupted every time he thought he'd finally —*

What? Have sex with a vampire who wants to kill me? Jesus, I have lost my mind.

"*A lot can happen when the sun dips down and the moon come out to play…*"

Fucking hell—*Vasilios was convincing. His words were drawing him closer, and the moan that tore through the empty bathhouse was full of raw arousal.*

Alasdair.

Not knowing if his presence would be detected or not, Leo crept closer, careful not to make a sound. Then, as he rounded the last column, he saw them.

Alasdair was pressed up against the end pillar. Nobody was with him, but he had his eyes closed and a hand rubbing his erection. It must have felt amazing too, because he was rocking into his palm as if he hadn't fucked for days.

Leo's own cock throbbed at the sight. Alasdair was as sexy dressed in a toga as he was in modern-day clothes. The only difference: his long hair, which was tied back now, showing off his spectacular face as the moon shone down and seemed to illuminate him.

Fuck this, Leo thought as he pressed his hand against his stiff length. As if he wasn't going to get achingly hard watching Alasdair masturbate only a few feet away from him.

But then the air shifted and practically hummed. Leo had felt this once before. This vibration of power that had only been present when Vasilios had been near—and aroused.

Leo kept his eyes on Alasdair as the hand he had been using to stroke himself was yanked away and pinned to his side. Leo swallowed, his eyes focused on what was happening, when Vasilios's voice sounded again.

"I have been waiting for you for some time, Alasdair Kyriakoús, son of Lapidos. Ise poli omorfos. A man worthy of my attention, if ever I saw one."

Leo squeezed his own cock at the words of praise. What must it have felt like to be worshiped so openly as Alasdair clearly was in that moment? He figured pretty damn good if his bucking hips were any kind of indication.

Then Alasdair demanded, "Show yourself."

Leo stared at the shameless picture Alasdair made while waiting for whomever was speaking to appear. Dying for some kind of release, Leo unbuttoned his jeans and slipped his hand inside. He was so fucking aroused by what he was seeing that he needed to do something to either get off or hold back the impending orgasm.

"I desire your presence," Alasdair panted, and when his eyes closed, his long lashes swept over his cheeks, which made

Leo's choice of fucking his fist or holding his climax off real easy. He started to fuck his fist.

"Understand, agóri. Once you really see me, you can never unsee me. You will be of my blood. Your life—tied to mine."

This was it.

That moment of passion, of desire so intense that Alasdair's mind was completely overtaken with arousal. The moment Vasilios had him.

Leo knew it, and so did the male vampire. He had Alasdair exactly where he wanted him. It was in the desperate cry falling from those delectable lips and the rawness of Alasdair's movements as he jerked his hips forward. And when Alasdair begged once again, a figure appeared.

Even with his back to him, Leo knew it was Alasdair's vampire by the power rattling the marble walls surrounding them. With the confident way he held himself and the short cut of his hair, it wasn't hard to make the connection. He hadn't done much to change his appearance in all his years, and neither, for that matter, had the sexy man he was pleasuring.

They were magnificent together, just as they had been in Vasilios's bed, and as Leo continued to watch, his feet moved him closer as if he were on autopilot. When he was finally standing beside the two of them, close enough that he could see Vasilios run his tongue along Alasdair's ear, Vasilios said, "Then open your eyes."

Alasdair's eyes opened, the stunning shade the same then as it was now. They even seemed to glow, but that wasn't from any supernatural reason—merely from desire. Then those sinful

lips Leo had felt against his own moved and Alasdair pledged a
vow.

"I am yours."

"Forever?" Vasilios asked as he raised his head, and the
covetous expression in his eyes solidified their undeniable bond.

Leo hadn't understood until that moment exactly how deep
their connection ran.

He knew what Alasdair's response would be, but as he
opened his mouth to tell Vasilios, the channel changed.

Present Day—Elias's Office

"I THOUGHT I would be disgusted by your kind."

As Elias continued to inspect her, Isadora felt a pain
in her gut, like his words were a knife stabbing her. Ever
since she had flashed her canines at him like a spitting
hellcat, he'd been studying her like a lab rat.

"I knew what I was looking for, was told I would feel
it. So I assumed I would be repelled. How wrong was I?"

She didn't dare take her eyes off him when he raised
a hand as if he were about to touch her, but at the last
minute, he took a step back.

"Nothing to say, Isadora? That's unlike you. You
never used to hold back."

"And you used to be a gentleman."

His laughter was full of disdain. "Yes, I suppose I was, wasn't I? But I didn't know *who* I was back then. And I certainly didn't know *what* you are." He slid his hands into his pockets, and Isadora cursed herself for noticing that he was as handsome as ever with his dark hair and odd-colored eyes. "Did you?"

The pain radiating up her arms made her clench her fists together as she fought against it. "Did I know what? About my being a vampire? Or are we still discussing my chatty tendencies?"

"You know exactly what I'm talking about," he bit out. "Did you know who I was when I pursued you?"

"Why should I tell you?" she challenged. "You have me tied to a chair, Elias. And *you* are watching me suffer. Excuse me if I don't feel like indulging you."

He shook his head, her ruse of innocence not winning him over. "Don't act like I wouldn't be dead on the floor if you were free. You're merely upset that I did it first. Don't make me hurt you."

"You already have."

She thought his face softened slightly but then he spun away from her. *Easier to punish someone if you aren't looking at them.* She knew that firsthand.

"Did you know who I was?" he asked again.

She glared at his broad shoulders, which were encased in his tailored jacket, and felt a strange sense of longing claw at her anger. "I had no idea. And I still don't. Not really."

He looked over his shoulder, disbelief in his eyes.

"Why would I lie? You talk as if I'm holding you at my mercy. But look at us, Elias. There are no shackles on you. If you want to end this, end it! You are your own master, and right now, it appears you are mine. But don't expect me to soothe your wounded pride."

He turned around and stormed over to her. Then he leaned down and touched his nose to hers. "And if I let you go? Then what?"

She swallowed, and the ache in her arms was almost outdone by the dry scratch of her throat. But there was no stopping years of instincts. "Then I will kill you."

Twenty-Four

1902 — London, England

"THERE. THAT ONE."

    Leo pressed the heels of his hands to his temples as his mind whirled and then came to an abrupt stop. He was now standing in a ballroom. A huge, rectangular one full of men and women dressed in their best finery. A string quartet played in one corner, and several young women were seated in another. A large chandelier with long, tapered candles lit the room, and men stood around the outskirts of the dance floor sipping from crystal scotch glasses.

    Christ. The dream has changed again, *Leo thought, and then he spotted them.*

Alasdair was standing in the corner of the room looking as handsome as ever in full black tails. Directly behind him stood Vasilios. They were so close they had to be touching, and from the smug expressions stretched across both their faces, they were enjoying the contact.

"There. See him? The Duke of Essex. He's looking very dashing tonight, and every time he passes, his eyes stray to you, agóri. Not that I can blame him. You're so very handsome in your evening wear."

Leo could tell by the way Vasilios's eyes tracked the man across the room that he was on the hunt, and he was more than enjoying using Alasdair as the bait. It was clear by the way Vasilios stroked a hand over Alasdair's shoulder, drawing the Duke's eye that he delighted in having others look at Alasdair and want him.

It was as if the fact that they found his possession appealing pleased him. But Leo also sensed that, if anyone dared to touch without his permission, they would likely lose their hand. Or their life.

"Are you sure you don't wish to go back to our room and—"

"You are hungry," Vasilios said. "You need to eat."

"I can wait."

"No, you have waited long enough. You must stop doing that. Testing yourself."

Alasdair scoffed. "It's hardly a test, Vasilios. I have been doing it for centuries. I am merely more selective than you."

"*Yes, but it seems so unnecessary when there is food readily available.*"

"*I know. But you spoiled me from the first. After tasting you, only something special will tempt me.*"

As the duke wandered by the two of them, he dipped his head in Alasdair's direction, and when the corner of Alasdair's lip curved up and his eyes glowed, the redheaded man straightened his shoulders like a proud peacock.

As he continued by, not wanting to appear conspicuous, Alasdair said softly, "I suppose he will do."

Vasilios raised the glass in his hand and took a long sip before he said, "So enthusiastic. You can always add a bit of excitement yourself, agóri. Tease him. Then take him. I'll wait here. Don't be long. I suddenly have a different hunger I wish to satisfy."

Alasdair grinned, and Leo caught the tips of his fangs before he shut his mouth and followed the duke outside.

Present Day—Alasdair's Bedchambers

ALASDAIR APPEARED IN his bedchambers and dropped Leo onto the king-size mattress in the center. He didn't want to leave him there unsupervised, especially with all the shit going down. But what other choice did he have? He wasn't going to take him to the Assembly Hall, where he could feel the Ancients were gathered, and that was where he needed to go.

He slung Thanos's arm over his shoulder and gave a final look at the man on his bed. With any luck, he'd remain passed out, or wherever the fuck he was, until he returned. Until then, he needed to get Thanos to the Ancients. If anyone could hope to heal his cousin, they could.

He faded them from his room to the Hall, and they appeared rather ungracefully. Thanos, a ragged mess, clung to him as he staggered to stay on his feet.

Eton winced as he stood. He had the same fair complexion as Thanos and was tall like him, but where his first sired was more muscular, Eton was lithe in frame. When his eyes zoomed in on the vampire Alasdair held propped up by his side, the shared pain their kind felt when their progeny was close to death was evident in his stance and expression.

Before Alasdair could begin to explain, Eton was at their side.

"I sensed something had happened but did not understand the severity. What is wrong with him?" he demanded, concern shining in the Ancient's eyes.

Just like he and Vasilios were dark in their coloring and nature, Thanos and Eton shared those same boyishly handsome features. Since they were charmers of both men and women, it was shocking to see Thanos so sickly and Eton so serious.

As the Ancient knelt down by Thanos's side, Alasdair wondered for the first time how the others would react should one of the three die. Was the concern in Eton's eyes for Thanos? Or his own safety?

"I don't know what happened, exactly." Alasdair glanced over at Vasilios, who was currently rounding the end of the podium and moving towards him. "I wasn't there," he admitted, and then he looked to the third in the room—Diomêdês.

He knew what he had to say next, and he didn't relish the reaction it was going to evoke. But he locked eyes with the third Ancient and stated loud enough to be heard, "Isadora—she is gone."

Diomêdês glared at him, his eyes changing to obsidian, and before Alasdair could blink, Vasilios was standing between the two of them, warding off Isa's sire with bared fangs.

"Step off, Diomêdês."

"Move aside, Vasilios."

Vasilios hissed and spat at the male glaring over his shoulder, and Alasdair knew that, if his Ancient hadn't been standing there, he would be dead on the floor.

Diomêdês's anger was clouding his common sense. All he was aware of was what he was pulling from Alasdair's mind—his first sired was gone, and he had been the one to let her go.

"If you kill him," Vasilios said, "you lose any kind of lead you may have. Not to mention I won't let you end his life, therefore ending my own. Think before you act, *adelfe*. Do you want that? To never see her again? Reach out to her. Can you feel her?"

While Vasilios tried to calm the rabid beast in front of him, Alasdair looked down at Eton, who was running a hand over Thanos's hair, showing more concern than he'd thought their kind capable of in that moment.

"He doesn't have much time," Eton stated.

"I know," Alasdair said as he crouched to look Eton in the eye. "His palm is fused in place. I cannot remove it to heal him. He was coherent before we faded. Told me it was a silver letter opener. So the amount is not much. It is the placement and the fusing that is killing him."

Eton frowned, his features more adult than Alasdair had ever seen. Usually, he was the most carefree of the three, younger in spirit even though he was much, much older than his looks suggested. But right then he had a worried frown on his face as he tried to devise a way to work out the complication before him.

"We need to remove the hand so I can get to the wound."

"But, to do that, you are going to tear the skin from his neck and possibly his face. And it's so deep, I'm not sure that *will* heal."

Eton grimaced and nodded. "I know. And he will hate me for it. But it will ensure his survival."

"And your own," Alasdair murmured. Then he looked into Eton's troubled eyes, which were now focused on him.

"You are right. It will also ensure my own survival. That may be selfish, but do not deny you wouldn't do the same." Eton stood to his full height and addressed the two Ancients still facing off against one another. "If you two are quite done here, perhaps you could help me save Thanos so we can then go and find Isadora. It's clear this war has begun, and we need to be on each other's side, not going at one another's throats like animals."

Alasdair raised his eyes as Vasilios turned and looked down at him. No words were said out loud, but he heard inside his mind, *Where is your yielding?*

Alasdair didn't respond, but he didn't have to. Vasilios's expression already told him that he knew.

Leonidas Chapel didn't know it yet, but when he woke, he would be a dead man walking.

1902—London, England

LEO FOLLOWED ALASDAIR *as he tracked the duke out of the room. When he reached the far end of the maid's hall, the duke glanced over his shoulder to make sure Alasdair was there—and he was.*

Leo was right beside him, matching him step for step as he strode after the man. It was supremely odd to be next to someone who was completely unaware of his existence. But that was exactly what was happening. He was in Alasdair's past, watching him like a moviegoer who'd bought tickets to a show.

The duke opened a door on the left, and when he slipped through, a growl rumbled from the male beside him.

Damn, even in a fucking hallucination Alasdair is turning me on. *That animal side of him, the side that was unlike anything he'd ever known, was both mystifying and tantalizing.*

When they reached the door the duke had exited, Alasdair pushed it open and they both stepped out into the night air. The sky was jet black, and the air was cool. A pungent smell was being blown over, probably from the river in the far distance. They were on some kind of estate, standing in the shadows on the side of the main house.

Alasdair lifted his chin and closed his eyes. He was sniffing the air, searching for the man, and then he spun to the right.

Scent caught, *Leo thought as he followed, his palms starting to sweat.*

He wasn't sure why he was so nervous. It wasn't like he was a part of this world, and Alasdair wasn't a threat to him. But he was fascinated with what was about to happen—and dreading it.

As they made their way down the side of the house, he was surprised that no sound could be heard but the faint rush of water.

They were walking over gravel, but his feet were making no sound, and Alasdair seemed to be gliding over it.

Those damn hunter moves of his. That stealth. It always helped with the surprise attack.

When they reached the end of the path, they stopped and Alasdair looked down the side of the house. Leo stepped around the corner, not worried in the least since he'd not been detected—and there he was.

The duke was leaning up against the side of the wall, one of his feet propped against the brick. After taking a draw from the cigar in his mouth, he blew the smoke out, and it curled up past his face before disappearing into the sky.

That low purr of Alasdair's vibrated through the air again, and Leo couldn't help himself from turning to look at the male beside him.

Alasdair was truly a sight to see.

His long hair was pushed back behind his ears, so Leo could see the strong line of his jaw and the arrogant tilt of his chin. The tip of his tongue came out to touch the corner of his lip, and when they parted slightly, his fangs descended.

Fuck me, *Leo thought as a rush of air left him. That mouth had been on his earlier, finally devouring his in a way he'd only imagined, and he wanted it back. He reached out to touch Alasdair's arm, needing his attention, even if it was the hunting, stalking kind, to be on him. But when he laid his hand on the sleeve of Alasdair's jacket, he felt nothing, and neither did the vampire. He was one hundred percent focused on his prey, and his jaw began to twitch as though he were holding himself back.*

Do it, *Leo thought out of nowhere. It was clear Alasdair wanted this man, and suddenly, he wanted to see him take him. Do it.*

As if he'd heard him, a whoosh of air ruffled his hair and Alasdair was over and in front of the duke in a flash —and Leo was quick to follow.

Twenty-five

Present Day—Elias's Office

ELIAS COULDN'T TEAR his eyes away from the woman— *no,* the female—bound to his chair. She looked terrible, which was hard to imagine of the Isadora he was accustomed to. This was a woman who'd captured his attention the first instant he'd seen her.

But that was before. Before his life had changed. And what he was seeing now was blowing his fucking mind.

Isadora was a vampire. Is, he corrected himself. *She is a fucking vampire, and not just any vampire—she is the one.*

"Although I'm flattered, I'm hardly thinking of you in the same light, Elias. But you needn't look so startled. I think, if anyone should be appalled at all of this, it should be me. After all, I'm over two thousand years old and you managed to overpower me. How did you do that, by the way? Or are we going to sit here forever in saturnine silence?"

Elias ignored that she'd read his mind and instead replied, "I'm still digesting the idea that I was created to eliminate a mistake. And that mistake was you."

"Excuse me. So, I'm a mistake?" Isadora asked, one of her perfectly shaped eyebrows arching. "I don't seem to recall you thinking that when you would worship me on your knees for hours at a time. So why not cut the bullshit and tell me who sent you, Elias."

Their eyes remained locked, and he caught a flicker of fear in their dark depths. Then he replied, "Someone more powerful than you."

1902—London, England

ALASDAIR HAD THE man cornered before Leo could blink. So he jogged after him and moved up beside them to get a front-row seat to what was about to happen.

Although he knew Alasdair fed, likely on other humans, Leo had never seen him do it. Well, except for the image he'd once pushed into Leo's mind that one time. But this…

This felt totally different.

Leo's adrenaline pumped through him, and he wasn't sure what exactly was driving him to feel the way he was.

The sensual way Alasdair stroked the back of his fingers down the man's cheek? Or the way the man straightened against the brick wall, allowing Alasdair to move in closer?

Sex and arousal were swirling around them as effectively as the smoke from the cigar, and then the duke dropped it to the ground, forgotten. His cheeks were flushed, and when Leo looked down his body, a solid erection was outlined in the duke's pants. It was obvious he was extremely attracted to Alasdair, who was now pressing their bodies firmly against one another. But if there'd been any doubt, the groan Leo heard when Alasdair placed his lips by the duke's ear dispelled it in an instant. Alasdair hadn't said anything yet, hadn't even touched the man, really, but Leo had the distinct impression the duke was ready to come.

Not that I can blame him, *Leo thought. Alasdair was a true creature of the night. He made a person want to do things and see things he'd never imagined, and Leo was hard just from watching him.*

"I saw you tonight," he whispered in the duke's ear. "Watching me."

The other man swallowed, and Leo wondered if he was nervous due to his arousal or because Alasdair gave off an overwhelming sense of danger. It was probably a heady combination of the two.

Alasdair's tongue came out then and traced along the man's jawline, and Leo heard his own breath catch.

"Is this what you were imagining when your eyes were greedily taking in every inch of me?"

The duke pushed his hips forward, making it clear which inches he was most interested in, and when Alasdair shoved him back and ground his hips over the man's, Leo reached down to palm his own cock.

This was so wrong. He knew that, but he couldn't stop himself.

Alasdair hummed and the noise seemed to stroke the nerve endings running along the length of Leo's dick. Because, even though Alasdair wasn't touching him, Leo felt as though that tongue and the hands now moving down to the duke's pants were all on him.

"It must get so lonely living in town with the duchess. Especially when you prefer cock over cunt. Does she mind, I wonder? Does she know?"

The sounds of rustling material and heavy breathing were all that could be heard—until Alasdair got ahold of what he was after. The duke's head fell back against the wall, and he jutted his pelvis out.

"Ahh…yes. It feels good, doesn't it?" Alasdair cooed as he trailed his eyes over the exposed throat in front of him.

Leo's eyes followed the same path, and he felt sorry for the man being so superbly manipulated—until he groaned again. Then Leo's sympathy went out the window, and fierce jealousy shot through him instead. He hadn't gotten this far with Alasdair, not once, and he was pissed off that he had to stand there and watch this.

"You are by far the most handsome man I have ever seen," the duke confessed.

A seductive sound that could've been taken for humor left Alasdair as he put his lips to the base of the duke's throat. Then the words, "Ne, I know," fell from Alasdair's mouth. And without any more talk, Alasdair lifted his head and struck like a cobra.

He sank his teeth into the side of the duke's neck, and a shout of agony came from the man who, only seconds ago, had been groaning for other reasons entirely.

The sound of Alasdair sucking and growling as he pinned the man to the side of the building should've appalled him. Leo thought he would have been terrified, but instead, his dick got harder.

He couldn't explain it, not if anyone had asked, but seeing this side of Alasdair was a hell of a turn on, and he wasn't sure what that said about him.

Alasdair's arm started moving, and Leo knew he was still stroking the duke's shaft as he viciously fed from him. Blood stained the duke's crisp, white shirt, and his shouts of pain changed to cries of confused pleasure.

Whatever horror had come from that initial bite had now altered into some kind of euphoric bliss. His eyes had rolled back, his hips were fucking against Alasdair, and he was drifting into a sweet, sweet death.

"Leonidas Chapel."

The unfamiliar voice was like a lightning bolt to his brain. It pulled him from his trancelike state and had him spinning on his heel to see if anyone had followed him outside. But no, no one was there. And when he turned back to where Alasdair and the Duke had been standing, all he saw was darkness.

Leo's erection subsided as fear of the unknown crept in. "Who's there? Who are you?"

"Perhaps the question you should be asking is: Who are you?"

A splitting pain shot through his head, and then a flash of Alasdair appeared before his eyes—him and the duke, just as they'd been a second ago.

Then the screams started.

Loud, fearful cries into the night air.

Alasdair clamped a hand over the man's mouth. The duke twisted and writhed against Alasdair, now realizing his life was coming to an end. Then Alasdair ripped his mouth away from his neck, brought both hands to the Duke's cheeks, and tore his head right off his shoulders.

Leo gasped at the gruesome action and covered his mouth as his stomach turned. Then the image disappeared.

"He is not what you imagine him to be. You have been shown this for a reason. You, Leonidas Chapel, were created to stop him and his kind. You and two others. We have been waiting for you."

But before Leo could say a word, he woke up.

Present Day—The Lair

ALASDAIR FOLLOWED BEHIND Eton and Diomêdês, who were carrying Thanos down the east corridor. Vasilios matched his stride step for step and hadn't said two words to him since his question back in the Hall. The truth was, Alasdair could sense his sire's volatile mood. He just wasn't sure what he was most disappointed about.

Leonidas's being back in the lair?

Isadora's having been taken?

Or—

Your bringing the human here in the first place, Alasdair. But perhaps we should refer to him by name, since we aren't quite sure what your young male is.

Alasdair turned to look at his sire, and when he didn't bother returning his stare, he lowered his eyes.

Oh, yeah. He's pissed.

Vasilios wasn't stupid. He would have seen everything he'd been trying to hide when he, Leo, and Thanos had arrived this evening. He'd been too preoccupied with his cousin's condition to concern himself with concealing his thoughts. So finally, it had all tumbled free.

The first meeting with Leonidas. His strange ability to paralyze him and see his past. The fact that he was now out cold on Alasdair's bed—

That is all rather interesting information. Don't you think, Alasdair? Vasilios interjected into his thoughts.

Alasdair's eyes flew up to meet the knowing ones of his sire.

Did you ever think that this may have been avoided had you told someone? Perhaps I should've let Diomêdês at you. It's the least of what you deserve. Vasilios gave a manic grin, seeming to derive enjoyment from that thought.

He couldn't blame him. He had been acting careless. Not thinking of the consequences of his actions when it came to Leo. But Alasdair had never felt such a pull to anyone the way he did with Leonidas, and even now, he felt it. It was almost as strong as the one to the male beside him.

Know this, Alasdair: I do not care if you find him more fascinating. Though I doubt that would be so if you would've stuck your cock in him already. He cannot live. And if you do not take care of it, I will.

Alasdair tried to ignore the anger at the words he'd known were coming, but he couldn't prevent it—it was there regardless. *I understand.*

Good. You have until dawn. Do whatever you must, but if I can hear his heart beating when the sun comes up, I will rip it from his body myself.

As they stepped into Thanos's bedchambers, all thoughts and discussion ceased as Eton placed him on the bed.

Vasilios took him by the arm, halting him, then said, "We shall discuss this more after we have seen to Thanos."

Alasdair gave a stoic nod. "This won't end well for him, will it?"

As the words left his mouth, Alasdair wasn't sure if he was referring to Leo or Thanos. Or maybe he meant both.

"No. I don't think it will end well for any of us. But for now, let us concern ourselves with your cousin. We need him, and as is, he is useless."

Alasdair walked over to the tray on the nightstand. Diomêdês had brought it in on their way there, and what was on it was enough to make even his skin crawl—a newly sharpened jeweler's saw and a pair of metal shears. Beside those items sat a bottle of alcohol, and beside *that* a syringe full of morphine.

What was about to happen would be horrendous. The wound was so deep it was almost a given that it wouldn't fully heal, and Alasdair only hoped Thanos remained unconscious for the duration.

"Let us begin," Eton said as he reached for the saw.

LEO WOKE TO the sound of screams.

Not the terrified scream of someone who was witnessing something frightening. But the agonizing cries of someone who was quite possibly dying. The loud noise was low, and as it tapered off due to lack of air, a ragged snarl grit out at the end of it.

The sound was what nightmares were made of.

He opened his eyes, not convinced he wasn't actually *in* a nightmare, and took in his surroundings. The room was dark from the lack of conventional lighting and the rich tone

of the cherry oak walls. Two lit candles hung on either side
of a door, and as the wax dripped down one of the long
tapers, he didn't have to think too hard to work out where
he was.

This had to be the lair.

That's what Alasdair called it, right? The place where
he'd first held him captive.

It had that same feel to it. But he'd never been to this
part before. This room was decadent—from the wicked
invitation of the massive bed he was lying on to the black
silk robe hanging over a plush, maroon recliner.

Leo scooted to the edge of the bed when another
shout from somewhere outside had him jerking to a stop.

"I'll fucking kill you! Kill you all!"

The shout was pained, the threat real, and it had him
dashing over to the door to pick one of the candles up in
case he needed to…

*What? Burn a vampire? Yeah, good one, Chapel. They're
immortal. I hardly think a single candle is going to do much.*

He pulled the heavy door open, relieved when it
didn't creak. The last thing he needed was to draw
unwanted attention.

"Fuck you, Alasdair! Just fucking kill me and be
done with it!"

The request, if it could be called that, was choked
out, and the gasping breath of whomever it was indicated
horrific pain.

When Leo reached the first door down the hall, Alasdair's voice reached his ears, "Hold still, cousin. Let us get it done so you can heal."

"I'll never *heal*," the first voice hissed. "Not from this."

"You will live, and that's what—"

"FUCK!"

The word was a thunderous bellow of suffering, and Leo reached for the handle. What the hell was Alasdair doing to this...

Wait. His cousin?

Leo twisted the handle and opened the door, using his shoulder to shift the heavy wood. When he stumbled into the room, three pairs of inky, black eyes landed on him. The figures hovering around a large bed were unfamiliar to him, but as he gazed past them, he saw Alasdair straddling the prone form of...*yes*, his cousin.

When Alasdair lifted his head and his glowing, green eyes found him, Leo's own widened. He had blood all over his hands and up his forearms. He looked fierce and wild, like an animal in the middle of a kill, but when Leo glanced at the other vampire, he realized he wasn't feeding from him. He was holding him down while one of the others—

His thought came to a halt as his eyes flicked to the saw in the hands of one of the unfamiliar males.

It was dripping with blood.

He then returned his attention to the figure under Alasdair, and the sight that greeted him was macabre.

Like something out of a horror movie.

The long hair of Alasdair's cousin, which he'd once thought a similar color to his own, was now streaked with blood, both dry and fresh. The pillow beneath his head was covered with the ruby-red liquid, but what was most grotesque of all was the man's face.

Where he'd once had a handsome and youthful appearance, he was now howling like a beast and flayed open like a raw piece of meat. From the crook of his shoulder and up his neck, or what was left of it, and to his cheek, the skin had been cut away—probably with the dripping fucking saw.

Still frozen with his hand gripping the doorknob, Leo tore his eyes away from the butchered flesh as his stomach somersaulted. He wasn't sure how much more he could take.

That was when Alasdair shouted in his head, *Get out of here! Run!*

The command left no room for argument, and even if he'd wanted to, the fierce expressions plastered on the other three vampires' faces had him pulling the door shut and fleeing for his life.

Twenty-Six

FUCK, ALASDAIR THOUGHT as Leonidas slammed the door to Thanos's room shut. The man's timing was fucking horrid. Up to his elbows in his cousin's flesh and blood, he could hardly chase the traitorous human down the hall. But Vasilios would have no such misgivings with leaving Thanos to die so he could track Leo down and put an end to him.

He needed to think and act fast if he wanted that honor for himself. Leonidas had to be eliminated, but not before he got some fucking answers.

"Vasilios," Alasdair said, knowing it would be much more effective than a voice in his head.

"He is awake," his sire stated, so slowly that Alasdair suspected he was about to be in as much pain as the man he was holding down was. "You said he was passed out, no threat."

"He was."

Vasilios kept his eyes on him.

Alasdair pushed into his mind: *It's the truth.*

"Go now. Take care of it. One way or another, that human *will* be dead by dawn," he vowed as he moved back to the bed with Eton and Diomêdês. "Thanos, we have one more infected piece of skin to remove. You will live, but perhaps you too will wish you were dead by sunrise."

Alasdair backed away from his cousin and the Ancients, and as his back hit the door, Vasilios said to Eton, "Don't let him move. This is going to fucking hurt."

THE SMELL OF burning flesh, where the silver was seeping through her skin and poisoning her forearms, was starting to make Isadora's stomach turn. Her head felt fuzzy, her limbs weak, and as her vision blurred, she said, "Tell me who sent you. How did you know what would stop us?"

The man she'd once thought would be her perfect equal came over to stand behind her. He leaned down and when his warm breath breezed over the back of her hair, she shut her eyes and remembered another time they'd been alone together in an office of his.

Ten years earlier

"DON'T TEASE ME, Elias."

The sexy man in front of her slowly got to his knees. Then he raised his head and gave her a grin that could rival the most immoral sinner—and she should know, having been sired by one.

"Don't tell me you aren't enjoying yourself, Isadora. Your sweet pussy tells me otherwise."

The door to his office was locked, and she had her back against it and a leg over one of his wide shoulders. Her black skirt was scrunched up to her waist, and when he'd gotten on his knees and pulled her lace panties to the side, a delicious throb had pulsed between her legs.

His tie was shoved over his other shoulder, and with his black hair mussed from her hands, he looked sexy as fuck.

"It's talking to you?"

One of his fingers traced a teasing line between her soaked lips and then dipped inside before he pulled it out and sucked on the tip. "Oh, it's saying something, all right."

A seductive laugh slipped free of her lips. "And what's that, Mr. Fontana?"

He grinned, the expression so fucking filthy she wanted to push him on the ground, rip his pants off, and sink her teeth into his neck. Then she wanted to ride the thick cock she'd swallowed only last night until she reached the orgasm he was withholding from her.

"It's saying," he whispered, angling his head until she couldn't see his eyes and could only hear him say against her pulsing cunt, "eat me."

"YOU AND I are made much the same, Isadora."

His voice in her ear pulled her from her memories, and she twisted her head until they were practically nose to nose. His eyes, that same unnatural silver they'd been when he'd realized what she was, still shone at her, and it reminded her that this was not the same man she'd once known.

"We are nothing alike."

"Ahh, but that's where you're wrong."

She pulled her face back from his. "Are you saying that you too are...vampire?"

The smirk on his face made her want to rip it off, even if it meant taking his head with it.

"No, but I'm happy to hear you finally admitting to it."

She swallowed. *Fuck him for having all the control. And fuck him for smelling so delicious.* "Then what are you?"

"Today, I am your master."

LEO SPRINTED DOWN the hall to the room he'd stepped out of minutes ago. He shoved at the door and thanked God that it opened. Then he slammed it shut and leaned back against it. His breathing came in rapid bursts as he tried to banish the image of blood and gore from his mind.

Jesus. How the fuck can I ever banish that? And how the hell am I ever going to get out of here?

Not only had the three with the black eyes looked like they wanted to murder him, but Alasdair's voice when he'd told him to run had been full of…anxiety. Which was worrisome. Alasdair wasn't one to worry. He was usually confident and ready to tell him that *he* wanted to kill him.

So, if he felt his life was in danger, the threat must've been real.

He let his eyes scan around the room again, searching for something he could push or drag over by the door to keep them out—but then he thought better of it.

They can fucking appear in a room. Like a bookcase is going to keep them out. He shook his head and decided to hide on the far side of the bed instead.

It was a useless attempt to avoid his inevitable death, he was sure. They would no doubt smell where he was the second they were in the room, or maybe even from outside, but he had to try. He huddled down and thought back to the erratic dreams he'd woken from.

What had they all meant? And if someone out there in the cosmos really thought he could stop the beings down the hall, they were fucking insane.

"Leonidas?"

Alasdair.

Leo didn't move a muscle as he sat with his knees pulled up to his chest and his arms wrapped around them.

"I know you are in here, *file mou*. I can hear your heart like the first night we met. Remember?"

Leo remembered, all right. He was starting to wonder if he'd ever be able to forget. The way Alasdair had chased him through the bathhouse and pinned him against the column would be forever engrained in his mind. As was the way his body seemed to respond whenever the vampire was near.

That night, Alasdair had told him that his heartbeat was like a beautiful melody as it beat: *Thump, Thump —*

"Thump."

The word was said so close to his ear that Leo's head snapped up, and he saw Alasdair standing directly beside him.

He looked awful. Leo took in the blood all over the chest and the arms of his shirt, and tendrils of fear twined around his nerves. He wondered what was about to happen as he stared up at Alasdair, but he didn't have the courage to ask. They hadn't exactly parted on great terms, and after what he'd seen in those visions, he wasn't sure what to expect next.

Sure, before he'd passed out in his kitchen, they'd been about to, as far as he was aware, make out. But *before* that, Alasdair had been accusing him of being someone he wasn't.

Fuck, maybe he was right.

"I am right. The question is: *Who* and *what* are you?"

The clipped and calm way he'd said that had Leo thinking his time was limited, and before he thought better of it, he scrambled up to his knees. Maybe begging would help, and fuck it, after what he'd seen and heard, he wasn't too proud, knowing death was likely coming for him next.

"I don't know. I swear. I have no clue what's happening to me. Or…or how I see the things I see."

Alasdair crouched so they were on the same level. "You know, I almost believe you."

"Because it's the truth," Leo rushed out, and then he did something he never would've dared to days earlier. He grabbed hold of Alasdair's shirt, not caring that it was covered in blood. "Earlier, when we…when I passed out, I had no control over that. I don't even know how it happened. Usually, it's quick, like a flash of a vision. But this time, I saw days. Different times, different moments. Why would I tell you that if I was trying to hide something?"

When Alasdair said nothing, Leo continued.

"I saw you in Greece. I saw your fiancée, for Christ's sake. Then I saw you with Vasilios, when you vowed to be his." Leo paused and twisted his hands in the material, pleading with Alasdair to hear the truth in his words. "I also saw you with the Duke of Essex."

Alasdair clasped his wrist hard. "How do you know all of that?"

"I don't *know*. But I know," he answered, hating that his voice wavered. Leo winced as Alasdair rose to his full height, making it impossible for him to do anything but stand. "Where are we going?"

"Be quiet." Alasdair strode towards a side door, where he flicked a light on.

Inside was a large bathroom with a tub, a shower, and a basin. As they entered, the door whooshed shut behind them without any assistance.

More freaky vampire shit.

Alasdair reached into the shower and turned it on, and as the water rained down on the tiles below, he faced him and removed his clothes.

Leo's mouth fell open, and he took a step back until his ass bumped into the sink.

"What are you doing?" Leo immediately wanted to take the words back. *Obviously, he's taking a shower, idiot.* It just seemed like such a…human thing to do.

Alasdair remained silent as he peeled his shirt from his body and tossed it aside. The hard expanse of his skin came into view, and Leo had to bite his lower lip to keep a sigh of pleasure from leaving him. He wondered if that skin was as smooth as it appeared—or as hard, for that matter.

When Alasdair's hand went to the button on his pants, Leo was horrified to find himself hoping, above all else, including his short time left in the world, he would unbutton them and push them off his hips. And when he did, Leo's breath caught in his throat.

He'd seen Alasdair naked that time in Vasilios's bedroom, but he'd been too overwhelmed to really look at him. That was *not* the case now. His eyes trailed down the ridges of his cut abdominal muscles to the thick thighs free of any hair. The cock jutting out towards Leo like a fucking arrow was impressive, long, and thick. The veins running its length made him want to get down on his knees and trace them with his tongue, and when Alasdair stood back up, he pinned him with a stare so effective it felt as though he had his hands on him.

You will stay here. Do not try to leave or you will regret it.

The voice in his head was the same as it had always been, but there was a certain edge to it now. One he hadn't heard from Alasdair since the first night they'd met. It both frightened and excited him.

"Tonight's the night, isn't it? You're actually going to do it. Kill me."

It wasn't a question, which was probably for the best. Because what he got in response wasn't an answer but a clear declaration of fact.

"Yes. I am."

Twenty-Seven

ALASDAIR BACKED AWAY from Leo before he did something stupid. *Stupid as in tear his clothes off and fuck him against the bathroom wall.*

When Leo had barged into Thanos's room earlier, Alasdair had thought he'd imagined him. He'd been thinking of him, and then, like some kind of warped apparition, he'd appeared. But when Vasilios and the others had also noticed him, Alasdair had known he was real.

Real and about to be very dead if he hadn't been able to hold Vasilios off.

As soon as Leo had fled the room, Alasdair's mind had gone into overdrive trying to think of ways to stave off the homicidal urge coursing through his sire. His best bet, as far as he'd seen, had been the promise to do it himself.

Leo was a threat to him and everyone he knew, but the thought of being the one to end his life troubled Alasdair more than he cared to admit. He'd pushed that aside, though, and swore to Vasilios that, by dawn, Leonidas Chapel would be dead.

"I know you don't want to do this."

Leo's voice cut into his thoughts, and the conviction in those words would've amused him several days ago. But the truth of the matter was, Leo was right—he didn't want to do this.

Two hands on his back shoved at him, trying to get some kind of a reaction. Alasdair was too quick for him, though, and he pivoted to grasp one of Leo's wrists. He yanked Leo inside the shower with him, and the wet material of his clothes stuck to Alasdair's naked chest, cock, and thighs. Then Alasdair closed his eyes and brought Leo's arm up to his nose to take the scent of him deep into his lungs.

As appealing as ever, Leo's blood called to him, and Alasdair rubbed his shaft over the soaked fabric of Leo's pants. He'd wanted this man since the first night he'd seen him, and Alasdair wasn't sure if that was due to who Leo was or *what* he was—and that galled him as much as his inability to let him go.

The rapid pounding of Leo's heart was steady and strong, and it made him long to taste the blood pulsing through his veins. But that urge would get him killed, and

he happened to be fond of his immortality, which, up until
recently, he'd never thought to question.

"If you were going to kill me," Leo whispered, "you
would've done it already."

Alasdair muscled him back to the wall of the tiled
shower. Leo's ass hit it first and then his shoulder blades
before he lifted his head and his light eyes collided with his.

"I'm biding my time," he said. "I have until dawn."
Then he watched in fascination as Leo's tongue came out to
swipe at the moisture that'd gathered on his lower lip.

"Until dawn?" Leo asked, and Alasdair found the
tremble in his voice extremely arousing. "Then what? You
turn into a pumpkin?"

Leaning in until their noses touched, Alasdair
whispered, "No. Then, if I don't do it, Vasilios will."

When Leo's mouth fell open, Alasdair knew he was
done denying his hunger—the sexual one, anyway. If he
only had until dawn, then he was going to take Leo any way
he could get him.

He swooped in and pressed their lips together. When
Leo's hands clutched at his biceps, Alasdair thought he was
about to push him away, but he didn't. He groaned into his
mouth instead and bucked his hips forward.

Yes. Let me in, Leonidas, he shoved into Leo's head,
and once Leo's eyes had shut and he'd replied, *Yes,* Alasdair
thrust his tongue between his lips.

LEO WAITED FOR that inevitable moment when the light would come. When a memory would hit and he would be torn away from the sinful pleasure of Alasdair devouring his mouth. But when nothing happened, he pushed aside past experiences, forgot what he'd been told of his future, and held on to the muscles pressing him against the tiles here and now.

It felt unbelievable to be at the mercy of this male. Alasdair's body was like granite. Literally hard as a stone all over, and just as cool. His hair was slicked back off his face, and the water sluiced from his dark head over his high cheekbones to trail down his neck. He was stunning, and even if he was the angel of death calling on him this final night of his life, Leo couldn't find it in him to care.

When Alasdair took a step back and lifted his head, his fangs appeared, and all Leo could think was, *deadly...he's so fucking deadly, but so damn hot.* He stepped forward from the wall, determined to touch what would inevitably kill him. He wanted to trace the polished surfaces of his canines and then run the pad of his finger over the pointed tips.

The growl that rumbled from Alasdair's throat made Leo aware that he was just fine with the idea running through his mind.

As he continued making his way towards him, he thought, *Yeah, come on, Alasdair. I'm not afraid of you. Not anymore.*

He'd decided to go with what he was feeling. And right now, he was aroused and fascinated with the male watching him.

As Alasdair ran his tongue along his teeth, Leo's hardened cock wept. Alasdair's eyes lit up like someone had flicked on a switch, and Leo had to clench his hands into fists by his sides. This beast of a man was focused entirely on him, and the light-headed rush he got from that was a high unlike he'd ever experienced.

Alasdair had been right. When under his spell, a person wouldn't mind being hooked up and fucked up by him.

Leo let his eyes trail down the tense vampire, and when he reached Alasdair's stiff erection, he couldn't help pressing a palm to his own dick.

What the hell. You only live once…right?

"If I'm to die in the morning," Leo said, taking another step until the water was hitting them both. "I want you to take me as you would your,"—*What did they call it again? Ah yes—* "yielding for the night. The kind with the handcuff. Not the collar."

Alasdair shook his head, and Leo knew that his meaning had gotten through. Then the vampire backed up faster than Leo had expected.

"No."

"Yes," he said, empowered by the conflict warring on Alasdair's face.

"No. And I don't *have* to wait until dawn to do what must be done. So do not mistake me for the bargaining kind."

Leo reached for his shirt and pulled it from his pants, the soaked material peeling away from his skin. "Then why wait?"

"Leonidas—"

"Yes, Alasdair?" It was strange. The more confidence he showed, the more it seemed as if doubt were creeping into Alasdair's mind. And Leo knew why. He didn't trust himself around him. He didn't trust himself to be able to resist the urge to feed.

"*Ti mou kanis?* I should just end it now," Alasdair said, his eyes narrowing on him, and as Leo unbuttoned his jeans he nodded in agreement.

"You could. Or you could fuck me like you have been wanting to since you first saw me. *Se thelo tora.* I'm not stupid. In fact, I'm extremely smart. Do you think I don't know you want it as much as I do—"

Before another word could leave his mouth, Alasdair gripped his shoulders, and Leo suddenly found himself naked and back in the bedroom they'd vacated, flat on his back in that massive bed.

"Well, that's handy. You even dried me off."

When Alasdair lowered his head, Leo shut his mouth. The tip of Alasdair's tongue touched the spot where his shoulder met his neck, and then he nuzzled his nose into the crook and inhaled.

"You are right, *file mou*. I've never wanted to feed from someone as much as I want to from you." The confession was tormented as Alasdair's nose brushed up his neck, and when a fang grazed his lobe, Leo arched his head away, giving Alasdair a view of what he wanted most. "But you will not fool me. I may want to taste you, but I remember what happened the last time I sank my teeth into your neck. So perhaps you are right." He pressed his entire weight against him, and every muscle, including that thick erection, aligned with his. "I will sink my cock inside you instead."

ALASDAIR ROCKED HIS hips over Leo's, and when he groaned and arched his body up, he moved down to nip at his shoulder.

"That's what you want, isn't it? I can smell it on you now. Your arousal, it's delectable."

"Oh fuck," Leo moaned, but the sound was muffled.

Alasdair lifted his head and gazed down into the lust-filled eyes staring back at him. "What was that?"

Leo punched his hips back up with more force, and this time his words were crystal clear. "I said, 'Oh *fuck*.'"

The powerful arousal mixing with Leo's natural scent made Alasdair's hunger intensify, and he snarled like a wild dog at the pissed tone of Leo's curse.

"How very true. We're *so* fucked. But it's too late to turn back now," he admitted, and then he let go to kneel between Leo's legs.

When Leo spread his naked thighs farther apart for him, Alasdair fisted his cock as he took in the feast splayed out on his bed. Then he reminded himself not to get used to it. It could only be this once. *Just this night.* And the only craving that would be satisfied was the one he was currently stroking. Not the one in the pit of his stomach.

Alasdair knew the only way he could do this was to keep Leo's hands off him, so he shifted down and pinned the man's hands over his head. Then he grazed the entire length of his body against the writhing one under him.

"I'm going to fuck you until the sun comes up, and when you finally close your eyes, you will welcome the relief I will give to you," he promised.

Leo's eyes flashed at him, and the fire Alasdair saw there made him want to pound him into the mattress. He had to give the man points—he was always courageous, even when faced with his own demise.

Then Leo wrapped his legs around his waist and replied, "Let's deal with that in the—"

Alasdair didn't let him finish. He was done listening. And instead, he crushed their mouths together.

GODDAMN IT ALASDAIR can kiss, Leo thought as his tongue tangled with the sexy-as-fuck vampire's. He thrust and tangled with him, playful and forceful at the same time, and when Leo lifted his head from the pillow to get a better taste, one of Alasdair's hands came under his head to hold him in place.

Leo sucked on his tongue, reveling in the deep moan that left the male weighing him down. The unreal pressure of Alasdair over him gave him something to rub his dick on as it made a sticky trail all over Alasdair's taut stomach.

When Alasdair removed his other hand to crowd down over him, Leo had no choice but to lie still as his dark angel trapped him against the bed. Alasdair's eyes glowed back at him before he dragged a tongue along his jaw, and Leo thought he would come right then.

"You need to stay still. Or this will be over before you feel my cock where you most want it."

The sensual words had Leo's breath coming in a desperate pant, but he made sure to keep his eyes on Alasdair when he replied, "Can't control yourself? I'm disappointed. I was sure someone as old as you would last longer than five minutes."

He wasn't sure, but he could've sworn Alasdair's lips twitched. However, he was too busy keeping an eye on the lethal teeth only inches from his face.

"You have a smart tongue, Leonidas. I wonder if it's as talented as it is talkative."

Leo's cock pulsated against Alasdair's as the implication of those words formed an image in his head.

"You also have a *very* detailed imagination. And a high opinion of your skill."

When Alasdair nipped at his ear, Leo's breath hitched, and then he asked, "Is that a bad thing?" He then purposely imagined, in great detail, Alasdair on his back and him sucking the hard cock he could feel against his own. He wanted nothing more than for Alasdair to slide inside his mouth and along his tongue. But before he could request it, their positions were reversed, and Alasdair had a hand on his shoulder, urging him down his body.

"No. It's not a bad thing if it proves to be accurate."

Leo looked at the devilishly handsome face daring him to put his money—*Huh*—where his mouth would soon be and smirked. He'd never had a complaint before.

He slid down the solid body under him, making sure to drag his aching cock over every inch, until he settled between Alasdair's solid thighs.

He pressed his erection against the mattress, trying to hold off the orgasm threatening, but when Alasdair raised his legs to plant his feet flat on the bed, Leo thought he might explode.

Only inches from his face was the most spectacular sight he'd ever seen, and soon, his mouth would be all over it. He could see every inch of Alasdair's cock, balls and ass, and if Leo had thought he was the perfect example of a male specimen before, he was now fucking positive men had been designed after him.

"You're amazing," he whispered.

And when an arrogant, "I know," met his ears, Leo smiled despite himself.

Yeah, usually, that kind of god complex irked the hell out of him, but in this two-thousand-year-old's case, it was fucking justified.

Leo placed his hands on the inside of Alasdair's thighs, and when he angled his head and swiped his tongue across his balls, the groan that met his ears was like a fucking symphony. He did it again, and when Alasdair pushed his pelvis close to his face, Leo continued to tongue his sac.

He thought Alasdair's skin would be cool like his hands had been. But he should've known better, because just as the vampire's tongue was a warm pleasure point, the tight balls, which were heavy and taut, were hot to the touch. It was as if, when turned on, Alasdair's temperature rose, and the thought of *literally* making him hot had Leo's desire skyrocketing.

He nuzzled his face in closer and drew his tongue up the underside of Alasdair's cock. Then he traced the veins he'd fantasized about, and when he got to the tip, he raised his eyes and saw that Alasdair's had changed to black.

Oh fuck, what does that mean? He didn't have to wait long to find out.

Alasdair widened his legs and told him, "They change with heightened emotions. Which usually leads to one of two things. The desire to kill and feed or..."

Leo wrapped his fingers around the base of Alasdair's cock. "Or..."

"The desire to fuck."

Leo dipped the tip of his tongue into the slit inches from his lips and then blew his warm breath over it. If this was to truly be his last moment in life, then, *hell*, he was going to make it count.

"Let's go with option number two."

ALASDAIR WATCHED LEO lower his lips down his shaft and tried to rationalize what the fuck he thought he was doing.

He could see the blond hair between his thighs and knew he shouldn't continue, but when Leo's lips tightened around him, there was no way he was going to stop.

He'd wanted this man for weeks now, and he'd been denying himself over and over. First the urge to feed, knowing what it would do to *him*, and then the desire to fornicate. To fuck Leo so hard he wouldn't be able to walk the next day.

And why? Because he hadn't known what Leo was. That wasn't the case now. Or was it? Did he really have any more answers than he'd had earlier? Or merely his own suspicions?

Something fucked up happened whenever Leo disappeared into his dream state. The human was learning things about him and Vasilios that could potentially threaten their very existence. But still, he didn't know anything more about *who* Leo was. And wasn't that the whole reason Vasilios had been upset over having lost Stratos as a valuable source? Why would he want to kill Leo? What could be more valuable than one sent to end them?

Yes…that's what I need to tell him. That's how he'd convince Vasilios to spare him.

The idea planted itself as his instincts urged him not to continue down this treacherous path. But it was no use. The lure of the flesh, of the immoral things he wanted to do to the man he'd become consumed with, were too strong.

His desire to push inside Leo's body *and* mind would not be denied. And when he shoved into Leo's thoughts and saw him imagining the same, Alasdair pulled his cock free of the lips surrounding him.

Get on your hands and knees. When Leo shifted to the desired position and looked over his shoulder, Alasdair added, *Se thelo.*

He moved so he was between Leo's legs, and then he bent down and scraped the tip of his fang over the curve of Leo's ass before soothing the sting with his tongue. Leo sighed and Alasdair saw his head arch back so his neck was stretched nice and long in sensual invitation.

Needing to distract himself, Alasdair traced his fingers up the shadowed line of Leo's crack then gripped the firm flesh of his ass cheeks and pulled them apart. He bit back a groan when Leo's tight hole came into view, right before he dragged a hot, wet trail over it with his tongue.

Leo cursed his name, and when he reached under himself to curl his fingers around his cock, Alasdair flicked his tongue over the small pucker a second time. The unholy cry that filled his chamber made Alasdair's fingers tighten, and the powerful taste of Leo on his tongue had him diving back in, deeper. He was determined to have this man writhing in his bed before he fucked him through it.

"*Kialo,*" Leo demanded in Greek, and Alasdair just about lost it.

He nipped at the sensitive skin and then ran his tongue along the dark crevice again, flirting with the puckered opening.

"I need something *in* me," Leo confessed as he dropped his forehead to the pillow.

Alasdair brought a finger up to where his tongue was teasing and slowly pushed the tip against Leo's body. When he shoved back, chasing his long digit, Alasdair pressed it firmer against his hole.

Is this what you want, Leonidas? And as he shoved the thought into Leo's mind, he entered him with his finger.

The pillow under Leo trapped his moan, but when Alasdair went to remove his finger, he raised his head and managed, "Yes. *That. Ksana.* I want more of that."

Loving the sound of his native language coming out of Leo's mouth, Alasdair decided to give *his* human what he had asked for. He slid his finger back inside and sucked the stretched skin that was widening for his entry. He couldn't wait to sink his cock in its place, and when he added a second and third finger and Leo started to fuck them like he was ready for a dick, Alasdair was more than happy to give it to him.

Removing his hand, he moved up to crowd over him, placing his hands on the mattress on either side of Leo's . "You always surprise me. You like my fangs against your flesh, don't you, *file mou*?"

Leo's heart raced at the observation.

Alasdair chuckled. "That's a resounding yes. Your body gives you away. Your cock, your heartbeat, the flush covering this creamy skin of yours. It all tells me you're dying for it. And really, you are, aren't you? Never more so than tonight."

As his words taunted the man under him, Alasdair felt an ache of his own, and it had nothing to do with the straining flesh between his legs.

No. His words, relaying death and the end for this human, didn't satisfy him as they usually would've. But before he could think any more on it, Leo shocked the hell out of him by rolling beneath him so he was flat on his back again and spreading his legs.

"You want to fuck me? Then shut up and fuck me. But you can look at me while you do it. You don't get to forget my face once you're done with me come sunrise."

He wondered if Leo had any idea that, right then, he knew he'd never be able to forget his face—not if he lived for another two thousand years.

Alasdair rubbed their cocks together and let his eyes close, deciding that it was best to keep that information to himself. Then the hands he'd been determined to keep off his body grabbed his hips and pulled him down for a harder massage, and when Leo's fingers moved over his ass to slip between his cheeks, Alasdair had to grit his teeth.

Once he got inside this man, he was going to bury himself there and finally find release from this all-consuming craving. What he wasn't sure of was what would happen when the sun rose, after which, all of this would end.

But for now, he had Leo under him, and Alasdair couldn't help but reach down between them and encircle their cocks, stroking a firm fist up both their lengths. He grunted when Leo shoved his entire body up, gliding the underside of his dick along his own, the sensation so unbelievable, Leo had him a hair trigger away from coming all over him.

"Enough," Alasdair finally rasped, not sure how much more he could take. "Especially when we both want my cock inside you."

His fangs appeared at the words, and Leo's eyes shifted to them, making Alasdair's cock throb harder against the man. He could hear Leo's pulse racing, and when he lowered his head, Alasdair goaded him.

"Do it."

Leo's eyes flew up to meet his as his body stilled under him, and then he raised a tentative hand. He traced the pad of his finger along Alasdair's lower lip, and when he sucked on the tip of it, Leo brought his legs up to wrap them around his waist. Alasdair released his grip on the both of them and snaked his hand down to push his own finger against the hole he'd widened earlier.

Then he dared Leo again. "Do *it*."

This time, Leo clutched his bicep, hauled himself up, and stroked his tongue over the pointed tip of his fang. Alasdair wanted to roar at the intense pleasure flooding his body, but instead, he withdrew his finger from Leo's passage and thrust it back inside the man responsible for his intense need.

Leo shouted out a raw guttural sound as he swiped his tongue over his tooth once more. Alasdair had miscalculated that move though. He never would've allowed it had he known the raging hunger it would evoke. The clawing need now scratching its way free of its tightly controlled confines had his finger now working overtime to stretch Leo wider.

Leo moaned under him as he pressed their lips together harder, and when he added a second finger to the hole being thoroughly worked over, Alasdair lost his grip on his inner savage.

Leo's eyes had shut and he'd let go of his arms to lie back and be used, and when he angled his head on the pillow and the vein in his neck pulsed, Alasdair told himself to get his cock in him or get the fuck out.

He yanked his hand back, his fingers slipping free, and Leo reached down between his legs to start feverishly tugging his cock. A low groan left Leo when Alasdair hooked his legs behind the knees and pushed them back, and when the head of his dick nudged Leo's tight entrance, his slate eyes locked with his and his mind screamed at Alasdair, *Tora.*

LEO CLOSED HIS eyes, hoping it would help to hold off the orgasm teetering on the edge. He wasn't sure why he was slipping in and out of English, but every time he did, the reaction from Alasdair was unreal. His muscles bunched and he looked like he wanted to sink his cock inside him and never leave.

When Alasdair had dared him to run his tongue over those deadly weapons in his mouth, nothing could've stopped him. The sharp prick of them against his tongue and the fingers Alasdair had been shoving in and out of him had made it close to impossible for him to hold back his orgasm.

But when Alasdair hiked his legs up and thrust inside him so hard his entire body shifted up the mattress, Leo was thankful he'd fucking waited.

The thick cock that was pistoning in and out of him filled him so well that he thought he might taste it on his tongue when Alasdair came. As it was, the male staring down at him was as frightening as he was appealing.

His jaw was clenched and his eyes were black with desire as his pace intensified. Then he bared his teeth to him, and Leo had never been more turned on in his life.

He knew that this vampire, that Alasdair, could and would likely kill him, but right then, as he looked up at him, he'd never seen anything more awe inspiring.

He tugged and pulled at his cock as Alasdair withdrew from him and then shoved home with another forceful thrust, and when Alasdair did it again, Leo's lips parted and a cry left his mouth.

Holy fucking *hell.* He'd figured Alasdair would be good at this. The guy had had over a couple thousand years to practice. But the smooth, solid strokes he continued to deliver into his ass had Leo's hole clinging to that wide intruder every time Alasdair pulled his hips back.

Leo squeezed his eyes shut, and for one sex-crazed moment, he imagined what it would be like if Alasdair were to lean down over him, plow back inside him, and sink those sharp-as-fuck teeth into his vein.

It was insane to wish he could be taken that way. *Insane* to wish he were normal and not a threat to the being who was so thoroughly fucking him. But in a way, Leo felt denied part of this experience.

He'd said that he wanted to be Alasdair's yielding. He wanted to be fucked and fed on by this male so completely dominating him, but he never could be, because he wasn't—

Human.

Alasdair's voice slipped inside him and had Leo's eyes flicking open.

HE WANTED IT. *Fuck, yes,* he did. He wanted nothing more than to sink his teeth into the creamy skin of Leo's neck. The urge, the hunger—they were riding him as hard as he was riding the body bucking underneath him.

Leo's muscles strained against his own, and the strength in him was a surprise. He hadn't expected the man to be a match for him—but he was.

He was raw, uninhibited, and demanding, and when Leo moaned in ecstasy, a hot jet of sticky fluid exploded between them, landing on his stomach and chest.

Alasdair squeezed his eyes shut. Another thing Leo was—irresistible.

"*Q theé mou.*"

He'd tried. He'd fought against every instinct he'd had to go to Leo. But as the man took him inside his body, Alasdair's control was slipping.

He shook his head and battled against the desire.

"Open your eyes," Leo demanded underneath him, tightening his legs around Alasdair's waist. "If you're imagining my death while you're inside me, the least you can do is look at me."

"I'm not," Alasdair snarled at him, shocked when Leo's lips curved into a devilish grin.

Oh, he likes when I snap at him, does he?

Alasdair lowered himself down until the sticky evidence of how *much* Leo had liked it slicked over his skin. Still hard and lodged inside Leo's hot hole, Alasdair swiped his tongue over the come marking Leo's skin. Leo's body vibrated against him, and he bit the hardened tip of his nipple. Alasdair then drew his hips back and gave a swift, sharp jab of them, plowing his cock back into Leo's waiting body.

"Oh fuck, Alasdair."

He groaned at the breathless curse and then said, "You like to risk your life, don't you, Leonidas?"

When Leo tilted his head and scraped *his* teeth along the stubble lining his jaw, Alasdair froze as he heard, "You can't risk something that's no longer yours to control."

Leo's words repeated inside his mind, and he started to pull out, only to have Leo threaten him.

"Don't you dare," he told him fiercely. "Don't you dare grow a conscience now. Not with *me*. I won't believe it."

Alasdair narrowed his eyes on the mystery beneath him.

"That's right. I've seen you, remember? I've seen you do the most atrocious things, yet, for some reason I can't explain, I want you more than I want to live to see tomorrow. So don't you dare think you can take my life without giving me *that*. Without letting me see how much you wanted me too." Leo paused and then invited softly, "Come. Come inside me. I want to watch you when you do."

Alasdair surged back inside him and put his lips to Leo's ear. "What are you? Some kind of spell weaver?"

"I keep telling you. I don't know," he replied.

Alasdair pulled out, and Leo moaned at the loss. When he thrust back into him and Leo's fingers dug into his shoulders, Alasdair buried his nose in the crook of his neck and closed his eyes. As his hips moved, he gnashed his teeth together in an effort to keep them from Leo's flesh. His climax was gripping his balls like a tight fist, and when Leo reared up and bit the side of his neck, it was all over.

Alasdair's shout was loud, his orgasm explosive, and the scrape of his brave human's teeth down the length of his throat had his come filling his tight little hole—just as Leo had requested. He couldn't remember a release such as this in a long time.

Silence filled the room. It was so heavy and thick that it was suffocating as Alasdair remained nestled inside Leo, half hard.

"Let me go," Leo pleaded, so softly Alasdair barely heard him.

"*Stamata*," he demanded, lifting his head to stare into the eyes that had captured him the first time he'd seen them. "Stop asking for what I can't give."

"Why? Why can't you give it? Just vanish us out of here. You've done it before."

Alasdair blinked down at him, shocked that, for one second, he'd contemplated doing that. "What you want. It can never be. This… You… You have been given to me, but only for a short time—" Alasdair stopped talking as Leo grabbed his arms and pulled himself up so their lips touched.

His tongue traced over his top lip, and when a shudder racked through Alasdair's body, Leo asked, "Why? Why can't I be like all the others? And be yours? I know you want that also."

He did want that. *Fuck*, and he'd never wanted it before.

He could see himself with this human. He could see many nights in his bed, many years with him as his yielding. But he couldn't have it.

Not ever.

"You are a threat to me. I cannot have you close. I shouldn't have had you at all."

"No," Leo denied adamantly. "I'm not a threat. I'm just me."

"Yes. And your blood—it will kill me. *You* can kill *me*. I'm over two thousand years old. Think about that, Leonidas."

Leo shoved at his shoulders, but it was no use. He couldn't dislodge him.

"I don't understand any of this," he said, his eyes flashing with confused anger. "Not you, not these dreams, and not the stupid fucking voice telling me I was created for some higher purpose. I didn't want *any* of this."

"What voice?" Alasdair demanded, pushing him back to the bed. He pinned him there with his unyielding grip, and Leo moaned when the cock inside him shifted.

"I don't know," he grit out between clenched teeth.

"There's a lot you don't know, *file mou.*" Alasdair's eyes moved to the tongue that darted out to moisten Leo's lower lip.

"I know. But I'm not lying. At the end of the last vision I had, someone told me I was created to end you. *Me?* Which is ridiculous. Don't you see? If I were a threat, why would I tell you all of this? I thought I was just a normal human—"

"Obviously, you were wrong."

"Maybe," Leo whispered, turning his head to the side. "Maybe I was."

Alasdair rolled his hips over Leo's, and the whimper that left him was full of mournful pleasure.

Leo was giving in. He had no more denials to give.

His human had finally accepted his fate.

Alasdair ran his tongue along the vein in Leo's neck. The easiest way to do this was a clean break. Painless, really, and over in a mere second.

It was time. He knew he had to do it.

And better to do it now while the rush of endorphins had Leo completely satiated. Then he heard it: the final soft plea from the man underneath him.

"Let me go, Alasdair."

"I can't. He will never let it be."

He knew that Leo understood exactly whom he meant. He'd seen his bond with Vasilios firsthand.

"And he decides?"

"He decides this."

"Because?"

The air around them seemed to crackle under the force of the presence entering it, and that could only mean one thing—Vasilios—who was now standing by the side of the bed.

Blood stained his hands and his arms, and his shirt was torn and close to rags as the Ancient ran his eyes down their entwined bodies. When they came back to rest on their faces, his top lip tightened, revealing the fangs that had been used on hapless victims centuries over.

"*Because* you are a crack in our foundation, human. A weakness in our bond. Our very existence. Alasdair knows it, and so do I," he answered right before he lunged for the two of them.

Twenty-Eight

"WAIT!" THE REQUEST that came out of Alasdair sounded more like a demand.

Leo's arousal turned to fear as the vampire who'd been over and inside him tensed and got in between him and his maker.

Vasilios was poised, on the brink of attack, and his sinister sneer made it clear he was ready to kill—him specifically.

"I do not *wait*. Not for you. Not for anyone, Alasdair. Do not forget whom you are addressing. Move off of him. Time is up."

Like a large cat sizing up its opponent, Alasdair slowly began to move. He crawled over him and shifted until he was upright and on his knees, directly between him and Vasilios. His muscled back and tight, rounded ass shouldn't have caught his eye in that moment, but after what they'd been doing, it was hard not to look.

On the edge of the bed, Alasdair bowed his head and stated calmly, "You said I had until dawn. The sun has not yet risen."

"I have since had time to change my mind. Move aside, Alasdair."

Leo reached for the sheets and pulled them up over his exposed body.

"I will not. You gave me your word."

"And now, I am taking it back," Vasilios barked.

Leo's eyes flicked to the male standing before Alasdair, and he knew that, should Vasilios want to, he could remove Alasdair from his path.

The tension in the room was born of defiance and disbelief and, on his part, abject fear. If Alasdair didn't get through to Vasilios, he would be dead.

And soon.

"Going back on your word is something you have not done in nearly two thousand years. What has changed?"

"Isadora. Her presence is quickly dissipating. Diomêdês can barely get a read. She was taken from the same place you took him. By a dark-haired male who knows *him*. He is connected, and we can't afford to waste time while you fuck him out of your system. So step aside, *agori*."

Leo's mind whirled at the words he was hearing.

The same place they took me from? A male? Dark hair…

Elias.

And suddenly, he had a plan. One that might help save his life, and perhaps the woman's—Isadora.

"Use me," Leo suggested. The two words had flown out of his mouth before he'd thought better of them.

When Alasdair slowly turned his head to look down at him, Leo scrambled to his knees, the sheet falling to cover his lap but otherwise baring his naked body.

"I can help you. I know where Elias works. I know where he lives. I can help your friend."

"She is of our blood, human. Not *just* a friend."

Leo shrank back from those words and the hate in Vasilios's eyes.

He was terrifying.

"Keep quiet," Alasdair said. His tone was low, but the command was clear, and though every instinct told him that being silent would be smart, Leo couldn't help the drive to fight for his own survival.

"I've been having dreams," he rushed on, looking around Alasdair's large shoulder.

When Vasilios's eyes focused on him and he bared his teeth, Leo thought he must be mad to continue, but he did so anyway.

"About you and him, back when he was a human. Back when you hunted him and made him—"

"Mine," Vasilios interjected.

"Yes, umm, when you did that." Leo nervously licked his lips, not really knowing his place. He'd just been caught in bed with this vampire's... *What do they call them? Lover? Mate?*

First sired.

The words were pushed into Leo's mind, and when his eyes flew back to Vasilios, he added, *Alasdair is* my *first sired.*

Oh wow. Okay. This guy's voice in Leo's head was like...like...nothing he'd known before. Alasdair's was hypnotic, made his cock ache and his heart pound. But this male—his voice was like a shot of pure adrenaline, and the power of it rushed through his veins like nothing he'd ever experienced before.

The highest of highs.

"I also saw you with him one night at a ball, with a duke. I keep seeing you and him together. But I don't know how. I swear. I'm not connected to anything—"

"Ahhh, but that's where you are wrong, *agóri*. Because you see, I saw *you* too."

Oh fuck. So that did happen. But how? It isn't possible. Yet, in the dream, Vasilios had looked right at him.

"Yes. I knew you were familiar, but I couldn't quite pinpoint it until tonight. When you walked into the bedchamber and your eyes went as wide as saucers—I'd seen that startled look on you before. You're connected to something much more powerful than you even know. And it is something we cannot allow to go unchecked." His eyes left Leo's and shifted back to Alasdair's. "Move aside, Alasdair."

Leo gulped and shut his eyes. The rush of blood in his head was loud and his hands trembled. If he was going to die anyway, there was no point in Alasdair getting hurt in the process. So he grabbed the sheet and pushed it aside before rising from the bed.

As his feet touched the floor, Vasilios was around the end of the bed and over to where he was now standing. His unforgiving fingers clasped his throat and held him in place.

Leo reached for the fingers even though it was no use. Then Alasdair appeared beside them.

"Let him go," he said.

Leo struggled to push his words past his constricted esophagus. "Don't listen to him. If you want to kill me, then kill me. But he's done nothing wrong."

"Neither have you," Alasdair said and glared at him, and Leo's eyes widened.

So the vampire does care if I live or die.

"Stop talking, both of you," Vasilios demanded and then yanked Leo forward. This close, he could see the light reflecting off the pointed tips of his fangs, and when the corner of his lip tipped up in a smile, Leo didn't know what to think. "You say you see these things when you put your mouth on *my* Alasdair."

"Yes," Leo rushed out.

Vasilios slowly tilted his head to the side, examining him. "And you defend him now, when you are to die."

Leo's eyes flicked to Alasdair, and he nodded.

"I think you want my *agóri* as your own. Is that what you want, Leonidas Chapel?"

Leo was about to say no when he heard, *Do not lie to him*, in his head—Alasdair.

"Yes, I want him. Who wouldn't? He's beautiful, and dangerous, and different from anyone I've ever met. He makes me feel things I haven't felt before."

Vasilios leaned closer and asked, "Is he worth your life?"

Leo squeezed his eyes shut. He wasn't sure what Vasilios wanted to hear, but he couldn't imagine going through life now knowing Alasdair was hurt or dead because of him. So, when a fang grazed his lower lip, he opened his eyes and said the only thing that came to mind.

"Yes."

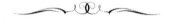

ALASDAIR STOOD TO the side of Vasilios and Leo, staring in disbelief at the fool human.

Had he really said that he was willing to die for him?

After all the threats, and all the violence, Leo was throwing himself at Vasilios's mercy. He didn't dare speak as the silence enveloped the three of them. The mood in the room was strange. It was ripe with fear, loathing, and…lust.

He could sense Leo's emotions easily enough. He was terrified of Vasilios—and for good reason. His temper was not something any smart being would provoke.

Vasilios's emotions, on the other hand, were harder to pinpoint.

Only seconds earlier, his intentions had been clear as day, but now, as he stood with his hand around Leo's throat and his mouth over his lips, Alasdair sensed something else. Something he'd only ever felt directed at him—lust.

Not the everyday feeling of want and desire. But the driving need, the craving to be consumed by the one he was currently touching, and the erection Alasdair saw when he looked below his waist solidified it.

Vasilios wanted this human. He wanted Leo. As much as he wanted *him* when he was near.

"Yes, you say? Hmm."

The sound of Vasilios's contemplation rolled over Alasdair, and then Vasilios looked his way.

"I do love a good self-sacrifice. What say you, Alasdair? Should we keep him? Should we *use* him as he so blatantly offered only moments ago?"

Alasdair's cock hardened at the sensual implications Vasilios attached to the word *use,* and then his eyes shifted to the human. Leo was watching him with the intensity of a hawk, and Alasdair wondered if that look was a plea for his life or a plea for death.

It didn't matter though. It was too late now.

He *was*, after all, a selfish being at heart.

Alasdair nodded, and Vasilios had Leo flat on his back and pinned to the mattress in a flash.

"Vasilios, take care. His blood—"

"Oh, I remember, *agóri*. I'm not going to drink his blood. He's going to drink mine." He loomed over Leo, and all Alasdair could think as he walked to the edge of the bed was—if Leo lived through this, the three of them would be forever tied.

There was no turning back now.

The End

Coming Soon

ISADORA

Masters Among Monsters #2

January 12th, 2016

Royalton
Luxury Resorts

Special Thanks

It has come to my attention that over the last three years my Special Thanks section seems to always include the same amazing people. This makes me one of the luckiest women on the planet, and if this is the only small token I can give, you will forever have a place in my Special Thanks.

I have been fortunate enough to not only find a wonderful group of people to help me achieve my goals, but I have also found a wonderful set of friends. The kind who are supportive, honest, and loyal to the end. They are women who have become my family and women I couldn't go a day without checking in with.

While each of them knows who they are, I would be remiss if I didn't mention what they mean to me and praise them for their individual talents.

Candace Wood. Really, nothing more needs to be said about you than: you are irreplaceable. However, you know me. I can't stop there. Not only are you the best friend and co-author a girl could have, you are an amazing editor, a brutal and honest critique partner, and one hell of a soundboard. You also have the ability to talk me back from insane story plots that I come up with in the middle of the night. You know what I'm talking about. **cough cough mass annihilation**

Thank you for the many hours you devote to pouring over my stories, and thank you for loving each of them so much that you eventually hate them. It takes tireless hours and meticulous eyes to get books to where they can be published, and I couldn't do that without you.

You teach me something new every day, and even if I complain about it, I promise deep down inside I'm thanking you for it.

Jen Gerschick. Cupcake. A woman who goes so far out of her way for others that she had five, yes, count them, *five* books of mine left unsigned after seeing me at a signing back in 2014.

Thank you for giving up your reading time to lend your eyes to my script before it hits e-readers. You are generous with both your heart and time, and I am so fortunate you fell in love with Cole Madison and found me to tell me so.

I also want to thank you for the many hours you spent running my street team so smoothly that it became an online "happy place" to everyone who went in there. Although we have shut the doors and moved on to a bigger adventure, I will always remember the Emporium for bringing many of our friends together.

Donner Byrd-Rodgers. My little antagonizer. I love that you always, for some unbeknownst reason, root for the underdogs in my books. Do you do that with other characters in books you read? Or am I the lucky one?

It reminds me daily that authors should always welcome constructive criticism. After all, that was what brought you to me—the honest question you had about one of my characters and the fact that you weren't afraid to reach out and tell me *your* opinion. Then, in the same conversation, you asked if I had a street team, and we have been friends ever since. That was a great day.

Please don't ever change your dry wit and unusual perspective on things. It always makes me think twice.

And, of course, thank you for reading my PNR book even though you are a scaredy cat like Candace. I expect a hug in Seattle and Florida, btw. Bye Felicia!

Stacy Wilkerson. Or should I curtsy, Queen Mary? Thank you for taking on the task of Alasdair. When I first came to you with it, you were one of the people who really encouraged me to dip my toes in the water of the unknown. You also had the same dirty thought in mind that I had, so I knew you had to be a part of this collaboration.

It makes me laugh so hard that when we first met I thought you were slightly insane. But over the last two years, I have come to learn that your emoticon addiction is just part of who you are.

Thank you for picking up Exquisite. Thank you for Twitter-talking to me when I had no clue what a re-tweet meant, and most importantly, thank you for being a kickass friend. I can't wait to finally meet you in Seattle next year.

Judy Zweifel. Now this is a woman who has so many sister's I'm not sure she has room for one more, but hell, I'm gonna push through anyway! You have amazing eyes lady, and I appreciate you putting aside things…including vacation time…to help me out! I can't wait to finally meet and hug you. I have a feeling 2016 is going to be the year I finally get to meet most of you. But for now I am beyond happy to call you my friend.

Renee Kubisch. Ahhh… I finally met you in the mother country. Getting to come back to Australia this year was the highlight of 2015. Putting a face to the name, a voice to the words, and a hug with a friend was more than I could've hoped for. You have two picky eyeballs in that awesome head of yours, and I've known it right from the beginning! Thank you so much for working your arse off for me on beta reads, and for the fantastic swag you made. You are one of a kind and a true professional. I am so fortunate to call you a friend.

Pavlina Michou. Or should we all call you the Greek Goddess? Thank you so much for your invaluable help with the names and phrases in this story. I literally could not have done this without you. I can't wait to hear you actually say these words in the correct form, because right now this Australian is trying to pronounce them in Greek, and I am sure I sound totally wrong! Thank you so much. You rock, woman!

Mickey Reed. My wonderful editor. It was such a pleasure to meet you this year in my new hometown. I want to thank you for all the hours and hard work you put into my stories—and let's face it, it's *a lot* of hard work. I've said it before, and I will say it again—you are a rock star.

Hang Le. I cannot begin to tell you how it felt to receive the cover for Alasdair. I had visions in my head of what I wanted, and I knew exactly what I did NOT want, but when you sent it through to me...my heart just about stopped. YOU NAILED IT!!!!!! Yes, it deserves all of those.
I still can't stop looking at it, and I've had it for weeks. It just makes me eager to get my hands on the next two. You are an absolute creative genius, and I feel so lucky to call you a friend and colleague.

Chasity at Rockstar PR. Thank you for taking a chance on me and helping me spread the word about Alasdair. You took a huge weight off my shoulders and handled it with the utmost grace. Thank you, for that. It has been a pleasure to work with you!

And last, but definitely not least, to my husband, who puts up with never seeing me except when I come out to eat. Thank you, Frank, for dealing with my irritable mood swings that often result in bursts of unreasonable behavior. Although you are a silent supporter and stay behind the scenes, you are my biggest cheerleader, and I truly couldn't do this without you!

Much love to you all,
Xx Ella

About the Author

About Ella

Ella Frank is the author of the #1 Bestselling Temptation series, including Try, Take, and Trust and is the co-author of the fan-favorite erotic serial, A Desperate Man. Her Exquisite series has been praised as "scorching hot!" and "enticingly sexy!"

A life-long fan of the romance genre, Ella writes contemporary and erotic fiction and lives with her husband in Portland, OR. You can reach her on the web at www.ellafrank.com and on Facebook at www.facebook.com/ella.frank.author

Some of her favorite authors include Tiffany Reisz, Kresley Cole, Riley Hart, J.R. Ward, Erika Wilde, Gena Showalter, and Carly Philips.

Want to get to know Ella better?

You can find her at **The Naughty Umbrella** on Facebook.

Manufactured by Amazon.ca
Bolton, ON

19233415R00192